Dead Ringer

A Teke Manion Murder Mystery

To : Meredith!
Thanks so
Much!
And Enjoy!
E
'23

Dead Ringer

A Teke Manion Murder Mystery

By Rod Sanford

Printed in the United States of America
First Printing 2022
First Edition 2022

ISBN: 9798841684954

Acknowledgements

I want to thank the folks I interviewed for their help on Colombian culture, coffee farm life, and the world of international smuggling. A special thanks to: Juana Perdomo(Romero) and Larry Romero. Thanks to David Romero who connected me to them.

Any representations that are slightly south of accurate were done for dramatic or literary reasons and do not represent an absence of respect for the subject matter.

Prologue

I, Teke Manion, was a pampered ass.

That was all I heard as I sat in a middle seat on something called Horizon Airlines. It was my third flight in the last twenty-four hours. On my first flight out of Raleigh Durham, I was in the middle seat in the back row. On my second flight, from Tampa to Miami, I was in the first row of ten. Now I was somewhere in the middle of a plane built when I was in grade school flying over the open Caribbean waters.

And my critical traveling partner?

My sworn enemy, Juan Diego "JD" Cruz, the enigmatic deputy sheriff of Manatee County. I begged him to take my employer's jet, which was waiting for me in Tampa, but he wouldn't have it. WorldSpan Underwriters had a Gulfstream jet waiting to take me home, and I was confident I could order a change in course, but no.

"I'm not asking WorldSpan for a damn thing," JD explained for the tent time, poking me in the chest before we started this crazy puddle jumping. "I'm asking you, Teke Manion, for your help."

I had just finished a golden opportunity that netted hundreds of millions of dollars for good old WorldSpan Insurers and Underwriters, and I was headed to Paris for a hero's welcome from the company and from Camille DeSoronne, my boss and lover.

I sent the pirate "booty" back to Paris with a US State Department escort and my apologies. Camille left about four voicemails, each one increasingly angrier. I left apologetic text messages, letting her know I was safe but that I would not be making it back home for a few days.

It kept me from having to explain what I was doing.

Nevertheless, when this was all over, JD and I were going to have a talk about buying plane tickets and upgrading seats.

What was "this?"

Deputy Cruz was the brother of my ex-fiancé, Soledad Marie Cruz. As you might guess, I wasn't his favorite person. Moreover, the last time we worked together, JD and I ended up shot and swimming for our lives in the Gulf of Mexico. At that time we had a mutual agreement that we never needed to cross each other's paths again.

Now we were back together like Tango and Cash for the only reason that would or could make it happen.

Soledad was missing.

She had flown out of the Southwest Florida International Airport three weeks ago for Medellín, Colombia. From there she had proceeded on a slow drive to the mountains of the Venecia Antioquia to the Lazaro Coffee estate. It was part of her new business venture.

JD explained that she had either called or texted him every day she was there. Her cell phone signal was spotty, so she used landlines or waited until she was in the larger cities to call. Over the last ten days, her calls and texts had stopped, and JD's calls and voicemails to her cell phone had gone unanswered.

"We always joked that if a week ever went by without us talking, the other one better come looking," JD explained.

"I can't get any help from the US Consulate, the State Department, or the local law in Medellín, so I'm going."

He needed help. Someone with international experience who knew how to investigate without being seen and handle himself if things went sideways. Fortunately, or unfortunately, that person was me.

He talked to someone at my Paris home office and found out I was finishing some interesting work in North Carolina, so he jumped on one of his snug, inexpensive little flights to retrieve me.

"What about this Lazaro family? Have you talked to them?" I asked as I fidgeted my backside in the narrowest plane seat I had ever experienced.

"I finally heard from Antonio Lazaro's secretary. She said Marie should be OK. Said she was in Cartagena working on the shipment."

"You don't believe them?"

"I don't know. I got the impression he was trying to posture. And it still doesn't explain why she hasn't called me."

I had witnessed the younger sister/older brother dynamic between Soledad and JD going back to when we were kids. JD was overprotective, but ten days with no contact concerned me as well.

"What is this business?" I asked.

"Mmmm, not sure. Something about wine."

"You said it was a coffee estate."

"Yeah, but I think they're branching into wine."

"Well, that's great, JD," I said, more irritated by the seat than the crappy intel. Like I said, I was pampered.

We sat back and endured the rest of the flight to Colombia.

To understand everything that happened after we landed, it's important to examine what happened about a week before JD retrieved me from North Carolina.

1

Based on the final report and briefing files of the Policía Nacional de Colombia, the National Directorate of Taxes and Customs, and WorldSpan Underwriters.

Lazaro Coffee Estate, Municipio de Venecia, Antioquia

The last light of a setting sun shone orange and gold over the hills of the Lazaro Coffee estate and the north casita. Several such squat dwellings dotted the 1,100-acre property.

They usually served as housing for the field bosses during the busy planting and harvesting seasons. Tonight, it was the site of a celebration by the principal stakeholders of an exciting new venture.

"A toast. To Lalvarez Wines!" Antonio Lazaro said to the group, holding up his signature malbec, the first issue of his new winery.

Soledad Cruz, sitting on his lap, took a full sip and kissed him hard, hugging him around his neck.

"Now that's how you toast a wine!" Wayne Kowl said, then took a sip and kissed his spouse and partner, Mario Romero.

The table was full of grilled chicken and fish served on a bed of peppers, onions, mangos, pineapples, and limes. The two couples were anxious but excited with anticipation and inebriation.

Antonio had started the winery and now ran it. He had convinced his father, Alexandro Lazaro, the owner of Lazaro Coffee, to let him use the small range of hilly land on the southern edge of the property, and he had pulled it off. Growing grapes and producing wine in Colombia was officially a thing. However, the humidity and select insects made it considerably more labor intensive than other places.

Antonio found the right combination of tough, disease-resistant grapes, an embrace of science, and a dedicated labor force on the estate that would do anything for the late Victoria Alvarez's baby boy. The southern hillsides were the highest on the property. The altitude and tree cover created what was known as a sub-climate that was favorable to grow wine grapes.

Antonio and Soledad met online. She was responsible for educating him and his staff on how to navigate customs, legal matters, and marketing hurdles to sell in the United States. At some point during their business dealings, it became more than business. Wayne and Mario had gone to college with Antonio. They owned a chain of wine stores and bars throughout California that Wayne had inherited from his parents.

This weekend they would ship one hundred bottles and two Flexi-Tanks of their Lalvarez malbec. The bottles were for marketing and promotions. The wine in the FlexiTanks would be bottled in California at a distributor picked by Wayne and Mario.

The four of them were loud and drunk on fresh wine, food raised on the land on which they celebrated, and the fruition of what seemed like endless years of work and coordination, which was now on the cusp of commercial success.

Antonio was ready to blaze his own path from the coffee legacy of his ancestors. Wayne and Mario were thrilled to be part of their friend's success, and the research told them they could be on the beginning of a hot trend. Columbian red wines were in their infancy but were gaining in popularity.

Plus, they missed Antonio from their days as idealistic college kids at the University of Southern California. For Soledad, this was a chance to use her international business degree the way she had planned. Over the last few years, she had arbitrated fair market deals in the States for cheese producers in Great Britain, alpaca sweaters out of Patagonia, and now wine from Columbia. Not only was this her biggest deal yet, it had also brought her love.

Antonio Lazaro-Alvarez started as only a business interest. At first she wasn't sure he could pull it off, the youngest son of a coffee empire trying to make a go of it in the wine business. Mutual business interest turned to admiration and then love. For the first few months, she flew back and forth. Then she closed her stateside housekeeping business and gave notice at the White Sand Island Coffee Shop and Bar to focus on Lalvarez Wineries.

An hour after dinner, Antonio and Soledad were in the casita alone. There was electricity but no television and spotty cellular service. Mellow guitar music filled the air, played by the workers as they sat around the campfires at the bottom of the hill near the bunkhouses. The first time they made love in that very casita, Antonio downloaded all kinds of music to play on his cellphone, but Soledad had told him to turn it off, and they listened to the songs of the workers and the music of nature. Ever since that night, she hated leaving him, hated leaving the hills of Venecia.

"Everything OK?" he asked as he laid in bed, his back against the Spanish cedar headboard. She was lying across him, her head on his stomach. Her legs were intertwined with his legs with a sheet half covering, half tangled between them.

"Of course," she said, then kissed the round mounds of his six pack.

"You didn't drink that much. You love the malbec. That's why I chose it."

"Yeah, I love it too much," she said, rising up and kissing him lovingly. "If I had drank as much as I wanted to, you would be talking to an unconscious woman right now."

"Lightweight," he said, then hugged her. "Sole, I can barely believe where we are right now."

"You mean about to get eaten up by night bugs in this casita?" she asked, laughing as she silenced his protest with a kiss. "I know what you mean, my love. I have never seen a man carve his own unique path in the soil of his ancestors. Do you know how proud I am of you, how proud I am to be a part of this journey?"

"It wouldn't have happened without you," he said. They kissed, and he felt her fingers deftly stroke him under the sheet.

"And it's soooo sexy," she said as she climbed on top of him. They added their own rhythm and music to the melodies of night and nature.

2

The Lazaro home complex sat on the northwest corner of the estate. The western wing belonged to the woman of the estate, Luisa Lazaro-Alvarez, the oldest child and only daughter of Alexandro. No one came to that wing without being summoned. That's why she was able to be there, undisturbed, with her lover.

Paulo Diallo stood out on the balcony, his tall, muscular brown body seeming to glow in the moonlight. The balcony was a walled structure that faced the wooded, hilly scrub land, occupied by coyotes and jaguars.

Luisa never got tired of watching his body, clothed or not.

Paulo was a descendent from the first families of San Basilio de Palenque—the first free town of former slaves in the Western Hemisphere. Tonight he seemed like one of those leery animals from the woods, on the verge of striking out at some unseen danger. The muscular curves of his tan back flexed and relaxed with every movement, and she wished he would return to bed and ease the craving that was reigniting inside her.

"You giving the coyotes and night birds a peep show?" she teased. He gave a barely perceptible nod. She sighed, realizing that if she was going to get any additional attention, she would have to leave the comfort of her custom-built king-size bed.

Stepping out onto the balcony, she slipped her arms around him. She was wearing her cream silk robe, but she kept it open, so her naked front could be against his naked, muscular backside. His body felt as stiff as the nut trees that shaded the coffee crop. The only indication he recognized her presence was his hand that covered hers as it rested on his flat, smooth stomach. She kissed his shoulder blades, tasting his scent and the salt of his sweat.

"Que esta mal, mi amor?" she asked, inquiring as to what was on his mind.

"Nothing," he responded quickly, but she could guess what was wrong.

"Paulo, you know this thing, this whole thing is more complicated than you and me."

"Mmmm-hmm," he said, still looking out over the darkness beyond the wall.

"If it were up to me . . ." She trailed off as she felt his hand drop from hers and his body stiffen slightly as he leaned away from her.

Luisa was not a soft woman, a pleading woman, or a woman trained in the art of softening the hardness of a man. She was raised with men. She competed with men, worked alongside them. Her beauty was that of a strong, handsome woman. She had a worker's tanned skin and athletic muscle tone but a beauty's fine features, including intelligent light-brown eyes, a perfect nose, and full lips.

The fact that he was the one who vibrated her feminine and sexual spirit was a testament to Paulo as a man. Nevertheless, this was something she did not do well. She walked back inside, flopped back on the bed, and reached for her Dannemann cigarillo.

Paulo walked back into the bedroom. She was laying on the bed looking introspective, focusing on nothing particular. Her beautiful form was enveloped in the smoke from the ancestral tobacco that she slowly exhaled from her nose. The whole scene invited him back to bed like a siren call to wayward sailors. His pride told him to get dressed and strongly consider never returning to this room.

"You thirsty?" she asked. He shrugged indifferently.

"Good, I'll make a drink for both of us," she said, laying the cigarillo in a ridiculously large ashtray. She moved from the room with that same long stride she used when she worked the fields, her satin robe flowing like a cape. Who was he fooling? He wasn't leaving.

Paulo Diallo was a fixture on the Lazaro Coffee estate. He came as a boy when his father was Alexandro's top field boss. Paulo had higher ambitions. He wanted to be a master roaster and taster, eventually packaging and selling flavored coffees under his own brand. Lazaro roasted their specialty holiday coffees onsite, but most of their product was roasted and processed by Venecia Roasting House.

Paulo and the Lazaro children played together, were separated by work and class as teenagers, and, as adults, fell into the familiar roles of employer and employee. Then Luisa began spending more time in the field, excelling in the crop sciences. It brought her in close contact with her old childhood friend. They were surprised by how well they had grown into their adult bodies even though they did not say so at first.

Over time they fell into a familiar friendship, sharing their frustrations, hopes, dreams, and passions. Alexandro wished she was in the office more, helping him run the company until Fernando, her brother and the oldest son, was ready to stop playing and get serious. She hated office politics, corporate cat-and-mouse games played by soft men and women who were too weak to do a job that required sweat.

Sometime over the last twelve months, friendship turned to heavy but secretive flirting and then a full-blown love affair. Alexandro was constantly parading milquetoast men to the dinner table in hopes of creating an alliance if not an actual love connection for her. She entertained them, several of them, for the longest time. It kept her father off of her back, and as men, they were very manageable.

After Paulo, however, she simply ignored them all.

Paulo was also a very popular catch in Venecia Valley. He was the "jack of all trades" at the largest coffee estate in the region. Alexandro consulted with him regularly on everything from equipment to crop quality, pest management, and worker disputes. Paulo was the one who convinced Alexandro to give Antonio the small southern hillsides for wine production, as the coffee there was seldom the best quality, and it cost far too much to harvest compared to other areas on the estate.

Luisa and Paulo had done a good job of keeping their secret. They knew Alexandro would not allow it. He would surely have Paulo fired and blackballed from working anywhere in the region. She would never let that happen to him. However, they missed having all the fun a couple could and should have, such as going to concerts, dining in public, and the joy of sharing their relationship with friends and family.

That night on the balcony, it was the subject of Paulo's ambition to be a master roaster/taster that was bothering him. Long before they reconnected, he went to the coffee academy in Bogota, graduating with the level of master roaster.

He had approached Alexandro on multiple occasions about being his onsite roaster/taster, but Alexandro wouldn't hear of it. He would let

Paulo second chair the roasting of the holiday brands, but that was it. He finally asked his secret girlfriend to speak up on his behalf, but she refused.

"How would that look?" she asked as she stirred her own drink with her finger. "I don't have a corporate reason to request that you leave your current role to become a master roaster/taster."

"Is it not in the company's interest to at least do some of their own roasting and processing?" he said as he slipped his boxers on and plopped down on the bed.

"He trusts Polonia at Venecia Roasting," Luisa replied, returning to the bed and handing him a dark rum over ice.

"It's not a matter of trust. It's a matter of having systems in place in case of future need," he said, animated now, gesturing with the drink in his hand. "We have multiple suppliers of everything from fertilizer to tractor tires."

"That's to create competition and keep the prices down," she said.

"OK, so why not in processing too? What happens if demand goes beyond what Venecia can handle? What happens if Polonia Meneses gets hit by a bus or has an equipment failure?"

She just looked at him.

"No, I would never do that. C'mon, Isa," he said, using a pet name for her that no one else ever used except him and only when they were alone.

"I don't know, my love," she said with a chuckle, attempting to lighten the mood. "You seem so adamant."

He didn't even smile in reply, so she hurried to fill the pregnant silence.

"When it comes to you, the number one thing is to keep this from my father."

"You sound ashamed of this all of a sudden."

"Don't be absurd," she replied. "I love you, but if news of our relationship got out, my father would banish you far from here and make it look like he had nothing to do with it."

"Banish?" he asked, genuinely surprised at the term. "Then maybe I should go."

He finished his drink and moved to get out of bed, but she snatched him back with a ferocity that surprised him. He fell onto his back, and in a one swift motion, she was on top of him, straddling his hips.

"You can't go, mi amor," she said leaning over and whispering in his ear, her long sun-faded hair caressing his face. "Because I have never been this healthy, happy, or productive. I love you, and I need you."

She took a sip of her drink and then kissed him, depositing some of her rum into his mouth. He drank it in heavily like he did everything about her. In his mind he had a ferocious verbal response to what she had just said, but it broke into a thousand pieces and blew away in the scirocco that was Luisa. He felt her deft touch as she reached down between her legs to his growing eagerness.

Yeah, another time, he thought, *another place.*

3

Fernando Matias Lazaro-Alvarez was in the back of his Venecia village coffee shop and private club throwing up in the bathroom. His custom-made Almacen Lord suit was still in decent shape given that he had been living in it for the last forty-eight hours.

It had started in Medellin where he was trying to gamble his way out of debt. Then trying to gamble his way out of more debt. Then he fled Medellin and traveled almost two hours to where he always went when he was in trouble: Venecia.

Municipio de Venecia Antioquia was a small village that was gaining notoriety as a tourist stop of majestic mountainous beauty. It was also the village just down the hill from the Lazaro Coffee estate, his home and birthright.

He could go to his father, but this would be the third time his gambling had gotten out of control. Sitting on the floor of the cramped toilet stall of his coffee shop, Fernando remembered his father's word on his future.

"I have bankrolled a high-end restaurant in Medellin and a coffee shop in Venecia. Either you make them profitable, or you will finally consent to come into business with me."

Fernando did not know what made him sicker: the third time being on the run from money lenders, the abject failure of two businesses in which he had been set up for success, or the thought of a life on the coffee estate. On more than one occasion, Fernando had thought of just running off to England or the United States and starting over, maybe under an assumed name. Then he had gambled away his runaway fund.

Just as morning illuminated the sleepy village, Fernando found peaceful sleep on the coffee shop bathroom's floor. It was cool and quiet. He started to dream about leaving the coffee shop closed for three days and sleeping the whole time. He just wanted to rest.

His dream was interrupted when large hands grabbed his lapels and yanked him to his feet. He was being dragged, but he could not get his eyes to focus. Those same hands slapped him twice, and his vision finally became clear.

"Munch, what are you slapping me for?" Fernando asked the oversized muscle. Munch just stood silently over Fernando, who was now sitting in the chair in his office.

"Nando, you left Medellin without saying goodbye," a voice said from the corner. It was Graves, Munch's partner. Fernando never saw one without the other. Munch was the big one, but short, skinny, slow-talking Graves was the real danger. He was the detached emotional being who was incapable of love, warmth, or even camaraderie, but it made him an excellent killer. And just like Fernando that morning, no one ever saw him coming.

"The problem is you left town owing the lady six figures. You promised you were going to make it good," Graves said. He turned his skeletal face with its tight, pock-marked skin toward the sun streaming through the office window and pointed a long slender knife held with bony fingers toward that same window.

"It's a new day, and you ain't made good."

Before Fernando could start lying, Munch punched him in the stomach. He fell out of the chair and curled into the fetal position. The thought struck him that they might kill him that morning. What surprised him was the twinkle in the corner of his mind that thought it wouldn't be a bad idea.

"Get up, Nando," Graves continued. "We ain't gonna send you home to Daddy all bruised up. We don't need that kind of heat."

Munch picked him up and pushed him back in his seat. Seeing the tears streaming down Fernando's face made Munch want to punch him again. Pitiful rich boy.

"She has plans for how you can work off your debt," Graves said.

"Yeah, how?" Fernando asked.

"It don't matter. Whatever it is, you're going to do it."

4

Three days later, on Monday morning, it was Lazaro tradition for everyone to make an appearance at the small dining table in the breakfast room. There was sausage, eggs, and various breads, but there was very little eating. Monday morning breakfast gave Alexandro Lazaro a chance to flesh out instructions to his children for the week. Such breakfasts were a lot warmer when Victoria, their mother, was alive. That was a long time ago, and the heartache was still too hard for Alexandro.

Luisa walked in first, all business in her beige fieldwork clothes. Paulo had slipped out of her room just hours earlier. She found it hard to sleep once he left. Six women from the fields followed her single file past her father, the kitchen, and into the back room. Each woman pulled a wagon of assorted decorations, dresses and sashes, electronic equipment and lighting, fruits of various kinds, and mounds of candy.

"What are you wearing? What is all this?" he asked as Alexandro watched the women with cool superiority. Luisa gave the women some final direction and a thank-you. They smiled broadly and then scampered out the back door, avoiding eye contact with Alexandro.

He was standing just inside the doorway to the dining room. Though only five foot eight inches, he seemed taller. He had a proud, manly Colombian stance with broad shoulders. He had his hair dyed and styled every week. He looked like a model for classic corporate dress wear.

"Good morning to you as well," Luisa said as she poured a cup of coffee for him and then set it at his placemat next to a platter of *bocadillo veleño,* a guava cube encased in a soft bread. She pulled his chair out, and he walked over and sat down. She leaned over and kissed his cheek.

"I'm in the field today. We have a good bean load to pick," she explained. "This will be the last production push before traviesa, our slow period."

"Yes, yes, but what was that parade of fieldworkers tromping their dirty shoes through my house?"

"Oh, Papa," Luisa said, hiding her chuckle behind her coffee mug. "It's for the holiday. Dia de la Independencia."

"I know the holiday is coming, daughter, the Independence Day of Cartagena," Alexandro said with a sigh.

"Good. Then you also recognize the ingredients for our Fiesta de la Independencia? The Pageant? The Bandos?" Luisa asked as if she were speaking to a child. "Surely, you wouldn't want to be the only farm not contributing to the holiday. The bad luck alone . . ."

"Yes, very well, Luisa," Alexandro said irritably. She was right about participating in Independence Day. Plus, he had forgotten all about it. "But I need you in the office today. We have contract extensions to review on field equipment, and the tax advisors want some time on the schedule today."

"Papa, you know Mondays are my field days. That was our agreement. Besides, you have an army of lawyers and yes-men for that."

"No! I need you there today," he said in that voice that made Luisa feel like she had no choice.

"I'll see what I can do in the afternoon," she replied.

"Why do you insist on playing in the dirt? In the elements—"

"With the common people?" she said with a sarcastic smirk. "Remember, these are the people you worked with when you started. The people Grandfather worked alongside as well."

"That was different," he said. "We're a different company now. We talked about this. I need you to help me—"

"Yes, help you keep things afloat until Fernando comes to his senses."

"Yes," he whispered, looking around to see if anyone was listening.

"Then I can go away and get married or something."

"You're being sarcastic. No one is going to marry you with that freckled, sunburned skin and frazzled hair."

"Now you're just trying to be hurtful. You can't be that backwards and still be my father."

"Backwards about what?" Antonio asked as he entered the room. He was dressed in work clothes as well, a brown slouch bag hanging off his shoulder. He kissed his sister and squeezed his father's shoulders before sitting down and filling his plate.

"And what are you dressed as?" Alexandro asked.

"Today we're loading and shipping wine. It's the first shipment from Lalvarez Wineries."

"That's wonderful, Tonio. I had no idea you were this far along."

Antonio reached into the bag that hung off the back of his chair and pulled out two bottles of wine. He handed one to Luisa and sat the other one in front of his father. Each bottle had a blood-red label. The letters L and W were in a classic old-world font. The rest of the lettering was cursive across a drawing of a wine bottle. All of that was over a faded relief drawing of the Venecia hill country.

"Impressive," Luisa said.

"Hmm . . . seems like a lot of expense on labeling. Good wine doesn't need such fancy labeling," Alexandro said, looking at the bottle but not touching it.

"Papa, what do you know about wine? I love the label. I'll try it tonight," Luisa said.

"Thanks, but I couldn't have done it without Wayne, Mario, and Soledad."

"Of course, the magical Soledad," Luisa said. It was her turn to roll her eyes.

"I like her," Alexandro replied with a devilish grin. "She has good ideas. Modern ideas. I may hire her for the coffee operations."

"No, no, Papa, she has a job with Lalvarez Wineries," Antonio said playfully.

"We'll see how much you like her when she has Antonio living in America half the year," Luisa said.

"What? Is this true?" Alexandro asked, alarm rising in his voice.

"Not in so many words, Papa," Luisa replied with a sardonic tone. "But in every conversation, she likes to let it slip out about how beautiful the beaches are in Florida, all the great airports, all the wine opportunities."

"So, she's proud of her home," Antonio said.

"She doesn't fool me, little Tonio; she has designs on you," Luisa said, pointing at him with a piece of toast.

"Well, that wouldn't be so bad," Antonio said, a goofy smile on his face. "Maybe she'll move here."

"Now that's an idea," Alexandro said.

"No," Luisa exclaimed.

The two men looked at her in surprise. She dropped her toast, stood, and turned to leave the room.

"I'm late," she mumbled.

She ran headlong into Fernando and Daniela Jasper entering the room. Daniela was the daughter of the family solicitor, Ernesto Jasper. She and Fernando have been on some level of involvement for the last five years.

In the collision, Luisa spilled her coffee on her work shirt. She cursed all the way out the door.

"No man is going to marry a woman who curses like that!" Alexandro shouted.

Antonio and Fernando laughed heartily.

"What are you two laughing at?" Alexandro said, looking at Fernando with a deadpan expression. "'Nando, you're late."

"I just got in from Medellin," he said nervously.

"I apologize, Mr. Lazaro, but I'm afraid I was the reason Fernando was late," Daniela said. "I've been after him to update his incorporation charter. I finally got him to slow down long enough to get it done."

Alexandro had already been told by his army of employees, acquaintances, hangers-on, and outright spies that Fernando's black Range Rover Velar had roared into the village in the middle of the night, but he decided to let it slide. It was good to see him with Daniela. Some sanity in his life.

"How are things, little brother?" Fernando asked. "Wine about ready to ship soon?"

"You know about the wine?" Alexandro asked in surprise.

"Of course I know about the wine," Fernando said.

"You do?" Antonio asked, just as surprised as his father.

"Yes," Fernando continued. "It's only been a dream of yours since you were in college with your cute little friends, Mario and Wayne."

"What do you think of the label?" Antonio asked. "Papa thinks it's too expensive."

"What? No," Fernando said, laughing as he examined the bottle. "Don't worry about it. Papa has but one single love: coffee. Everything else, not so much."

"Thank you, Nando. Soledad and I spent a lot of time on the design."

"Yes, when are we going to meet the famous business partner from America?"

"You're the only one who hasn't met her," Alexandro said. "I may only know coffee, but at least I've met my son's girlfriend."

"Girlfriend? Oooooooooo," Daniela and Fernando teased.

"Stop it! Both of you. I have wine to pack today."

"Today?" Fernando, asked, choking on his coffee. Alexandro handed him a cloth napkin with a look of disdain. "I was talking to the shipping captain at the garage. He said you weren't shipping for another week."

"Yes," Antonio said with a chuckle as he held up a bottle of malbec. "Like you said, we're ready to move forward. We're ahead of schedule, so Soledad left for Cartagena early this morning. Wayne and Mario will be heading down to the wine warehouse to supervise the loading to transport in a couple days."

Fernando jumped up, wiping spittle from his face. He mumbled something about unpredictable millennials and then hurried from the room. Daniela followed, a confused look on her face. Antonio and Alexandro watched him go and then looked at each other in bewilderment.

5

Anise Constaneda-Rodriguez was a card shark, illegal casino boss, loan shark, extortionist, and a dealer in stolen goods, but none of that paid like her latest venture. She controlled the pipeline of stolen goods between Cartagena and Buenaventura, two of Colombia's main ports. The back roads, ramshackle storage houses, and secret forest clearings, were all protected by a rag-tag army of roughnecks, down-on-their-luck farmers, bankrupt fishermen, and corrupt police officers. Illegal logging, rogue mining, and the hunting of endangered species moved through her pipeline.

Ever since she was a teenager, she had been surrounded by men who were notorious for their treachery and their skills with deadly weapons. They also resented working for a woman.

As she moved up the ranks with her own crew, many of them were older men who were loyal to her father. They were not criminals, but they were tough guys who knew how to handle themselves. If she was going to stay alive in this world, she needed something extra.

That's why her largest payoffs were to select poorly paid police officers and local government officials who were in trouble. She raised their standard of living and showered their wives with beautiful albeit stolen clothing and jewelry. She used her father's name and bribes to put their children in the best schools. They became men of importance and, therefore, they were ferociously loyal to her.

For those who did try her, she had her two "assistants": Graves and Munch.

Munch was in his late twenties, well over six feet tall, and three hundred pounds. His hands were massive from working in the oil fields and, later, the docks. Munch had a loud voice, a loud walk, and a loud punch.

Graves, however, was the dangerous one. He was twenty years older than Munch, skinny, drawn, short, and quiet. When he did speak, his voice sounded like it was being dragged over charcoal. He was deadly with a gun and silent and scary with a blade. People never saw him coming, and he never needed a second shot or more than one slice.

Munch and Graves were cousins from one of the first families in the region, a family that lost their home during the land grab orchestrated by the Lazaros and their rich friends. That family no longer existed. Now they worked for Anise.

She was the daughter of Hector Rodriquez, an elected magistrate in the central Colombian region. He had been a man of the people, winning his position due to his popularity and his ability to walk the fine line from the Kipling poem. He walked with kings but kept the common touch.

To that end, Hector entered into an agreement with some select estate owners to consolidate coffee-growing properties to create larger operations. It was going to be good for the Colombian coffee trade. Sure, it meant buying out some smaller operations, a version of eminent domain, but Hector was convinced it was what was best for the region and Colombia as a whole. He was also convinced he would be the political head of a new commercial center of the country.

However, once the large estate owners got what they wanted, they turned their back on Hector and the elected officials who helped them. They were drummed out of office, accused of corruption, and replaced with newcomers who were loyal to the estate families. One of those families was the Lazaros.

Hector eventually died of alcohol abuse and disenfranchisement in a dank, dark apartment in Bogota, right in front of his fourteen-year-old daughter, Anise. Her mother had died years earlier.

For Anise, the next seven years were times of unspeakable hardships and an emotional barrage that was either going to kill her or make her what she eventually became: a shrewd gangster who ruled her destiny with money, a gun, or the latest weapon—information.

Once she opened her gambling houses and prostitution dens, the extortion business almost fell into her lap.

The weakness of men, she thought as she sat in her flat in Medellin.

It was the multiplier of all her income. It was the world that circumstances offered to her, and she was going to show that Constaneda blood would persevere. This was how she had made her money for the last ten years. It had made her rich and given her influence, but in the process, it had stolen her spirit and made her dead inside.

Then a new fly got stuck in her web: Fernando Lazaro-Alvarez. He was loud, arrogant, and losing big in her gambling houses. Once she confirmed who he was, she could not believe her luck.

The standard plan for soft marks like Fernando was to find their fatal flaw—gambling, drugs, underage children, same-sex prostitutes—whatever threatened their squeaky-clean family name and heritage. Once she found it, she worked it like a cow's udder. Like the cows, the marks leaned into the process, a little extortion for a continued secret walk on the wild side.

This presented a new opportunity, one that filled her head with orgasmic feelings. Fernando Lazaro-Alvarez, son of Alexandro Lazaro, heir to the Lazaro coffee empire.

Alexandro Lazaro was part of the consortium that had used her father, then threw him out of office and blackballed him from any form of government. Now she had a chance to destroy one of those names.

She had him right where she wanted him.

"The stupid son of a bitch actually tried to skip town, like I wouldn't find him back in Venecia, under Daddy," she said to herself.

Munch and Graves had found him in his coffee shop. She told them to bring him to a house she owned at the north end of the village about a block away from the park. When he arrived, she put him to bed and locked him in the room. Munch and Graves brought clothes from his apartment. She fed him the best food for two days. Then on the third day, she had Munch and Graves bring him downstairs, sober, well fed, and wondering what was going on.

"Anise, I know I owe you a healthy stack of cash, and I promise I'll make it good," Fernando said the minute he came down the stairs and saw her sitting in the screened patio off the kitchen. She was dressed in her trademark Dolce & Gabbana suit and Manolo heels, stirring her tea and looking sorrowful.

"Nando," she started with a sigh, "you're one of my favorite customers. One of my favorite people."

"I am?" he asked, not expecting that response. She laughed and motioned for him to join her at the small patio table. Fernando plopped into the seat but kept looking over his shoulder.

31

"I get it," she said. "Munch and Graves, right? I sent the muscle after you, but you misunderstood. I wanted them to look after you. You left my club drunk, driving like a crazy man. I sent Munch and Graves after you to make sure you made it home OK."

"You did?" Fernando said, pouring a ridiculous amount of sugar into his tea.

"Nando, I could use a man like you in my organization."

"Really?"

"And we can find a way for you to work off your debt."

"Well, are you sure you can afford me?" he asked, sitting back and crossing his legs.

It was all she could do not to roll her eyes. Ruining the Lazaro name was going to feel so good.

6

As it turned out, Luisa didn't get to the field that morning. Alexandro guilted her into coming to the office instead. A two-hour morning meeting turned into half a day. That afternoon she was determined to get her life back.

Paulo had the horses ready just outside her wing of the estate, a white Peruvian mare for him and a . chestnut Criollo gelding for her. As they rode out together, the lady owner and her lead field boss, everything seemed right on the estate. She missed being out amongst the crops. She missed being with Paulo. He was a master horseman. He and his mount seemed to move as one.

They worked their way south from the stables on the northeast end. The estate also kept a small farm with chickens, a few milk cows, goats, and a two-acre garden.

They stopped at the covered cuttings, Luisa's experimental plant splicing. It was her laboratory where she was creating a coffee plant with better resistance to disease and insects.

Next, they found what they called the prime picker group. These were the best pickers, the fastest and most experienced to pick beans at their ripest point. Coffee beans ripened at different times. Inexperienced, eager pickers had a tendency to pick beans too soon. This group included some of the oldest pickers on the estate. Some of them had worked there as children when Luisa's grandfather was still alive.

After that they watched workers burning a portion of the field, giving it a rest. Coffee pulled a lot from the soil. It was standard practice to rest a portion of the land every year to keep from exhausting the soil. In this part of the field, the coffee plants were over twenty years old. It was time to plant new ones. It is where her experimental cuttings would go next year.

As she and Paulo rode along the main trail that divided the estate north and south, they heard the crack of a pistol, faint but distinct. She and Paulo looked toward the sound and then back at each other.

"You hear that?" she asked.

"It was a handgun," Paulo said. He barked instructions to one of the burners, a long-term estate hand who favored Paulo, probably a cousin. The field hand ran and untied a nearby horse. He and Paulo steered their mounts toward the sound of the shot. Luisa made to follow, but Paulo cut her horse off, making the gelding rear up slightly.

"Luisa, let us check it out," Paulo said, his eyes firm with determination. "It'll only take a moment."

"But that came from Antonio's vineyards," she said.

She maneuvered her mount around his and struck off down the trail between the fields. Paulo cursed, then mumbled some instructions to his kinsman. The field hand drew his Colt revolver and then took off after her.

When they entered the vineyard along the crop rows, Luisa shouted her brother's name, but Paulo shushed her. He reached into his long saddlebag and pulled out a short-barrel rifle. He also handed his Colt revolver to Luisa. She opened it to check the bullet load. Paulo instructed his kinsman to stay on the trail by the grapevines.

Following the trail past the terraces of grapevines, Luisa and Paulo came to the small warehouses. One of the buildings held the aging wine in barrels. The other one held the fully aged wine, some bottled and ready for shipment.

Guns drawn, Paulo and Luisa entered the first warehouse. No one was there, but the smell of gunsmoke was heavy in the air. They searched both buildings but found no one.

"It doesn't make sense," Luisa said. "Antonio was supposed to be moving his product today, or maybe it was yesterday."

"Was he using Lazaro trucks?" Paulo asked. She nodded. "Then where are they?"

Paulo looked around and then walked over to the wall next to the large overhead door. A clipboard was stored on a shelf there. Paulo read the pages attached to it.

"Yeah, according to this, cases and tanks of malbec are supposed to be in Cartagena in several days," he explained.

"Right," Luisa said, remembering. "Antonio's little girlfriend was already headed there."

"Where are his partners?" Paulo asked. "The Americans?"

"I don't know," Luisa said. "Paulo, can your man stay here on guard? I want to head back to the house and find Antonio. I have a bad feeling about this."

Paulo rode back up the trail from where they came to give his man instructions. Luisa rode to the opposite side of the buildings.

A river ran along the western border of the Lazaro Coffee estate. Its source was somewhere high in the hills of Venecia. By the time it got to the vineyards on the southwest corner of the estate, it was more of a lazy stream that rose and fell with the level of rainfall. On the opposite bank of the stream, the forest started for several miles to the western edge of the Lazaro Coffee estate. During that time of the year, the trees were full of parakeets and yellow tanagers, the air alive with their chirps and songs.

Luisa decided to take the trail along the stream. It was uphill, but it was the shortest way back to the main estate. As she cleared the buildings, her horse started to buck and spook. She focused on the ground, looking for snakes. There was nothing. Then she smelled it: the pungent odor of fresh blood. She had smelled it before while hunting wild game. This was different but close enough.

She dismounted her horse and stood close, making soothing sounds in the horse's ear. She held the revolver up close to her face and cocked it. She kept her head on a swivel. Then she saw a man's body about ten feet into the woods, leaning against a tree. She could see at least three holes in him, not counting the bloody hole where his left eye used to be.

She left the horse, sweeping her surroundings with the revolver as she splashed clumsily through the water to get to him. It was one of the Americans. Wayne, not Mario.

"Don't talk," she said as she reached him, pushing his arms down. He was delirious and trying to move away from her. "It's Luisa; I got you."

"M . . . M . . . Mario," he struggled to get up before he coughed up globs of blood and mucus.

"I don't know; he's not here," she replied. Wayne grabbed her wrist with a bloody hand.

"He ran. You got to find. I tried to stop them but couldn't hold them."

"Them? Who?"

Wayne tried to stand but failed. He went rigid, unable to talk anymore. All he could do was murmur. Then he pointed to something behind Luisa. She was not one to get caught from behind. She swung around behind the tree, raising the revolver and ready to squeeze the first two rounds on general principle and taking count afterwards.

Boom! Boom!

The .45-caliber explosion filled the air, sending birds flying, animals running, and poor, dying Wayne to moan. She peeked around the tree trunk. Paulo was lying on the ground, his hands over his head, but otherwise untouched.

"Paulo, sorry!"

"Sorry?" he shouted, rising to his feet. He motioned for her to lower her weapon as he sloshed across the gurgling stream. Then he bent down to inspect Wayne.

"M . . . M-Mario, still out there," Wayne gurgled.

"Who did this? How many?" Paulo asked urgently.

"Don't exert him; we need to save his energy," Luisa said, applying pressure to Wayne's chest wounds and sending an explosion of blood from his mouth.

"Isa, he's not going to make it," Paulo said. "They hit his lungs, sending blood through his windpipe."

"Two . . . two men," Wayne murmured between coughs. "Tried to stop but couldn't. M . . . Mario ran out there." He pointed a limp, bloody finger west into the forest.

Paulo got lower until his face was even with Wayne's, who was shaking uncontrollably. "I promise I'll find Mario," Paulo whispered. "Te prometo, mi hermano."

Wayne managed a nod. Paulo shouted for his man, who was standing guard. He rode up on his horse. Paulo ordered him into the forest to find Mario and cautioned him about possible gunmen.

Afterwards, things went quiet. Paulo whispered a prayer over Wayne's still body, and Luisa sobbed softly as the birds continued to sing in the trees.

7

Antonio was all over the place when Luisa found him in his makeshift office on the estate. They called the local authorities, sheriff and deputies who were more experienced with livestock disputes and fights between local teenagers than murder. They seldom handled anything as serious as homicide.

Luisa tried to reach their father. His phone went to voicemail. She called his personal secretary. No one seemed to know where he was. All they knew was that he was out for an appointment.

"I have to go search for Mario," Antonio said, heading off to change his clothes.

"No you don't," Luisa said, pushing him back down. "Paulo and the deputies will look for Mario. There are killers out there."

"And they killed Wayne. He was my friend. Wayne came down here to help me, and now he's dead."

"I know, little brother, and I promise that we'll find out who did this, but we have to be smart."

Just then Fernando barged into the room.

"What the hell is going on?" he asked, his voice full of emotion and his eyes wide. "I just talked to the deputy out front."

"Where have you been?" Luisa asked. "Where's Papa?"

"I don't know. I was just leaving for the coffeehouse, and I . . . Is it true? Is Wayne dead?"

"Yes, and Mario is on the run. I got to call Sole. The shipment has to be halted. The suppliers . . ." Antonio stopped and paced, trying to control his emotions. Fernando stepped in front of his brother and hugged him for a long time, soothing him. Luisa wasn't sure what she was seeing, but she just watched.

"Lazaro One, come in."

It was the walkie-talkie resting on the charging station. Luisa walked over and picked it up.

"Lazaro One, come back," she said.

"This is Team Paulo. No sign of Mario or the others. Still on the search," Paulo said.

"Where are you?" Luisa asked.

"Along the southwest border, working our way back to the estate. When we get back, we'll have to deal with the wine shipment. Trucks, cases, and tanks are still sitting out in the access road, waiting to be loaded."

Luisa looked at Antonio, who shook his head.

"Wait," Fernando said, holding a hand up to Luisa. "Antonio, I want to propose something."

"Nando, I hear what you're saying about business, but I . . . I just can't."

"You don't have to. We can do it together. Just hear me out," Fernando said, grabbing his brother by the shoulders. "You stay here. Find Mario, and handle your friend's remains. Let me get your shipment to Cartagena. I'll meet Soledad in Cartagena, and I'll direct the shippers."

"No, Nando, you don't even know her. I need to speak to Papa and—"

"Brother, this is your time," Fernando replied, almost shouting. "If you call Father, all he's going to do is shut down your operation, control the news so it doesn't affect the coffee business, and your little wine operation will never see the light of day."

"So, what should I do?" Antonio asked, his eyes full of tears.

"I know I haven't been around a lot, but I am your older brother. Be guided by my council. Stay here and do the right thing by your friends. Paulo will give you all the assistance you need. Let Soledad and I handle the product. Trust me with your baby. Let's show Papa we're the masters of our own destiny. That we don't need to go to him."

Antonio looked at his sister. "Luisa, what do you think?"

Luisa was still surprised by Fernando's initiative. "It can work," she said finally. "Paulo and I will give you all you need. I've tried calling Papa, but he's not answering."

"Of course it can work," Fernando said, grinning broadly. "I need you to give me the OK, little brother. This is your show. I promise I won't let you down."

The siblings sat silently in the home office.

Luisa wanted to get back out on the property to help look for Mario and protect Paulo's blind side. Antonio had at least eight things on his mind at the same time. His heart was breaking for his dead friend. Fernando was trying to look sincere, hoping they wouldn't realize what he was doing.

"OK, Nando. I'm trusting you," Antonio said. "I'll let Soledad know you're coming."

"No," Fernando said, almost too excitedly. Antonio and Luisa gave him a quizzical look. "I mean, not yet. Wait until you have news of Mario. If you tell her too soon, she'll want to return to the estate. We need her to focus on the shipment with me. I can't do it without her."

"That actually makes sense, Antonio," Luisa said, thinking she had enough to deal with without the perky Soledad with all her take-control "American-ness." "Let Fernando tell her. By the time he gets to Cartagena with the shipment, you and I will have news of Mario."

Antonio eventually allowed himself to be led by his older siblings. He got into his riding clothes and followed Luisa out on the hunt for Mario. Luisa was on horseback. Antonio, two farmhands, and one of the local deputies rode on horses and all-terrain vehicles.

Fernando took his pickup truck down the main trail to the wine operation. Two trucks were parked next to the buildings. Fernando got out of his truck and called for the driver. Two hulking, shady characters stepped out of one of the wine buildings. They tucked their guns when they saw Fernando.

"We thought you were more unexpected company," one of the drivers said.

"What happened out there?" Fernando asked.

"Don't know," the other driver said. "Munch was supposed to meet us here. You said no one was going to be here."

"They weren't, but how did they end up shooting people?" Fernando asked, his voice hoarse with emotion.

"Not our problem. You want to talk to the boss lady, or you want to move the product and pay your debt?"

"Who do you think you're talking to?" Fernando asked, getting in their faces. "This is my family business."

"Either show us the barrels we need to move or tell us to leave, but get out of my face before we add to the body count," one of the drivers said.

39

"Don't threaten me," Fernando said, showing a rare case of machismo. "Ask your boss if she wants me dead before I repay my debt."

The two drivers pulled their guns, not saying a word. Fernando leaned back instinctively. Then he stepped forward again. The drivers just looked at him with non-blinking hooded eyes.

"Hey," Fernando said with a nervous laugh, "we're all on the same side. Follow me. I'll show you the wine."

Alexandro Lazaro laid back in the wide king-size bed, smoking a Don Tomas cigar. He was in one of the private residences of Polonia Agapitos-Meneses.

Polonia, fifty, was the most affluent and politically powerful woman in Venecia Valley. Her Venecia Roasting House, started by the family of her deceased husband, processed three fourths of the coffee beans harvested in the Venecia Mountains. She and her husband and Alexandro had been associates for years. Polonia and Victoria Lazaro had been in the same social circles and charity committees.

Polonia and Alexandro became friends and then lovers for practical reasons. Both of them were lonely after the death of their spouses. Victoria Lazaro had died from a brain aneurysm. Gorge Agapitos had died of a heart attack on his yacht during a fishing trip.

Neither Alexandro or Polonia were ready to be identified with a new significant other. However, they shared a bed regularly, where they discussed their competitors, allies, regulators, and workers. Aside from the sex, they had discovered the benefits of regularly comparing notes.

The coffee producers and processors in central Colombia were a small, close-knit, but understandably competitive group. Most of them were like the Lazaros, a multigenerational operation almost one hundred years old, run by the founder's male descendant.

Venecia Roasting House was the anomaly seeing as it was a processing operation run by a female and did not grow its own coffee beans. Polonia had made herself irreplaceable because she was local. Most other roasters were closer to the shipping cities of Cartagena or Buenaventura.

In addition to roasting, she also graded, labeled, and packaged product. Once growers released their crop to her, she could handle everything else.

She educated her roasters and tasters, paying to send them to the best schools all over the world, in exchange for exclusive contracts.

Lastly, her relatives, the Meneses family, had worked in Colombia's ports for sixty years. From the guard staff at the main gate to the quartermaster bookkeeper's office, to the loading foremen, they had a hand in all aspects of the ports' business.

If there was a problem with a shipment, Polonia could make a single phone call and be one person away from the solution. She even used her connections to settle shipping issues with those who processed their coffee crop with other roasting houses. Like her husband before her, Polonia was a necessary step to move coffee through Venecia Antioquia.

That afternoon, Alexandro watched her small, tight body move from the bed to the kitchen and back in her matching lavender bra and high-cut French panties. Her shoulder-length auburn hair framed a face with strong Spanish and Caribbean tribal features. Her brown eyes seemed to glow in the natural light that filled the room. She had a wide smile and full, rich lips that gave her face a youthful appearance.

She reminded Alexandro of the beautiful girls who danced in the cafés during Venecia festivals when he was a young boy. He thought she was the sexiest woman he had ever known, and he had known a lot of women before and after his wife.

She walked around in her underwear making afternoon coffee with heavy cream and spice for him and tea for her.

I really could watch her all day, he thought.

"I love it when you're like this," she said as she placed the tray on the bed and handed him a cup. "You're just smiling."

"What? You make me sound like a clown," he said, taking a sip.

"No, never," she replied, her hands on her lace-covered hips. "But you walk around like a balled-up fist. Like all you estate owners. But when you're with me, you're . . ."

"What?"

"Happy. Generally happy," she said, then turned around to give him another full view of her.

Alexandro let out a low laugh. He placed his cigar in a large crystal ashtray. He patted the side of the bed next to him. Polonia slid in next to him. He grabbed her by the face, pulling her close. He kissed her full and long on her lips. Her kiss tasted like Asian spice, lemongrass tea. His kiss was a combination of sugared coffee, fine tobacco, and his sandalwood cologne.

"Yeah, happy," she said as she pulled away. She sat on her haunches and picked up her tea, taking a sip. "So, who's watching the store today?"

"Nobody," he said, sipping his coffee. "Luisa was there, but—"

"But she wants to be in the fields," Polonia said, finishing his line. "When is Fernando going to take over?"

"I don't know. I don't know. He'd rather run his restaurant in Medellin and the coffeehouse in Venecia."

"How's that going?" she asked. "Is he profitable?"

"Huh, hardly. But he's a Lazaro. He'll come around."

Polonia was silent, but Alexandro didn't miss it.

"What? What do you know?" he asked.

"Nothing, baby," she said nervously. "You know I hear things here and there. He has a rough crowd in that place sometimes."

"Aaaaggghhh," Alexandro said with a wave of his hand. "He's young. I used to do my share of dirt when I was young."

Doing the mental math, Polonia put Fernando's age at just shy of forty, but she sipped her tea and stayed silent. She had intimate knowledge of all three of Alexandro's kids.

She knew Fernando was in money trouble with gamblers. Again.

She was the one who finally convinced Alexandro to let Antonio have the land for the winery.

Antonio had even come to her for advice on how to secure shipping container space for his wine on his own, so he didn't have to ask his father.

She tried to tell him that his daughter, Luisa, preferred to be in the field than the office.

Alexandro was a lot of things, but above all, he was proud. If she had personal knowledge of his family before him, his pride could not take it. They were his greatest love and his biggest blind spot.

8

"A nise! What are you doing?" Fernando asked the female smuggler/
loan shark/extortionist, spittle shooting from his mouth, some of
which landed on the skirt of her Carolina Herrera suit. They were in
the back office of Teresa's, his restaurant in Medellin. It was one of the
popular places for tourists who came to Medellin. Fernando was in his
chair behind the office desk. Anise was sitting on the opposite side, her
legs crossed. Her permanent backups, Munch and Graves, were standing
behind Fernando's chair on either side of him.

"Graves killed Wayne and Mario."

"I didn't kill nobody," Graves said, his face half in shadow. "The fool
went after the gun."

"Then how did he get three bullets in his chest?" Fernando asked.

Anise, her face blank, turned back to Graves.

"We fought for the gun. He got his finger on the trigger, and it emp-
tied the clip. Most of them went into the wall and the floor. Three of 'em
hit the wine guy."

"But none hit you? Graves, do you think I'm a fool?" Fernando shouted. Munch just shrugged at the question and kept looking at his nails.

"But that is a good question, Nando," Anise said, brushing her skirt
with a handkerchief. "Do you think I'm a fool? You owe me over 950
million Colombian pesos or just under $250,000 US dollars. As a way
of working off that debt, you were supposed to allow us room in the

coffee shipment!"

Munch stepped forward and pressed his gun into Fernando's temple. Fernando raised his hands and sat back in his chair.

"Now imagine my disappointment when I found out that my property was going in Junior's wine shipment," Anise said.

Munch smacked Fernando with the barrel of the gun, sending him sprawling to the floor.

"And now I ask you, what are you doing?" Anise continued.

Fernando got to his knees, holding his hands up for capitulation and protection. "Anise, just hear me out. I'm with you. But you got to know the scrutiny on coffee shipments is deeeeep and wiiiide." Fernando said the last words with hand gestures and a deeper voice. "My brother's shipment is so small, and it will go under the Lazaro flag. We won't get noticed."

"OK," Anise said, looking interested now. "But when you don't tell me ahead of time, and your happy puppy of a brother jumps the timetable, then the consequences are on you, right? *Right*?"

"Yes, I agree," Fernando said as Munch stepped closer, extending his gun hand.

Anise stood and moved Munch's gun off to the side, away from Fernando's sweaty face.

"Nando, we're good. I like you. We have a good time, but business is business. So, tell me how you're going to fix this, and I won't have to send Munch and Graves onto the Lazaro Coffee estate to kill your father, sister, and brother, ransack your estate for everything of value, and set it ablaze. Afterwards, I'll send falsified documents to the media making it look like you hired people to kill them for the insurance money."

"Th-th-that won't be necessary," Fernando said, rising slowly to his feet, his eyes wide with fear. "I have your guys picking up the shipment and putting your product in the FlexiTanks while my brother and the field hands are looking for Mario. Just please don't kill them."

Munch bumped Fernando's head with the butt of his gun.

"What about my product, Nando?" Anise demanded.

"I'm going to Cartagena to meet the shipment and Soledad to make sure that things get off OK."

"Who's she?" Anise asked.

"Antonio's girlfriend and partner in the wine business. I got Antonio to hold off telling her and convinced him to allow me to help him with his shipment. Anise, I got it under control."

Anise gave him a severe, murderous stare. Munch stood to Fernando's left, his gun just out of sight. Then, as if with the flick of a switch, she smiled and stepped back. Then she turned toward the door, Munch and Graves moving in her wake.

"OK, Nando," she said, her voice even and low. "We'll do it your way. Get my product onto the ship and to our customers in the States."

"Of course, Anise. Don't worry," Fernando said, recovering his composure.

"Mi amor, I never do," she said as she closed the door behind her.

9

Soledad arose early on the tenth day and headed for the cargo hanger where their wine was to be delivered and placed in their assigned cargo box. It had been the hardest week and a half of her life.

Something had gone wrong at the winery. According to Fernando, Antonio was handling it, but he needed her to stay in Cartagena and receive the shipment.

It started on days one and two; she only spoke to Fernando, Antonio's older brother, whom she had never met. She had not heard good things about this brother, but that was from Luisa, who didn't seem to like anyone. She wanted to be strong for Antonio, to show him he could depend on her.

On day four, she rose early and headed to the port. On the way she realized she had not talked to her brother, JD, for some time. Cell service was outrageously expensive. She got an international calling card and tried to reach JD. When it went to voicemail, she left a short message.

"Hey JD, it's Sole. Just wanted to say hi."

Sometimes the less said to her brother, the better. She had promised to stay in touch, but if they had a conversation, he would pull out everything that was happening. And then what would she say? She didn't know what the emergency was, but she knew what JD would do. He would be down in Colombia, guns blazing, to "rescue" her and drag her back home from the "trouble she had gotten herself into." He would disregard all the good work she had done. Plus, she hadn't told JD about Antonio and her.

I just want to have one serious relationship without my big brother looking over my shoulder.

No, this was big-girl business. If she didn't handle it correctly, no one would ever trust her. Not JD and not Antonio, and she needed Antonio's trust more than ever.

Day five was the worst. All alone, she finally got the nerve to do what was in the back of her mind for the past month. With all the wine business going on, it was easy not to think about it, but now she was alone with her own thoughts. She had taken several pregnancy tests, and they came back positive every time. On top of that, she hadn't heard from Antonio yet. It would have been a nice evening to get drunk in her room and go to sleep, but . . .

Day eight was the second time she heard from big brother, Fernando.

"Good news, Soledad Marie. The shipment is on its way. I'll meet you in Cartagena, and we'll get thewine on the ship."

"That's great. Is Antonio around? He's not answering his phone."

"That's my fault. I told him I would stay in touch with you, and I failed to do so. My apologies."

"That doesn't instill me with confidence," Soledad said sourly. "I've been waiting for over a week."

"Aaaahhh, you must remember, this is Colombia. Sometimes things move slowly. Not like in the United States."

"I didn't think manners were extinct in Colombia," she mumbled, then remembered that she wanted to be there for Antonio, so she shouldn't insult his brother.

"OK, Fernando, what's next?"

"I'll be there tomorrow, and I'm sure in a couple of days you will hear from Antonio. He's in the field on some family business. Phone service is not the best in the hills of Venecia."

"What about Wayne and Mario? The American partners?"

"They're with Antonio," Fernando replied. "Perdoneme, Señorita, but I must tie up some loose ends here if I'm to meet you tomorrow. I can answer more of your questions when we meet. Goodbye."

So, on the tenth day, Soledad rose early and headed to the port where her shipment of wine was scheduled to be loaded. She was met by a larger-than-life Fernando Lazaro-Alvarez.

He was dressed in off-white linen pants and a stiff navy-blue cotton windbreaker over a tight long-sleeve sailing T-shirt, all very expensive material. He was taller and slimmer than Antonio. Even though he was less than ten years older, his eyes looked like that of a much older man. Expensive clothes couldn't hide skin that was suffering from a lack of time outside.

"Soledad Marie! At last we meet," he said, his arms outstretched.

"Just Soledad," she said as she allowed his hug. "Good to meet you, Fernando."

"Call me Nando," he said, smiling broadly as he released her. "You're practically family."

What has Antonio said about me? she wondered.

"Come, let's get a coffee and talk. This must be so exciting. My little brother in the wine business. Oh, my father is livid."

"He is?" Soledad asked, looking concerned. "Antonio told me that Señor Lazaro approved of this."

"Oh, he did," Fernando said. "But secretly, I think the old man assumed it would fail, and Antonio would lose interest. But here we are! About to ship our first batch to the States. So exciting for us all."

Our first batch? she thought. *Since when did he lift a finger to produce wine?*

They walked away from the port toward the small commercial square nearby. It contained one of the quartermaster stations, a few warehouses that also sold shipping supplies, and a few eateries. There were some bars, but they only opened after sundown.

"Where's Antonio? What's the emergency? And why haven't I heard from Wayne and Mario?"

There, she got it out. She had struggled with whether to say anything. She wanted to look like she was in control, like what Antonio needed, but she had to know.

Fernando motioned for her to follow him to the nearest table. They sat, and almost instantly a waitress appeared to take their order.

"OK, you got questions. I understand," he said and then paused.

Soledad just stared at him, eyes wide in anticipation.

"There was an accident at the winery," he said. "I don't know what happened exactly, but Wayne was injured."

"Oh no," Soledad said.

"Mario has been offline trying to take care of him. Antonio feels sick about the whole thing. He's making sure Wayne and Mario get what they need. At the same time, he wants to uphold his commitment."

"His commitment?"

"To his business," Fernando said, as if that should be obvious. Then he leaned in close, as if he was about to share a secret. "And to you."

"Me?" Soledad said, not expecting that.

"Yes, Soledad Marie, you. He wants so badly to be his own man. For himself and for you. You know that, right?"

"Yes."

"OK, you two are close to pulling this thing off. This wine thing?"

"Yes."

"Then you two got to push through. That's business. Nothing gets in the way of the business. How do you think our coffee empire lasted this long through emergencies and unforeseen circumstances?"

"I guess not," Soledad said contemplating what he was saying.

Their coffee orders arrived. Fernando took a sip that seemed more theater than thirst.

"That's why I'm here," he said. "Soledad Marie, I just want to be part of the success. You and Antonio are sooo close. Let me help you. I promised him I would."

"Well, I haven't talked to Antonio in over a week," Soledad said plaintively.

"Oh, well," Fernando said, looking sorrowful, "that may be my fault. I promised him I would reach out to you. Then I had to secure the shipment and get it rescheduled. That took some days."

"You were supposed to talk to me?"

"Five days ago," he mumbled into his cup.

"Five days!" she said, louder than she meant to.

"I'm sorry, but I really want to help."

"By leaving me here wondering for five days? Where's Antonio? Tell me now."

"In the hill country around our property. They're on a search, which is why his phone doesn't work."

"Searching? For what?"

"Wayne," he said, taking another long sip.

Soledad stared at him, not blinking.

"It's like I said, I don't know all the facts. Wayne was hurt and was somehow lost in the hills. Mario and Antonio and some of the hands went looking for him. Antonio promised to stay and help."

"I should be back there helping them," Soledad said.

"Well, he knew you would say that," Fernando said, speaking in a rapid whisper. "But you see, if that happens then the shipment will sit at the winery or at the port in Cartagena for months. There are distributors in the US waiting on the shipment. That window only stays open for so long."

With all the cloak and dagger and worry in Colombia, Soledad had forgotten about the commitments in the US. She rubbed her forehead, an involuntary show of stress in front of this man whom she was not sure was an ally.

"Soledad Marie, can I make a suggestion?" Fernando asked. He tried to sound trustworthy, but there was an undertone of mendacity to Soledad's ears. Nevertheless, he was Antonio's brother. If she couldn't trust him, who could she trust? Maybe it was some of the stories of irresponsibility that Antonio and Luisa had shared with her that clouded her judgment.

"Sorry, sure," she said, realizing an uncomfortable amount of silence had passed since he last spoke.

"We have a couple of days until the wine arrives. Let me stay here with you during that time and help you get that product on the ship."

"Don't you have a restaurant to run?" she said reflexively.

"I got good people. They can handle things for a couple of days."

Soledad had to stifle a cynical snort. She knew the restaurant lived in the red but for infusions of cash from the coffee operation.

"Antonio is in Venecia doing everything to help Mario and poor Wayne and get that wine to the port. He has every employee on the estate lending a hand. He's depending on you to get it on the ship. Let me help you both."

He had a point, she thought. She did feel all alone before he showed up. At the end of the day, there were things he knew that she didn't know. He was Antonio's brother, and if something crazy happens, she would just have to deal with it.

"I guess I don't have a choice," she capitulated, and Fernando clasped his hands in gratitude. "But at some point I need to talk to Antonio. Talk to someone who can put me in touch with him."

"Of course, as soon as he comes out of the hills," he assured her. Then there was silence as they drank their coffees.

"So, what are we going to do for the next couple of days?" Soledad asked. "I don't want to be away from the port."

"Don't worry," Fernando said, grinning confidently. "I have a plan."

10

Later that same day, just before midnight, JD and I landed in Medellin from North Carolina. We rented a relatively new Jeep Wrangler and spent the night at a clean but modest local hotel near the airport.

After having some time to digest the situation, I still couldn't figure out how these two missed each other for ten days.

I had JD call Soledad several times from his cell phone. He kept getting the recording that his phone was out of network. I had him call from my cell phone. I had an international calling plan. I got a recording that her voicemail was full.

"So, how many voicemails did you leave for her?" I asked. JD just shrugged and said he had lost count.

"Besides, if I overreacted by bringing you, I don't want her to find out I brought you with me unless I tell her first."

That made sense. I was sure the last person she wanted to see was her ex-fiancé while she was trying to handle her business.

"Let me hear her voicemails on your phone," I said.

"I haven't gotten any in the last ten days," he replied.

"Then let me hear the ones before that," I insisted, taking the phone from him.

We connected to the Internet at the hotel. Then we had to remember JD's password for the voicemails on his antique iPhone 4. We eventually got down to it.

"Hi JD. I just wanted to check in. Talk soon!"

"Hey, big bro, talk soon."

"Hey, it's me. Later."

There were a few more like that but nothing special.

"What about texts?" I asked.

"We do it, but her more than me," JD explained. "I'm better at just picking up the phone than doing a lot of typing."

"But in the last ten days, did you try texting her when you couldn't get a hold of her?"

He looked confused, so I broke it down for him. "JD, it appears you have been missing each other because you don't have international calling, and she's in a spotty cell zone, but if you've been sending her texts, she'll get them as soon as her signal is strong or she signs onto a Wi-Fi network."

"I did send her a text or two but nothing lately," JD explained.

"Send her a text now, from my phone. I'm sure of the signal."

He typed a message and sent it.

"Are you sure she wants to be found?" I asked. "I find it hard to understand why she wouldn't be in touch with you after all this time."

"Exactly, Manion," JD said. "That's why I did all this."

Early the next morning, we went to Teresa's, Fernando Lazaro's restaurant. It didn't open until 11:00, so we sat in the Jeep a few doors away and waited until someone showed up. Teresa's was on Carrera Road between Calle 11 and Calle 12, in the El Poblado district.

There were hotels, storefronts, real estate offices, and restaurants of every kind. All sorts of morning workers moved up and down the block. Central Colombia was entering the wet time of the year, characterized by dry mornings and wet afternoons. It was cloudy but warm. Street vendors at the end of the block filled the air with the scent of pork, eggs with onions and cilantro, and fresh arepas.

With ten minutes to go, a black Chevy Tahoe with oversized wheels eased around the corner and came to a stop in front of the restaurant. I sensed JD's eyes flick to the side of my head and back to the door of Teresa's. I kept my eyes on it as well. I had a feeling that things were about to take a turn.

After a few seconds, the restaurant door opened, and three people came out. One was a well-dressed man who looked about forty years old. He seemed nervous and fidgety. The next was what could only be described as a big guy. Big body, big head, big hands. He opened the door to the Tahoe and stood by. Then came the woman.

"It's Sole," JD said, pointing.

It did look like Soledad. The long brown hair, tan skin, the confident walk. However, she was dressed in a $1,000 business suit, $700 shoes, and wearing heavy makeup. While I was trying to figure out what I was looking at, JD was jumping out of the car and running for the Tahoe.

"Hey, wait!" I said, leaping out after him.

"Hey!" JD shouted as he hurried up the street.

The woman who looked like Soledad glanced at JD marching up the street and then nonchalantly eased into the Tahoe. The big man turned toward JD and then reached into his humongous sports coat.

"Gun!" I hollered as I watched things unfold, suddenly remembering my combat training from Rudolph Lemieux, the former Foreign Legion recluse under whom I had studied.

Whether due to my call or his own police training, JD reached the suited giant and locked his hand in his jacket. While they wrestled for position, I jumped off the fire hydrant and caught the big man with a roundhouse kick that spun him around.

JD shoved him to the ground and relieved him of his gun. I was back on my feet with my forearm in the well-dressed man's throat.

"Manion, check on my sister," JD said while holding the big man's gun on him.

I shoved the dapper one against the wall and pointed at him to stay where he was. Then I turned and bent down into the Tahoe's open door.

"Soledad, don't be afraid. We—"

That was when she put one sharp, expensive heel in my throat and pushed me to the ground. Then she closed the door, and the Tahoe sped off.

"Who the hell are you guys?" the well-dressed man shouted, staying against the wall.

"What did you do to my sister?" JD yelled at the big man, who could not take his eyes off the gun barrel in his face. "Why is she running from us?"

"Your sister is Anise?" the well-dressed man asked, bewildered.

"No, Soledad Marie Cruz," I said.

"Are you . . . Señor Lazaro?" JD asked.

"Y-yeah."

"Then you know my sister, asshole. Why did she kick my man out of the car and take off?"

We heard sirens, and all of us froze. Big boy tried to get to his feet, but JD kicked him back down to a prone position.

"I don't know who you guys are, but I'm Señor Fernando Lazaro-Alvarez. Your 'Soledad' is my brother's business partner."

"That was my sister in that Tahoe," JD said. "I know my sister."

"That wasn't your sister," Fernando said coolly, adjusting his lapels.

"Manion?" JD asked, looking at me with something bordering on desperation.

"Yeah, I didn't see her face for a long time, but I saw what you saw."

Then the police came around the corner. I left the sidewalk and stepped into the street with my hands up. JD pulled the clip from the gun and pitched it in one direction. He racked the firearm to empty the chamber. Then he joined me in the middle of the street. JD instructed me to kneel while keeping our hands up.

"What have you got me in?" I said as members of the Policía Nacional de Colombia—Medellin Region—pulled us to our feet.

Needless to say, all the Zen that Alexandro found with Polonia was erased when he returned home the next day. It took Luisa, Antonio, Fernando, and even Paulo to convince him not to shut down the wine operation. He was convinced that Wayne and Mario had brought the "criminal element" to his estate. Speaking of Mario, no one had found him. Antonio was paying for extra men to comb the entire mountain for his friend—or his friend's remains.

In the end, Fernando assured him he would help Antonio through his "trouble." He promised his father that none of this would reflect badly on the Lazaro coffee operation or the family's reputation. In the end, Alexandro liked seeing his oldest take charge of things.

Maybe something good will come out of this tragedy, he thought.

"OK, Fernando," he said. "You will take charge of this. Luisa, take some time away from playing in the fields to give him whatever assistance he needs."

"I'm sorry, Papa," Antonio said in a small voice. He was truly sorry for bringing this to his father's doorstep, second only to his sorrow for the loss of his friend.

Alexandro just looked at him in silent exasperation. He wanted to scold him for getting into this foolish wine business, to tell him that this was why new things were not always the best thing. In the end, however, Antonio had always been his baby boy, a surprise to him and his wife, and his anger couldn't exceed his heartbreak for the boy.

Later that evening, Paulo made his way to Luisa's end of the estate. She was in a foul mood, pacing around the large, ornately carved wooden table and chairs in the dining area between the sitting room and the bedroom. The last light over the western hills shone through the windows that faced the same walled balcony that extended to her bedroom.

Paulo had tried to get her to eat something. It had been a crazy thirty-six hours. She had found a dying man in the woods, a man she knew. She had almost shot Paulo, and they had been in the hills around Venecia all day looking for Mario. Instead of finding her exhausted, she was furious. In place of her dinner drink of the most recent malbec from Antonio's stock, she was taking angry but copious swallows of a very expensive Asian whiskey that she had bought on a trip to Japan some years ago. She had been saving it for a special occasion. Paulo didn't think this was what she had in mind.

"Did you hear him? Now he wants me to back up Fernando," she said. "What a joke. I found the body, dammit."

Paulo nodded as he poured himself a small portion of the whiskey in a crystal tumbler. He stuck his nose in the glass as he took the first sip. The smokiness of ancient Nipponese fires filled his senses. As she continued her rant, he felt fatigue edge into his muscles. He took a seat in one of the dining room chairs.

"Did you hear what he said? 'Take some time away from playing in the fields.'"

Paulo nodded again, looking into his drink and striving not to display the concern he felt inside.

"That old man doesn't appreciate anything I do. The research? The new disease-resistant crop that kept us in business when every other estate was losing money?"

"The relationship with the workers," Paulo said, half in jest, as he pointed to himself.

"Yes," she replied quickly. Then she blushed, struggling to hold back a smile. She wanted to stew some more.

The truth was that Alexandro was far removed from his workers. This was indicative of his reign.

His father and grandfather had kept on an almost first-name basis relationship with many of the workers. They knew their children's names, remembered anniversaries and dates of passing. Luisa kept that going now when she could because the Lazaro men were way too busy.

"I think you're missing the big picture," Paulo said. "Your biggest complaint is that you don't get enough time in the field. Now Fernando seems to be taking charge. That frees you up, doesn't it?"

She took another gulp and then stared out the window. "*Seems* to be taking charge is right," she said. "I'll believe it when I see it."

Paulo sank into his own thoughts. Throughout that week he had been working up his nerve, getting his speech together to approach Alexandro about promoting him to a roaster/taster position. He had been talking to Luisa about it for over a year, and it had gone nowhere. Señor Alexandro and Paulo's father had been more than employee and boss. They had been friends, or so Paulo thought.

What's the worst that could happen? he asked himself. *Alexandro says no, and I go back to doing what I've been doing? Or do I?*

Señor Alexandro had a reputation for being hot-headed at times. He could be rash and then have too much pride to walk back any rash decision. Paulo couldn't imagine the old man being mad enough to fire him, but . . .

While Paulo was weighing his options, JD and I were being interrogated by Detective Mateo Meneses-Osorio in the office of the Policía Nacional de Colombia in downtown Medellin.

"Gentlemen, I must admit, I'm having a hard time following your story here. You seem to imply your sister has been kidnapped and that she did not recognize you when you called to her in front of Teresa's?"

"Right," JD said.

We were behind a dull metal table sitting on chairs made of the same material. Our hands were cuffed and chained to hooks on the table legs. I had to lower my head to scratch my face.

"And Señor Manion, you say she kicked you out of the vehicle when you addressed her?"

"Right," I replied, though a little less confidently than JD. The more I thought about my vision of the Soledad in the fine clothes, hat, and designer shoes, the less sure I felt. The woman looked like Soledad but somehow slightly different than I remembered. I chalked it up to the amount of time since I had seen her last. I had known JD and his sister since we were in grade school, but I had never seen Soledad dressed like that.

We had been there for several hours. We had been given a box lunch of something called *salchipapa*, a mix of sausage, fried potatoes, cheese, and a really good red chili sauce. We had a chance to make phone calls. JD called the American consulate. I reluctantly put in a call to World-Span Underwriters in Paris.

Thankfully, I got the office of our general counsel and explained my situation. Sort of.

I explained that I had been arrested and gave them the city and the detective's name. They explained that they would work on my release. I was assured that we had legal partners in the region.

Day turned into evening, and evening turned into night. JD and I were still in that same interrogation room.

"Hey, Mateo, what's up with those two in room seven?"

Detective Meneses didn't look up from his paperwork to answer the question. It was asked by Detective Ramona Valez, but she answered to "Padilla." She never told anyone why. She always worked alone and spent a lot of time behind closed doors with department captains. Since the crazy cocaine days of Medellin, law enforcement was always on the lookout for corruption amongst its rank and file. Everyone assumed Padilla was an informant for the brass. Either way, Padilla never chitchatted with anyone. If she did initiate conversation, it was for a purpose, usually to get information.

Here she is, starting a conversation with me, Meneses thought.

"It's nothing, Padilla. A couple of Americans being held on an assault charge."

"Really, who?" she said, plopping down in the perp chair in front of Meneses' desk.

"Who, what?" Meneses asked, trying to read her facial expression. All he saw was wide-eyed innocent curiosity.

"Who did they assault?" she said, rolling her eyes and waving her hand as if to say, "Crazy Americans, right?"

Meneses picked up the smell of expensive perfume, chewing gum, and flavored vape smoke. He stared at her without answering, then started shuffling through papers on his desk.

"Look, Padilla, I've had a long day. Here's the prelim report. If you have questions after that . . ."

Meneses handed her the arrest sheet. Padilla almost snatched it from him.

"Oh, snap, they mixed it up with Anise Constaneda? Surprised they're still alive," Padilla said, whistling through her teeth. "Says here they thought it was a relative of theirs."

"Yep," Meneses replied, still typing on his computer.

"Then why did they attack her?" Padilla asked.

"You said it yourself; anyone running up on 'Anise the Thief' is crazy. These two found themselves in a fight before they knew it."

"Do they still call her that?" Padilla asked, her narrowed feral cat eyes looking up at Meneses.

"That's what I call her," Meneses said. "Anyway, she's not pressing charges."

"Then why are they still here? An American police officer and a . . . what is this? An insurance salesman?"

"Insurance investigator," Meneses clarified. "They thought Anise was the policeman's sister. They say she looks like Anise."

"Hmm . . . you know, they say we all have a twin in this world," Padilla said, continuing to peruse the report.

"Hadn't heard that. Good to know." Meneses was getting irritated by the shady detective's shameless prying.

"So, you letting them go tonight?" Padilla asked.

"No. We got orders to hold them overnight and release them in the morning."

"Orders from whom?"

"From Captain—None of Your Business," Meneses answered. He leaned back in his chair and closed his laptop. He stared at Padilla in such a way that she knew the conversation was finished.

Actually, the order to hold them overnight was a pain. It meant Meneses had to stay later to make sure they got dinner and someplace to sleep. He also had to invent some reason to hold them overnight that would satisfy a fellow law-enforcement professional. However, his captain had explained that the orders were a favor from some very important people.

Cruz and Manion were talking about going to the Municipio de Venecia the following day to talk to the Lazaro family. Meneses didn't know any Lazaros well enough to warn them, but he knew someone who did. He scrolled through his phone until he found his cousin's number—Polonia Meneses.

11

Arnie Rutledge was FBI legacy. His father was a young agent assigned to the Hillside Strangler case in Los Angeles in the late 1970s. His uncles were on the Elizabeth Smart kidnapping in 2002.

Arnie had been with the bureau's Southern California division for over ten years. He met a nice girl at work. Her father was a lifer field agent in the Denver office, catching counterfeiters. They got married and had two children.

It was an All-American existence. However, the big case, like the ones that made his father's career and got his uncles promoted, had eluded him.

That's why he took the new assignment. Switching to the Bureau of Alcohol, Tobacco, Firearms and Explosives, he would be in Colombia for up to two years, working with the Colombian custom authorities to catch smugglers who were moving illegal goods into the United States. It started with drugs but had since turned into everything from lumber to precious metals, bootleg medicines, and human trafficking. The number-one suspected smuggler was a woman named Anise Constaneda. The authorities knew she was behind some of the biggest shipments but could never connect the links back to her.

If he could help the National Directorate of Taxes and Customs (NDTC) bring down the Constaneda smuggling operation, it would make his career.

It had been almost a year, and all he had done was watch the Constaneda warehouse and her residence in Medellin's Envigado district. The NDTC team and the maritime authority were still watching the ports and her ships as well as the airports. At first Arnie thought it was about glory and recognition. After all, the action would probably happen at the points of exit. After several months, however, he began to think that maybe some of his Colombian peers were supplying intel and access to the Constaneda operation. He expressed those sentiments to his superiors back in the US.

What he didn't expect is that it would get back to those same hardworking Colombian officers whom he worked with every day. They let him know that they were aware of what he had said about them.

From that point on, it had been the loneliest time of his life. He was far from home, not really liked or trusted by anyone he worked with, and it seemed like he had no support from home. He reached out to his uncles who said they would try to see what the lay of the land was, but they also scolded him for what he had done.

"Dammit, nephew, if you had concerns about the crew down there, you should have come to me or your dad first, not blab over official channels!"

During a celebration of Día de la Raza (Spanish Columbus Day) a year ago, he had met Detective Ramona Valez. She was local police but was clearly impressed with his US federal status. She liked that he didn't look like an American federal agent from the movies. He was just under six feet tall with thinning brown hair and an average build, but he had intelligent eyes behind round wire-rimmed glasses.

"It's why I know you're so good at what you do," she explained that night over tequila shots. "They don't see you coming. Look at all these macho officers, so proud of wearing a badge, you can smell it on them from a mile away."

They laughed as they watched the Colombian and American agents at a private bar party in a drunken but macho swagger.

"It's why I'm one of a few female detectives in Medellin," she explained. "They don't see me coming."

Arnie had to agree. Unless she approached and engaged someone, she was easy to forget or miss altogether. She had a round, average face, short hair in no particular style, and a nice body that was masked in slightly oversized and comfortable but unflattering clothes.

He actually declined the suggestion to take her back to his hotel suite where he had lived for the last several months, but he did run his mouth enough about the surveillance on Anise Constaneda so that Padilla could bargain back into the life of her former lover. Anise had let her back into her life and occasionally into her bed. Padilla knew she was being strung along to bring more information, but she didn't care. Anise was worth it.

Just when she was settling in for the long haul of endless dreary conversations with the American agent, Padilla was invited into the surveillance van on a rainy Friday night just down the street from Anise's warehouse. She introduced him to national drink, Aguardiente del valle, and Agent Arnie Rutledge introduced her to a maudlin air of loneliness and boredom. On their third shot, she shoved her tongue into his mouth out of impatience, and in an instant, he was on top of her.

That night became the start of a weekly humping habit and a tawdry tradition. Each time, Padilla got all the information she needed on the surveillance of Anise Constaneda. Arnie never told anyone about his "dates" with the plain yet beguiling female detective with the determined, almost desperate look in her eyes. Had he mentioned it to someone, anyone within local law enforcement, he would have been warned about her checkered reputation.

They met in the afternoon that week in a hotel room just across from Anise's office complex.

"Any new movement this week?" Padilla asked as she lay naked on top of the sheets. She blew cigarette smoke and took another long pull off an ice-cold Septimazo IPA. The television was broadcasting a Colombian version of an American reality show about former child television stars competing in a baking show with their former costars.

"What do you mean?" Arnie asked, looking out the telescope and making notes. "There's always something to report."

Padilla snorted to stifle a laugh. Arnie turned around to look at her.

"Sorry, Rutledge," Padilla said, holding her hands up and rising to her knees on the bed. Arnie could not keep his eyes off of her small, round breasts. "I meant no disrespect, but we haven't seen Constaneda in weeks."

"That's not true," he said, agitated. "She just wasn't around on the days you were here."

Padilla tapped her head with the palm of her hand as if to say, "Duh, I should have known that."

She fell back on the bed, letting everything on her body move freely. Arnie dropped his pen and went over to the bed. He laid his head on her chest.

"Sorry. I guess I'm just not made for surveillance," Padilla said sulkily.

"It's all good," he mumbled between kissing and biting her nipples.

"But here's my question," she said, gritting her teeth through the pain. "Who's watching her when she's not in front of you?"

"Oh," he said, eager to answer, "my Colombian partners."

He proceeded to explain the location of all the surveillance teams, including the ones on the ports. She flipped him onto his back and returned the favor while he gave the names of the team members. She licked his entire groin wet while he explained the twenty-four-hour rotation. Then she rode him to glory in four minutes. Just before he went to sleep, he explained how they were sure they were going to have enough evidence to bust Anise within the next week.

12

The next morning, JD and I woke up stiff, hungry, and in a sour mood. We had spent the night in a spare conference room instead of a jail cell. They found a sofa, and we slept on at either end.

"This is insane," I said. "We're not under arrest, but we can't leave."

JD nodded. "Yeah, something's not right here."

"Well, you're the lawman. Can't you give them the international cop secret handshake?"

"Very funny, Mr. International. Not even sure why I brought you."

"You called the State Department?"

"Yes, Manion, I called the local US consulate. They told me they would work on it and get back to us."

I rolled my eyes.

"Well, who did *you* call?" JD asked.

"WorldSpan Underwriters. Who else?"

"And. . .?"

"They are working on it."

"Ha!" JD said.

After a bit of silent stretching and back muscle cracking, we were greeted by Detective Meneses who entered the room.

"Good morning, señors. You slept well, yes?"

We just stared at him in silence. Meneses laughed. "We can get you some coffee. You'll feel better afterwards," he said and then turned to leave. Then he stopped as if he had forgotten to say something. "By the way, you've been released—conditionally."

"We have? Both of us?" JD asked. "The consulate came through."

"Uh . . . no," Meneses replied.

"Wait, what conditions?" I asked.

"You;ll see."

"Did you find my sister?" JD asked.

"Uh . . . no."

"What's the condition of our release?" I repeated.

"I am," a female voice behind us answered. JD looked bewildered. I didn't even turn around.

"I was told you know the lady, and she has come a long way to assist you," Meneses said, suppressing a laugh.

"Bonjour, mes amies! You have been sprung, as they say!"

While I was eager to leave, to find out what happened to Soledad, the thought of facing Camille DeSoronne on that side of the Atlantic was frightening. She *never* came to that side of the Atlantic. I knew this would not be good.

Smart and confident, she had been one of the managing partners at WorldSpan Underwriters for the last decade. She was one of the youngest to make directing partner. She was fearless in the boardroom. Her cunning was wrapped in an unapologetic feminine charm that was no less lethal. She was not a woman impersonating a man. She was a woman who had found a way to succeed on her own terms, and for the last six years she had been my boss and my on-again/off-again lover.

Camille was from the Bordeaux region of France. Tall, slim, and beautiful, with prominent cheekbones, she had skin that tanned easily, short blonde hair, and a wide Cameron Diaz smile. In a nutshell, she was the walking personification of what American men thought a sexy French woman looked like. Most of the time I had no idea why she was with me. I was just glad she was. Usually.

She was flashing that smile now, but there was no mirth in her eyes. She was wearing a custom-fit two-piece suit that was a shade of yellow that caught the light flecks in her cognac-brown eyes.

I had let the silence linger too long. She broke eye contact with me and turned to JD. "Camille DeSoronne, WorldSpan Underwriters," she said, shaking JD's hand. "You're . . . ."

"JD Cruz. Deputy Cruz."

"Right, the brother of the missing Soledad. Let's see if we can get you some answers."

In her heels she was an inch taller than JD. She took him by the arm and turned to follow Meneses out of the conference room/bedroom.

"Let's go, Manion," she said over her shoulder as I stood there, riveted in place. "We have work to do."

Meneses and Camille led JD and me to a small office, where our files were processed and closed, and we would be released.

"Señor Cruz, I understand you thought the woman in question was your sister, Soledad?" Meneses asked, even though he knew that already. JD nodded.

"The lady's name is Anise Constaneda, a local businesswoman," Meneses said, opening a beige folder and rotating it in front of JD and me. JD pulled up a picture of his sister and my ex-almost fiancé on his cell phone and held it up to the picture in the folder. I heard Camille make a verbal noise of interest behind me.

While the differences between the two were evident, the similarities were uncanny.

"A true doppelganger," Meneses said.

"What?" JD asked.

"Everyone is supposed to have a twin somewhere in the world," I explained as JD ran his hand over Anise's picture, "but we seldom get to meet them."

"Well, I guess we owe Ms. Constaneda an apology," JD said. "What kind of business requires her to roll with bodyguards?"

"Bodyguards aren't that rare in this part of the world," Meneses explained. "Officially, she runs an international shipping business, but—"

"But she's currently under surveillance by the National Directorate of Taxes and Customs, the Policía Nacional de Colombia, and the United States ATF for her alleged role in smuggling and illegal logging and mining," Camille said.

We all turned to look back at her. Meneses just nodded in agreement. The room was quiet as we digested the information. I could feel Camille's eyes glaring at the side of my head.

"Well, where's my sister?" JD finally asked.

Meneses shrugged. "We're not sure."

"And why is someone like that and who also looks spookily like Soledad also doing business with the Lazaro Coffee people?" I asked. "That was a Lazaro at the scene, right? We were headed there to talk to him."

"Right, Fernando, the oldest son," Meneses said. "Is that your sister's partner?"

"No, it's the other brother, Antonio," JD said. "They're in the wine business."

"Wine? At a coffee estate? Hmm . . . Then you want to go to the Lazaro Coffee estate," Meneses said. "It's where Antonio and the rest of the family operate. You were at Fernando's restaurant, Teresa's. I don't think it's attached to the rest of the family."

"You seem to know a lot about the Lazaros," Camille observed.

"They're a well-known family, very respected."

"But one of them hangs out with a suspected smuggler?" JD said. "Doesn't sound very respectable to me."

Meneses closed his files and started signing some papers. "Things in Colombia are not as white and black as they are in America, Deputy," he said, not appreciating JD's inference. "You're free to go. We'll keep an eye out for your sister. We have the number for Señorita DeSoronne's satellite phone."

"Let's go, gentlemen," Camille said. "We need to get cleaned up before heading out to the Lazaro Coffee estate."

On the way out, they all shook hands with Meneses and promised to keep in touch with any developments. Meneses held his polite smile until he noticed Padilla standing one office away, pretending to be engrossed in a folder of mugshots. Meneses shook his head when he noticed the folder label was upside down.

He went back into his office, closed the door, and locked it. Going to the farthest corner from the door, he pulled his cell phone, selected a number from his contact list, and waited.

"Hello, my cousin," he said, almost in a whisper. "Just a heads up about a curious situation. One that involves your special friend, Señor Lazaro . . . Yes, I know you're just business friends, but the next time you see him, let him know some Americans are in town looking into his business."

"OK, gentlemen, we can get you cleaned up and head out to Venecia Valley," Camille said as she stood on the front sidewalk of the police station. She waved to a private vehicle to pull up.

"Wait," JD said. "Look, I appreciate your help. Camille, right? But I asked for Teke's help, not WorldSpan. If you don't mind, I'll go it alone from here."

Even I looked at him like he was crazy. Just as I was about to tell him how stupid he was, Camille placed a hand on my arm. Then she opened the car door and turned to JD. "Call me Camille, JD, and I understand your point. I don't want to do anything to disrespect your wishes, but I'm afraid you're stuck with me."

"Oh, really," JD said, feeling very disrespected.

"Yes, really. You were released under my recognizance, not your own and not the US State Department, *mine*. That means you're under my auspices, and unfortunately, I am WorldSpan. So is your friend, Manion, despite what he thought when he agreed to help you. Now, this is your show. We'll follow your lead, and we'll put WorldSpan's resources at your disposal because Manion has involved himself, which means he has involved us. Now, unless you want to head back inside the police station and wait on the US State Department, I suggest you allow us to tag along."

JD looked at me and then at Camille. "Don't know why a big insurance company would do that without sending me a bill," he said.

"It's simple. We have an investment in your friend, Mr. Manion. We care about his safety even if he doesn't care about it himself. Hence, because he's invested, we're invested."

JD finally moved to get into the car, and we followed in silence. Camille sat in the front passenger seat, and JD and I sat in the rear seats. The driver moved back into the metro Medellin traffic.

"And for the record, Camille," JD said, looking out the window. "He's not my damn friend."

In true WorldSpan fashion, Camille had our luggage from the hotel and moved it to a private AirBnB home she rented in the El Poblado district. JD complained again about being handled until he saw his room and bath.

He tried to call Soledad on her satellite phone, but it didn't connect.

"She must be somewhere with absolutely no signal," Camille said. "That's not unusual in the mountains."

Eventually, he went to clean up, change clothes, and prepare to head for the Lazaro Coffee estate. As much as he grinded on me, I hated to see him leave Camille and me alone. Now I was going to get mine.

Camille and I went into the primary bedroom. She opened her suitcase and began laying out clothes and toiletries. Then she set up her laptop and portable satellite Internet router, moving back and forth through the luxurious suite as I stood there, feeling unsure.

"It's good to see you," I said, knowing I needed to start somewhere. I was looking forward to getting my cussing out started and done. I deserved it. She didn't stop moving or look my way. I repeated my opening line, louder this time.

"Good to see you too," she said, still moving around the room.

"Camille, I should have called, but JD just showed up. He was desperate, and—"

"And you, being the great Teke Manion, just had to go?" Camille asked. She was in the bathroom by then, running water.

"No. At the time I thought it would be a quick trip. I thought we would find her hanging out with friends, and it would be a laugh all around."

She peeked out of the bathroom. Her pained expression signaled to me that I should shut up.

"Tekelius, why do you think I'm mad at you?" she asked, her beautiful eyes squinting as if she had just found a dead skunk in the bathtub.

"Um, because I took off to help find my ex-girlfriend instead of coming home after the Graves of Gold," I said carefully after hearing her use my full name.

"Graves of what?"

"That's what they called it in North Carolina," I explained, speaking about my last assignment where I almost died from a nineteenth-century booby trap while recovering pirate gold.

She re-entered the bedroom. I started to talk, but she held up a slim, manicured hand. She checked her laptop and entered some information. In a few seconds she turned from the screen with all the sexiness she didn't realize she exuded all the time. I just stood there.

"So, you think I'm upset about your old girlfriend? The girlfriend you ran from to come to Paris and WorldSpan?"

I stayed quiet.

"I was dispatched by WorldSpan when our primary operative went missing. The same operative who had just completed an assignment that landed the company and our client a record-breaking return but also put said operative in mortal danger, an operative who suffered a life-threatening injury."

"It was just a cut to my leg," I said, but it even sounded stupid to me.

"I came here because the directors at WorldSpan are divided. Half of them think you're the Indiana Jones of insurance salvage recovery. The other half suspect you're mentally unstable and should be suspended, and your role as 'expeditor' reevaluated. They have suggested that maybe you pocketed some of that 'grave gold' for yourself."

"That's bullshit," I said, my anger growing.

"Of course it is, Tekelius," she replied, her angry French accent still sounding good to my male American ears. "People in corporations are jealous and competitive. Then you disappeared, sending the gold back with those fools from the US State Department. Next the directors asked me where you were. And what could I tell them? *Nothing*, which is what I got from you."

"I'm sorry. I didn't think it would take this long."

"I don't care if it took a year. The issue is that I had no idea where you were. I looked like a fool to the directors."

"I'm sorry."

"Remember when you accepted this new job? I asked if you were sure you could do it, and on your first job, you ghosted the company."

She was right. I had not thought about any of that. I felt bad about putting her reputation at risk. Until that moment I had thought of the trip as a kind of vacation that only affected me. She was on a roll.

"I started with the people in Benoitown. No one knew where you went. By the way, a Ms. Babbineaux was very concerned about your well-being. Then I moved to White Sands. You're not liked in that town, except for a talkative little bartender. I even hunted your brother down."

"You talked to Tommy?" I said, surprised. My brother was a guitar phenom who played all over the world. He had inherited the parental gift. Half the time I didn't know where he was.

"Yes, and you know what he said?" Camille continued. "He told me not to worry. That you'll come wandering home like a straggling dog."

"Hmmph, he did, did he?" I made a mental note to discuss that with him when I saw him.

"Yes. It made me mad, but in the end, he was right," she said. "Now, let's get ready."

She started removing jewelry. Then she opened her robe to finish undressing. I kicked off my shoes and looked around the room.

"Where's my bag?"

"Oh, you thought after all this you were going to shower and change with me?" she asked.

"But, Mila," I said using my nickname for her.

She walked over to me, her robe open, showing her black lace panties and bra. I was instantly homesick for Paris. She removed her Brazilian-cut underwear and held them dangling from her index finger.

"You will get showered and changed in the other bathroom when JD is finished," she said, smiling for the first time. Before I could beg and whine, she threw a perfect panty strike to my face. I caught them while trying not to shamefully inhale.

"You see, Tekelius, I have instructions from the WorldSpan directors to bring you back to Paris as soon as I find you."

"Oh," I said, trying to focus on what she was saying and not on what I was seeing.

She closed and retied her robe. Then she pointed to her laptop. "I'm due for a video update to headquarters in five minutes. I don't think you want to be seen in the camera shot."

When she turned to her laptop, I turned to leave.

"Leave the underwear, Manion," she said while placing a headset over her ears. "You're still on probation with me as well."

13

For almost five minutes after she woke up, Soledad was not sure where she was. She remembered that she was in Cartagena, but this didn't look like her hotel room. The bed was round and king size and seemed to float.

"Where is . . . what?" she said, getting out of bed. Her feet were bare, but thank God, the rest of her was in the clothes she had been wearing the day before. Then she felt the rocking again. She went to the window.

"A boat? I'm on a boat!" She paused for a moment to think. "Wait, where's Fernando? Whose boat is this?"

She looked out the window again. The ship was docked. She tried to make out other landmarks when a face suddenly appeared on the other side of the window.

"Good morning, sister!"

Soledad jumped back, rubbing her eyes. Then the distortion of the nautical glass gave way to recognition. "Fernando! Get in here!"

He continued to grin and wave.

"Now!" she said, banging her fist against the window. Fernando jumped back and scrambled to his feet.

In a minute he knocked on her door. She opened it and found him standing there with suitcases in his hands. She grabbed him by his arm and pulled him into the room.

"OK, mister, where are we? How did I get here?

"Easy, easy," Fernando said, his grin still wide. "Is this not a beautiful ship? We are less than ten slips away from where our wine will be loaded." He pointed to the window. "See that reddish brick building? The receiving house, yes? I met you there yesterday."

Soledad let out a deep sigh of relief. She turned back to Fernando, who was smiling expectantly. That just pissed her off again.

"Whose boat is this?" she asked.

"It belongs to a friend of mine. We came here last night. Don't you remember?"

"No, I don't remember," Soledad said. She looked off into space, trying to recall the previous day. "Wait, we were at the coffee shop. Then we went back to the clearing house in the quartermaster's office. They gave us a space to use."

"Right, we called the estate," Fernando prompted.

"We couldn't get Antonio. He was still in the hills. We spoke to Luisa. Then it gets fuzzy."

She started to pat her clothes and look around the cabin.

"We went to dinner, the little place suggested by the harbormaster," Fernando explained.

Soledad had no recollection. She turned over the bed linens. Then she went into the adjoining bathroom.

"Where's my phone?" she asked.

"Uh, I'm not sure. You don't have it?"

"No, and I need it. All my information is on it."

He shrugged. "You did get a little drunk."

"Me? No!" she said, trying to remember. Knowing her condition, why would she drink?

"I was surprised as well," Fernando explained. "You were worried about Antonio. You had a small glass of aguardiente and some mango nectar. Then before dinner came, you were dozing off."

"What?"

"And slurring your words."

Soledad frowned in confusion, still trying to remember.

"I didn't feel comfortable letting you go back to your hotel alone," Fernando continued. "So, I brought you here to where I am staying." He spread his arms to reference the entire cabin.

Soledad looked around, pondering his words. Then she noticed her suitcase behind Fernando.

"That's my luggage. How did—"

"Just a little friendly persuasion to the maid staff, and they packed you up and delivered it here."

"But why would they give my things to a stranger—" She stopped when Fernando held up her driver's license, passport, and laptop. She snatched them out of his hands.

"Sister, don't be mad. Remember, I'm on your side. I promised my brother I would do everything to help you."

She shook her head. "I just wish I could remember."

"Look, you've been under a lot of pressure. I think you were just tired."

"Maybe you're right," she replied.

"I would like to think it's because you knew someone had your back," Fernando said. "Or at least that's what I'll tell my niece or nephew years from now."

Soledad looked at him, the import of his words striking her. She wanted to hide her expression, but it was too late. He had been given a clue, and now he was sure.

"Don't get mad, sister," he said. "The maid who packed up your room saw the kit and congratulated me. I had to tell her you were my fiancé."

"I just found out myself," she said as she plopped onto the bed.

"Antonio doesn't know?"

She shook her head.

"Don't worry, Soledad Marie. My lips are sealed."

She gave him a dubious look.

"I promise," he said, crossing his heart. "But I know he's going to be over the moon when he finds out."

"You think so?"

"Of course," he said, kneeling in front of her.

"What about your father?"

"You kidding? The old man has been after us for grandchildren for years."

"Luisa won't like it; I don't think she likes me."

"Luisa doesn't like anybody unless they're a coffee plant or a horse."

They both laughed at that. Then a memory struck her. "What did she say about Antonio, Wayne, and Mario?"

"Antonio is well. They haven't found Mario, and Wayne is still under medical care. They're still in the hill country, but they found a landline in a local village and called the estate."

"Did he ask about me?"

"He didn't get a chance. Luisa told him that we were in Cartagena awaiting the shipment."

"What did Antonio say? Was he pleased?"

"You know my brother. When he's focused on a task . . ."

That was true. Antonio was so enthralled in this wine business. So many things could go wrong. Nothing had though, and they were about to ship their first varieties to the US. It had started out as a project of interest and profit but was now one of love as well. She believed in the potential and promise of every grape from the Lalvarez Winery.

She was about to remind Fernando again to be quiet about the pregnancy when she heard more voices on the deck. Soledad also heard footfalls, and the boat rocked slightly as people came up the gangway.

"Aaaahhhh, sister," Fernando said, "get showered and dressed. Then meet me on the main deck. I want you to meet a special friend."

14

That same morning, I woke up from a surprisingly good night's sleep. The previous evening, we had a quiet dinner and watched a bit of television. We had JD send emails to Soledad in a continuous attempt to find out where she was. Camille had me in quarantine, so I slept in the third bedroom. I came out ready to go, ready to find Soledad and get home to Paris.

In the living room, I saw Camille's laptop open and working. The screen was alive with lines of text appearing and disappearing. It appeared to be downloading something. I looked around and found her on the balcony adjacent to the living room. She was dressed in dark pants and a sleeveless red silk blouse. She would have looked inviting except for the expression on her face and the cigarette between her lips. When she saw me, she stomped the cigarette under her designer heel and walked back into the room under a head of steam.

"Sit down, Tekelius," she said, pointing to one of the chairs next to the laptop. The tone in her voice signaled that this was a shut-up-and-comply situation.

"The more I thought about this missing girl, the more something didn't add up," she said as she stood over me. "How have they not spoken to each other in over ten days? Not by voice, text, voicemail, or email?"

"I know!" I replied. "I thought that too, but—"

"But instead of looking into it, you just flew off to Colombia like the

American Superman and got arrested," she said, looking at me with no affection in her eyes. I tried to appear appropriately contrite.

"In addition to using WorldSpan to bail you out of jail, I have used our IT abilities to hack into the Cruz family's phone accounts."

"What?" I said, standing up. She shushed me and motioned for me to sit down. "Mila, how did they do that? Is that legal? I mean—"

"Please, this is low-level stuff," Camille said as she typed on her laptop. She seemed to be temporarily stopping the download. With a few more keystrokes, she brought up a folder with a list of files.

"Buenos dias," JD said as he came out of his bedroom. He was dressed in jeans and a beige collared shirt with the sleeves rolled up to his elbows.

"Perfect timing, Deputy," Camille said. "Have a seat. We have some questions for you."

JD felt the heaviness in the room. He took the chair next to me as Camille continued. "First, we're committed to reconnecting you to your sister. I can't imagine worrying about a sibling in these crazy times."

"Thank you. I have been worried," JD said.

"Especially since you haven't talked in over ten days," she said.

"Exactly. We keep missing each other, and the international cell service is crazy," JD said with a chuckle. "I just want to make sure she's OK."

"But there's another reason for that ten-day absence, isn't there?" Camille said..

JD looked confused. I shook my head. This was not going to be good.

She turned to her laptop and moved her cursor over a file on the screen and clicked the mouse.

It was an audio file, and the following is what we heard.

"Sole, what the hell? I've been trying to call you."

"JD, I returned every call. I left a message."

"I called seven times, Sole. I got one message from you!"

"But my message was the same. I'm good. So I didn't repeat myself."

"Now you're being a smartass. I'm just concerned. It's dangerous for a woman traveling by herself."

"Isn't the world dangerous, period? But you assume because I'm a woman, I'm not being careful."

"When you don't return my phone calls? Yeah, that's being real careful. When are you going to finish your little wine thing?"

"I'm not sure, and it's not a wine thing. It's a—"

"It's just like all your other nickel-and-dime ventures. More adventure than profit."

Silence, followed by the sounds of a woman crying.

"Sole, Sole, are you crying? Look, I'm sorry. I was—"

Click.

Camille and I looked at JD. His face bore an expression somewhere between surprise and agony.

"That's why the long time with no contact. You two had one of your classic fights?" I asked. I turned to Camille. "When I checked his voicemails and messages earlier, he must have deleted some of them, so I didn't catch on. That's why her voicemail box is full with no call back. You two were having it out."

"They've done this before?" Camille asked.

"It's what they've always done!" I said, getting up and pacing. "Ever since we were kids, this one always bossing Soledad around. Soledad always giving as much as she got."

"And yet," Camille said, putting her hand out to stop my pacing, "you didn't think to ask or check on that. You just followed him down here blindly."

I didn't have an answer for that. It was my turn to look thunderstruck.

"Alright, Señor Cruz, your turn to talk," she said, turning back to JD.

"Yes, we had a fight," he began, accentuating his speech with hand gestures. "She was going down to Colombia more and more. I wasn't sure where she was getting the money. She said it had to do with wine, but I never heard of wine being produced in Colombia."

"It's a small industry here, but it's growing," Camille said. "See? I do my homework." She motioned for JD to continue.

"Well, I didn't know that, but I did know that tourists, especially female tourists, were getting caught up in some shady crimes. Getting mixed up with the wrong people. Soledad is still somewhat naïve about these things."

"You mean like going into business with a one-hundred-year-old coffee family? Sounds really shady, JD," I said sarcastically.

Camille gave me a look that told me to shut up and let her speak.

"So, you had a fight, and she cut you off. Now, you're scared that you messed up, and if she's in trouble, you want to get to her before it's too late."

Those last few words from Camille brought misery to JD's face and tears to his eyes. I had not seen that coming.

JD nodded jerkily, then got up and walked out onto the balcony.

Camille and I sank back into our own thoughts about the situation.

About a year ago, I was swimming for my life in the Gulf of Mexico with JD, who had a bullet in his body, and I swear he looked better that night than he did at the moment.

Several minutes later, he came back inside. "Sorry for the lies," he began.

"Not a problem, JD," I said, cutting him off. "We're here now, and I'm still on board. Let's go find our Sole."

We looked at Camille. She slowly lowered the lid on her laptop. Then she smiled at us with wet eyes. I hadn't noticed that before.

"I guess we're all on board," I said.

We had a breakfast of pineapple, kiwi, strawberries, apples, sausages, assorted cheese and arepas. Then we were off to the Lazaro Coffee estate. Camille turned in her luxury sedan and upgraded our Jeep to a Wrangler Sahara. JD and I argued about who would drive, but I won out, as I was a WorldSpan employee. JD road shotgun, and Camille took the backseat. Even in Colombia's hot, humid climate, she was the cool French beauty.

Within fifteen minutes we were out of the city and into the lush foothills of Venecia Valley. Even though it was the middle of the day, I felt the temperature drop as we negotiated the two- and one-lane roads to the Antioquia countryside. Heavy brush along the hills bordered the twisty paved highway. The view was occasionally broken up by reddish rock and soil, clothes hanging on a homemade line, or a huge transport bus rushing by in the opposite direction.

About ninety minutes later, we reached the central square of the Municipia de Venecia. It featured colorful antiquated buildings with Spanish architecture, nothing less than fifty years old. Most of the people wore gray and beige work clothes, some with wide-brim straw hats. There was an outdoor market in a small park in the center of the square. By then I had discovered I had a hidden gringo's fixation on Spanish and Portuguese street food. Empanadas, fruit juices, and arepas were being sold alongside every kind of meat, tamales wrapped in green leaves, and *chupe de papa*—potatoes covered with cheese, meat, or a salsa-type mix. Desserts came in all shapes and sizes. Some resembled donut balls, and some were flatbreads covered with jams and soft cheeses. I wanted to try a little of everything. My love affair with the *salchipapa* street dish in the city was over.

As we walked around, one thing was obvious: the three of us were the talk of the square.

Coffee estates in Central and South America actually did a fair amount of tourist business, but they were usually run by carefree young folks wanting to enjoy time off the beaten path. Despite our attempt to dress down, we were too official looking to be anything but trouble. Besides, we were also stopping every half block to catch our breath due to the altitude.

"OK, JD and I will head over to the street market to get directions to the Lazaro Coffee estate," I said. "Camille, you can hang out here or head to those stores and do some shopping like a real tourist."

For once I got no backtalk. Maybe we were forming a decent team.

JD did the talking, being fluent in Spanish and able to stumble his way through Portuguese. I got schooled that salchipapa was more of a city street market food and somewhat paled next to the countryside's fresher fare. They were right. As I enjoyed a bowl of pineapple, mango, passion fruit, and dragon fruit, JD got directions to the Lazaro Coffee estate. Our phone coverage was spotty at best, so we had to just remember the directions, landmark by landmark.

"So, you think we fooled anyone in town?" Camille asked as we got back into the Jeep. She was carrying several bags of newly purchased items.

"Not in the least," JD said. "Ten to one, they're finding a landline and calling the Lazaros to tell them about the three Americanos headed there."

"Good because I'm ready to get some answers," I said, feeling like we were getting close. "Camille, how about you hang out in town and chat up the people at the local restaurant and stores? Throw some cash around and see what you can find out?"

"You think they'll talk to me?" she asked.

"Sometimes it's what they try hard not to say that speaks the loudest," I replied.

She looked around until she spotted a place called Elevacion Hair salon.

"I think it's time I got some maintenance," she said pointing to the storefront with colorful writing on it and ladies sitting out front with their hair in rollers, drying in the mountain air.

Giving JD a turn at the wheel, he took the curves out of town like he was ready for business. About fifteen minutes later we turned off the main road at a sign for the Lazaro Coffee estate. About a half mile in, the road forked. We took the left fork for the main estate, which we could see in the distance. The right fork went to something called Lalvarez Wineries. The road wound through rows and columns of coffee plants that were taller than the Jeep. I spotted workers throughout the rows filling straw baskets with ripe coffee beans. Occasionally, one of them would turn to look at us, but for the most part, we were a non-entity.

We weren't surprised when we were met by four men on horseback about one thousand feet from the estate. They appeared to be Latino and wore the same beige work clothes and wide-brim hats as the others. We pulled to a stop, and one of the four came forward. Like the others, he did not smile. Rifle butts peaked out of saddle holsters at their sides. The one moving forward also had a pistol with a long barrel in a holster strapped to his leg.

"Beinvinedos, señors, Welcome to the Lazaro Coffee estate."

He was well built, taller, and more prosperous looking than the rest. He had a mix of Latino and African features and coloring. His voice was cheerful, but his eyes were intelligent and leery. They didn't communicate fear. On the contrary, it was a confident caution that seemed to say, "I wish you would . . ."

The entire time he stared past JD and directly at me.

"Thank you for the welcome," JD began. "I'm Juan Diego Cruz from America. I'm looking for my sister, who has been down here for work. I have not heard from her in some time."

"Your sister is in the coffee business?"

"Uh, no. She was here for the winery. If we could speak to Señor Antonio Lazaro?"

The rider asked a few more questions, and I had to give it to JD. He stayed even keeled and polite. It was obvious to me that these men knew who Soledad was. The question was whether this was a stall for time or a tell that we were going to have to do things the hard way.

I heard a squawk as if from a walkie-talkie. One of the riders answered as he kicked his horse to saunter out of earshot. A few seconds later, he called to the rider who had spoken to us.

"Paulo!"

He broke off his conversation with JD and turned to look over his shoulder. He looked irritated, I'm sure, in part, because now we knew his name. I couldn't suppress a smile. The other rider rode up and whispered something to Paulo, who asked his partner if he was sure. I looked inquiringly at JD, who never took his eyes off of Paulo, the proud guardian.

"Gentlemen, I have been instructed to escort you to the main estate," Paulo said in a loud voice that only emphasized his aggravation. "Please follow the men to the main house."

Before we could thank him, Paulo rode off in one direction, and the other three riders galloped toward the estate, waving for us to follow.

"The plot thickens," I said. "What was all that about?"

"I don't know," JD replied, "but that guy was no joke."

In a few minutes we pulled into the circle drive in front of the expansive estate. It was a sprawling structure with a combination of Spanish Hacienda and Southern Antebellum architecture. The front was accented with floor-to-ceiling windows that opened like doors. I saw grand sitting rooms inside. There were large multi-story wings to the left and right. The windows on the ends were smaller but more numerous. There were balconies all around the wings, probably off bedrooms.

JD and I jumped out of the Wrangler and onto the pavement, instinctively moving to the front door. We were not going to be turned around without some effort. To our surprise, the main door opened, and a well-dressed young man in wire-rimmed spectacles appeared, ushering us inside.

"Beinvinedos, señors, come in. come in."

He introduced himself as Chico, the personal assistant to Señor Lazaro—the owner, not one of the sons.

"My boss is aware of your presence and will be with you momentarily. He is finishing up some business."

"That Paulo's a scary guy," I said by way of making conversation. JD gave me a dirty look.

Chico smiled. "Don't mind him. He's the field supervisor and a close friend of the Lazaro family."

"I didn't know the coffee business needed so many guns," I said.

"Well, when you have an estate this size, you must be ready for any kind of unannounced guests," Chico said with what my friend Gerald Williams called a "shit-eating grin."

We settled down in a large sitting room ,and a housekeeper brought us water, coffee, some kind of bread, fruit, and on a separate tray, cigars.

"So, this is good cop/bad cop?" I asked.

JD didn't answer right away. He was obviously taken in by the opulence. His eyes kept moving from the frescoed ceilings to the huge furniture to the artwork that seemed to cover every square inch of the walls.

15

Soledad quickly showered and frantically searched her luggage for something presentable to wear. She could hear voices on the deck. There were laughs, shouts, and maybe some arguing. Even though she could not make out what they were saying, it felt invasive, like someone would walk through the door and discover her half dressed.

She was giving herself a last once-over in the mirror when someone knocked frantically.

"Coming," she said. Then he stepped inside. Fernando was smiling, but that was the only happy thing about him. His wide eyes were dancing all about, and he was sweating profusely. His usually dapper clothes, which had seemed perfect minutes earlier, now looked bunched and wrinkled.

"Are you ready for my surprise, Soledad Marie?" he asked, holding his hand out. She instantly noticed the large and expensive gold hoop earring in his left ear. Soledad flicked it with her finger, and Fernando flinched in pain.

"Come on," he whispered. "It's a long story."

She walked past him and up on deck. Whatever the surprise was, she wanted to face it on her own terms.

The vessel's name was Largate, which meant "Get out, hop off, or beat it" in Spanish. It was a ship in every sense of the word. The main deck was over one hundred feet long and a third as wide. Fernando called it a

SuperFast class of yacht, as if that meant anything to her.

There was so much glass and white fiberglass that the glare blinded her when she reached the top of the steps. Soledad stood still to allow her eyes to adjust. The voices she heard had moved inside.

"Everyone is in the main salon," Fernando said, taking her by the hand. They walked along the teak wood deck on the port side to a large interior room. About fifteen people were inside, dressed in high-end white-and-blue boating attire. They smiled at Soledad but mumbled to themselves.

"Soledad, it is a sincere pleasure to meet you," a woman's voice said. It came from behind the crowd. Then, as if choreographed, the group parted to reveal the speaker. "Nando said we were twins, but now that I see it, I may cry."

The woman, also well dressed and wearing oversized shades, rushed forward and hugged Soledad for several seconds. They stared at each other, Soledad stupefied, and the woman snatched off her glasses while the room went silent.

"Señora Soledad Marie Cruz, may I present Señora Anise Constaneda-Vargas," Fernando said, stepping between Soledad and the near twin standing in front of her. "Anise, this is Antonio's business partner and fiancé, Señora Soledad Marie Cruz from Florida, USA."

"Nando, get away from us," Anise said, waving Fernando away. Then tears streamed from her eyes.

"Señora Constaneda, it's a pleasure. Your vessel is breathtaking."

Anise just stood there, tears streaming from her eyes.

"Are you OK?" Soledad said, reaching out to her and rubbing her shoulders. She finally looked at the others. There were a few security guard types, all muscles and dark suits. There were also a handful of men and women who could only be described as beautiful people, dressed in expensive casual clothes with three-figure haircuts and studio tans. They all murmured to themselves while pointing at the two women.

"Soledad, forgive me. I'm fine. Nando told me that he had met my twin," she said, wiping her eyes and smiling. "But come on; it's Nando, so I didn't believe him."

With that everyone on the boat laughed. Soledad laughed as well.

"When he told me how he had kidnapped you on the boat, I was so mad at him," Anise said, wiping her eyes with a tissue. Then she crumpled the tissue and threw it at Fernando, who was standing just a few feet away. The beautiful people began making castigating noises at Fernando, who stood there looking confused.

"It's OK," Soledad said.

"No, no," Anise interrupted with a devilish smile that Soledad found familiar and disconcerting. "I told Nando that if he was going to act like a pirate, he should at least look the part. We held him down and pierced his ear to give him that pirate's earring."

Soledad was shocked after realizing they were serious. Fernando turned his left ear to her to show off the bling and the line of dried blood from the hole in his ear. He shrugged, and all the beautiful people cheered with a sense of accomplishment. Anise grabbed Soledad by the shoulders and turned her until they were facing each other.

"My sister, you're Antonio's woman, yes?" she asked, and Soledad nodded. "Listen to me. If you're going to deal with these Colombian men, you have to make sure they respect you," Anise explained. "You have to keep them honest, or they'll walk all over you."

All the ladies made agreeable sounds in response to Anise's statements.

"Now, Antonio is a sweetheart, and he obviously has good taste, and," Anise reached over, stuck her finger in Fernando's hoop earring, and pulled, "Tonio is the better of the Lazaro brothers."

Laughs all around.

"But take it from a Colombian woman, you have to keep them in their place."

The ladies clapped, and the men just waved them off. Then the security guys came in with glasses of champagne. Everyone took one.

"A toast!" Anise shouted, raising her glass. "To Lalvarez Wines!"

The crowd cheered.

"And to sisterhood," Anise added, wrapping her arm around Soledad and squeezing. "And to a bright future," she finished, and everyone drank. Soledad took a fake drink, holding the glass to her lips.

Afterwards, everyone found places back out on the sundeck to hang out. Fernando stepped up, but Anise pushed him away.

"Soledad, I have some news," Fernando said. "From the estate."

"Antonio?" Soledad asked.

"No, he is still out in the hills, but the wine shipment is packed and on the truck. It will be here in a couple of days."

Soledad was clearly disappointed.

"This is good news," Anise said. "I know you want Antonio here, but Nando said there was some trouble?"

Soledad nodded.

"Honey, that's business. Antonio will handle it. You have to get that wine on the ship, right?"

Soledad nodded.

"Big-girl time, yes?" Anise said with another grab of her shoulders.

Soledad nodded again.

"I know Nando, here, isn't much, but I promise you, we're all here to help you. I won't let my twin fail!"

"Thanks," Soledad said with a deep sigh. "I appreciate it."

"Come on, let's dive into my closet. We'll get you a swimsuit and something to lounge in."

Over the next three hours, Anise and Soledad hung out in an even larger cabin, and Anise gave a polished explanation of her "export" business.

They repeatedly reveled in how much they looked alike, noting minute differences. Soledad showed her a scar she received from softball in ninth grade. Anise noted that her own chin was a little longer, and her makeup belied skin that was damaged beyond her years. Anise also rolled her birthdays back a few years to be equal to Soledad in age. Soledad could tell she was younger than Anise but was too polite to verbalize it. She was still a beautiful woman, and the resemblance was uncanny.

It was during that fun girl's afternoon that a sinister plan germinated in the smuggler's mind.

16

After sitting in the grand receiving room of the Lazaro Coffee estate for hours, it felt like lounging in a museum. JD and I considered making more of a ruckus, complaining about the wait, but then we thought about Paulo and his posse. We didn't even talk that much. We were overdosed on food, drink, and time.

I walked outside several times and watched nature working around us. The estate was not the buildings. Despite all their splendor and architectural precision, the buildings were the anomaly. The estate was the nature, the hills, the birds, the rush of water. Man, and his grand domiciliary manifestations, was a distant second to that beautiful picture.

I thought about Soledad. What did she think when she saw this? How did it affect her? I wondered where she was.

Until then I had thought this would be a quick turnaround. JD was worried, but he and I would go down to Colombia and find Soledad hard at work, as always. She would be embarrassed and pissed at her brother and bewildered by my appearance, after which I would catch a flight home to Paris.

Since our arrival, we had been arrested, given the runaround, and held up by armed estate hands, and we still hadn't found Soledad. In addition, we had found a Soledad look-alike with a member of the family that our Soledad was supposed to be visiting.

Now, we had been kept waiting for hours and fattened until our senses were dull.

The feeling I was getting was familiar. The last two times I ignored it, I almost paid with my life. Now I recognized it for what it was. It was the first instinct that something was wrong. Mortally wrong. My holistic teacher and combat instructor, Rudolph Lemieux, told me that feeling was a gift that I should be proud to have and exploit. I would have to take his word on that one.

I asked Chico if I could use the satellite phone to call Camille. The call didn't go through, and I was instantly suspicious for the hundredth time that day. I tried Soledad's number and got the same result.

Just before 5:00, we heard footsteps and voices approaching. We recognized one as Chico, Señor Lazaro's assistant. The other had to be the man himself.

He was of medium height and impeccably dressed. He was a throwback to how American executives dressed in the 1950s or 1960s—cufflinks, tie clip, handkerchief, custom-tailored three-piece suit in seasonal material. He wore rings on three fingers and an oversized but very expensive watch. He smiled at us when he entered the room, but his eyes said something totally different.

"Excuse us, Don Lazaro," JD began, speaking just above a whisper. "We do not mean to intrude on your hospitality. It is just that we are looking for my sister."

"Come now, Señor Cruz, I am no nobleman. There are no dons here," he said and let his face go into a smiling frown like he had never heard the term before. He and Chico shared a chuckle. "Please, Señor will do just fine. Now, what is this about your sister?"

He sat on the sofa across the expansive room from us, and Chico handed him a drink. We remained standing.

"Yes, sir, Soledad Marie Cruz. I believe she was working with your youngest son, Antonio, on a wine venture." JD proffered a photo of Soledad on his phone.

Alexandro leaned slightly forward, barely looking at the picture or JD. Then he leaned back and sighed. Feeling his attitude creep up past my ankles, I decided to take a seat. He shot me a look that showed he didn't like that. Good.

"And you are?" he asked with barely controlled disdain.

"Teke Manion, a family friend," I said at a volume slightly above conversational. "But I'm sure you already know that, Señor Lazaro. It has been several days since we have heard from Soledad. We thought maybe you could help us."

"I can't. I run a coffee estate. I know nothing about wine."

"Then maybe we can talk to Antonio," JD said. "I understand that they are working closely on Antonio's wine business."

Alexandro sipped his drink and then stared at us for several seconds. "Antonio is not here. A few days ago, one of his American friends was killed. Another one of his friends ran off into the hill country. Antonio and some of my men are trying to find him."

"Killed? How?" I asked, jumping to my feet.

"Was my sister with them?" JD asked, fear in his voice.

"Nooooo," Alexandro replied as if our questions irritated him. "She was not here. You know, this wine business hasn't made a dime, but already it has caused my business great trouble. Gunplay and bloodshed on my estate? It's disgraceful. If this is what this business brings, I won't have any part of it."

"I don't know what to say, Señor Lazaro, except that my sister isn't a part of anything illegal. The Cruzes are an honorable family steeped in law enforcement in the United States. I am a deputy in Manatee County, Florida." JD pulled out his badge and credentials to show Alexandro.

"Ah," he said and all but spat. "Cruz! A common name."

That would have been fighting words for JD any other time, but for some reason, he was giving this rude old man deference beyond belief. So, I said what had to be said.

"Hey! We're sorry for the trouble you had, but we need to find Soledad. If she's not here, and Antonio isn't here, where is she? Tell us that, and we'll be on our way."

With that he smiled. It was not a nice expression.

"I believe my other son, Fernando, is going to help her get the wine shipment on the ship to America. As far as I'm concerned, the sooner, the better."

"Fernando, yes, we met him in front of his restaurant. He was with a woman, um, Anise Constaneda," JD said. I knew that was not a good idea as soon as he said it.

"You?" Alexandro shouted, his eyes wide and his face full of contempt. "You're the two who attacked my son at his restaurant?"

"It was a misunderstanding Señor Lazaro," JD said. "The woman, she looks a lot like my sister, and—"

That was as far as he got. The door from the front veranda flew open, and Paulo entered with a few new players. They looked official.

17

The day was unforgettable.

Soledad started that morning unsure and in a strange place. The day got even stranger when she met Anise Constaneda, who was practically her twin. Then from the time they met, the day got as "dream good" as it had been strange.

They spent that afternoon marveling about their appearance. Anise lived like Soledad thought a successful, confident woman lived. They laughed, sharing stories about their respective childhoods. They both had older brothers who bullied and then protected them. They also had relatives who were in law enforcement or government. Their mothers died when they were young.

Throughout the day people knocked on Anise's cabin door, and her phone rang. She dispatched orders in a succinct fashion. She knew every facet of her business. She didn't need to have a meeting or consult a committee. She answered questions and never let the mood wane.

"Tell me the Lalvarez Wine story," Anise said as she laid on the bed looking up at Soledad, who was still trying on clothes from the voluminous closet. There was no way Soledad could refuse. It was like telling the story to herself.

She started with the video meeting where Antonio discussed his dream of a Colombian winery, producing red varieties to rival Argentinian, Chilian, or Brazilian brands. At that time his first vintage had been barreled for a year. He was another year from bottling, but he was as confident as a man could be with no product to sample.

Anise sat riveted and secretly envious as Soledad detailed each subsequent visit. Soledad had gone from exploratory vacationing to officially advising to emotionally, intellectually, and strategically invested in her lover's dream. It was a dream Anise could have had, long before the betrayal and misdirection pushed her into the underworld.

"Why didn't you tell your brother about Antonio?" she asked.

"I did but just about the business part. I wanted to make sure the other part was going to last beyond the initial launch."

"I get it," Anise said. "I've heard relationships based on intense experiences never work. Sometimes the pressure and constant stress of working on a project can make strange bedfellows."

"Yeah, right," Soledad said, laughing in recognition of the familiar line from the movie *Speed*.

"Then after the project, things could go sour."

"Oh, I know," Anise said, rolling her eyes. "It happened to me."

"Really?"

"Twice," Anise said in a confessional tone, holding her hand to her heart.

"Oh my god, Anise?" Soledad said.

"What?"

"It's just . . . that you seem like you have your stuff together and that you would be immune to that. Who broke it off?"

"The first time, I did. The second time, she did."

"She?" Soledad said, unable to hide her giggle.

"It was a very special project," Anise said with a nonchalant smile and a wink.

Later, she sent Soledad out on deck to catch the sunset with the others. Her bathing suit was as white as Greek limestone and a tad more revealing than Soledad liked. Anise gave her a silk wrap and pushed her out the door.

"I have some calls I need to return, and I must get some sleep," Anise said. "Then I want to call the harbormaster and lend my name to that wine shipment. Make sure he gives it the attention it deserves."

"But that's not really the harbormaster's job," Soledad said.

"Oh, my twin, I assure you," Anise said with a devilish grin, "his job is what I say it is."

A few moments later, Anise heard Soledad laughing and talking to the others on the deck. Anise found the satellite phone and called a number. A woman answered. Her voice was still as sexy as the night she seduced Anise the first time. Anise had been an operative for a small-time smuggler whose name and the location of his remains had been long forgotten.

"Thanks again for the heads-up," Anise said.

"Anything for you, baby," Padilla replied. "You on the boat?"

"Yeah, and so is she. The resemblance is spooky."

"She may look like you, but she ain't you. Not where it counts."

Anise rolled her eyes and stayed quiet. She could hear street sounds on the other end of the phone. Padilla was always out somewhere. Despite her suspect character, Padilla's voice and shameless flirts always affected Anise, making her feel soft inside.

"What else can I do for you, Neecy?" Padilla asked, purposely using a secret nickname that she had created for Anise.

"What's my status with the authorities?"

"The same," Padilla said, sounding bored. "Several patrols are watching your warehouse, your personal residence, and your big, sexy boat."

"Any raids planned?"

"No, but they're watching the lumber you're moving in and out of your warehouse. I have to say, your crew is pretty sloppy. They didn't even cover the load or come in after dark."

"Yeah, I know."

"Baby, the minute you try to move that illegal lumber out of the country, they're going to bust you," Padilla said, irritation in her voice.

"Is that so?"

"Yes. They're going to put a tracker in your shipment and confiscate it the minute you start to move it."

"Let me guess," Anise said excitedly. "Then they'll swoop down and arrest me wherever I am as part of an international task force to combat smuggling."

The phone was quiet except for the street sounds on Padilla's end.

"You think you're smarter than you are," the crooked cop said.

"Oooohhh, baby, don't think I don't appreciate the intel. I hope you didn't have to 'swallow' too much pride during your sessions with the feds."

"To hell with you, Neecy," Padilla said, irritated now. "I'm putting my job and my career on the line for you."

"No, no, I'm paying you to play nice with the police, to leverage your unique 'talents' to the benefit of my business. Now, are you sore at me, baby, or just sore?"

Anise knew she had gone too far. It was one thing to pay Padilla to sleep with cops to get inside information. However, she had said it out loud, thrown it in Padilla's face, and that was a no-no. The American agent was the easiest target—away from home, married with two kids and no 'fun' in his life. To him it was just sharing interdepartmental intel with local authorities. With benefits. Nevertheless, it was bad business to remind her paid agents of the dirty work they did, but Padilla had pissed Anise off with that "Neecy baby" crap. Those days were long gone.

She said those things to get a rise out of me. Well, she got a rise, alright.

"Is there anything else?" Padilla asked.

"I don't know. Is there?"

"Anise, you called *me*, remember?"

"Oh yeah, I guess not. Tha—"

Before Anise could finish, Padilla hung up. Anise chuckled. Then she punched in another number, this time to her warehouse manager.

Things were in place.

18

It had been a relaxing day in Venecia for Camille. After Teke and JD left for the Lazaro Coffee estate, she spent time at the Elevacion Salon. Then she settled in the small market and restaurant called Zena's. The other coffeehouse, owned by Fernando Lazaro, was closed. It was the coffeehouse for tourists. Zena's was where the locals and fieldworkers went.

It was run by a no-nonsense, fifty-something Colombian woman named Zena. She did the cooking while her children took orders, collected the money, and bussed the tables. She had a son, Andres, age sixteen, and a daughter, Seynah, age twenty.

For the first hour, they served Camille with quiet dispatch. By the third hour, it was the slow time of the afternoon before the laborers returned from the fields. As was her habit, Zena put her cabbage with sausage and pork adobo on slow simmer and took a much-needed nap in the back storage room.

Camille entertained Seynah and Andres' questions about Paris and other parts of Europe, and she listened intently to their plans for the future. Andres wanted to get on the estate and work his way up to being a field boss or a truck driver, like their older cousin. Seynah couldn't wait to get out of the hill villages and travel to anywhere but Colombia.

Zena reappeared in the late afternoon. Camille couldn't tell if her stern expression, efficient actions, and the loud clatter of pots and pans indicated if she was upset about something or if it was part of her routine in anticipation of the evening business. Her children snapped back into their duties, saying little and avoiding eye contact. Camille finished her last coffee, closed her laptop, and prepared to leave.

She had not heard from Teke and JD. She tried to use her satellite phone to call Teke's cell, but it didn't go through. She tried to pay her check, but Seynah and Andres were not around. Camille brandished several 100,000 Colombian peso notes at the front counter. Zena looked up from her cooking and gave a quick nod. Camille left the cash, which included a hefty tip, on the counter.

The village's central quad was filling with people again. Music wafted through the air from one of the corners. It was not an actual band but rather a few men playing songs by Carlos Vives, crooning melodically but mournfully about unrequited love. As she sauntered past the shops in the square to get a closer listen, she heard someone hiss at her from a side street.

"Señora DeSoronne, I'm glad I caught you," Seynah said. She was against the side of a building. From that vantage point her mother could not see her from the front window of their restaurant. Camille guessed that would be the only person Seynah would fear seeing her talking to the female stranger. Camille looked around to see who else may be watching. Making eye contact with no one, she slipped between the buildings where the young server girl was hiding.

"Call me Camille," she said when she reached the teenager, who showed genuine fear in her eyes but also a level of anger. No, not anger. Defiance.

"I'm a good girl; I do what my mother tells me each and every day."

"Of course," Camille said. "I know that."

"My mother, she is suspicious of strangers, and there has been talk about you and your friends."

"What kind of talk?"

"That you had something to do with the murder at the Lazaro Coffee estate," Seynah explained.

"What murder?" Camille asked, urgency all over her face.

"The American who was shot."

"Shot? Killed? Which one? How do you know this? My friends just went up there today," Camille said, her voice going well above conversational as she grabbed Seynah by her shoulders.

"No, Señora, not your Americans. This was last week. The Americans who were helping Señor Antonio Lazaro with his wine business. One was shot and killed. The other was lost in the hill country. No one knows what happened."

Camille stepped back, releasing Seynah. She was breathing hard to stem the lightheadedness she felt. They stayed that way for a few seconds. Camille needed to think.

"OK. What about the lady, Señorita Soledad Cruz?" Camille asked while trying to process that Teke was once again involved with dead bodies.

"Oh, yes, I believe she and Señor Antonio Lazaro are more than partners, if you know what I mean," Seynah said with a knowing smile.

"Yes, yes, yes, but where is she? Was she hurt?" Camille asked, barely maintaining her composure.

"I don't believe she was hurt, no, but I don't know where she is. She has not been seen since before the shooting."

Camille nodded, thinking about what she had just been told and what she should do about it.

"Camille, did you mean what you said about helping me get to Paris to study?" Seynah asked. The question caught Camille off guard.

"Yes, of course. You and your family have been excellent to me and my friends. How old are you?"

"Twenty," she said quickly. "but I'll be twenty-one in four months."

"Good for you," Camille said. "Let me guess: your mother doesn't approve of you straying away from home?"

Seynah did not answer, just looked down at her feet. There was an extended silence in the alley.

"Wait a minute," Camille said, her brain continuing to work. "Why are you telling me this now? About the killing? I've been sitting in your place all day."

The fear returned to Seynah's young face. "Like I said, Camille, my mother is suspicious, but you've been so nice, so . . ."

"What, Seynah? What do you know?"

"Your friends who left this morning? I heard my mother talking to her friend whose son works at the local police department."

"Yes," Camille said, fearing rising in her again.

"They've been arrested."

"Arrested? For what?" Camille said before thinking. She waved it off as Seynah shrugged. "Never mind that," Camille continued. "Just point me toward the police station."

Seynah pointed to the building on the opposite corner with a Colombian flag draped in the front. Camille turned to run in that direction. She stopped after a few steps and turned back to Seynah. "I can't help you with Mama, but I promise to help you get to Paris if that's what you want. Thank you for your courage."

Camille opened her leather satchel and pulled a business card from the inner pouch. She signed the back of it, handed it to Seynah, then kissed her on the cheek and ran across the quadrangle toward the police station.

It was an old Spanish façade with pale beige paint. The tip of the parapet walls was festooned with carved wood. The symmetrical windows were similarly adorned. Camille thought it could just as easily be an apartment or a set of business offices.

When she got inside, it took several minutes to find someone who spoke Spanish slowly enough or English well enough for her to have a conversation.

Eventually, she got an audience with Constable Munoz—no first name.

Munoz was big. Worldwide Wrestling Federation Big. Everything from his head to his feet seemed to be supernatural in size. He had short black hair, heavy eyebrows, and a toothy grin that emerged as soon as he appeared.

"Let me guess," he began. "I arrest two Caucasian Americans for the first time in five years, and now a sexy overdressed French woman shows up. I can connect the ends."

"I'm not sure what that means, Deputy—"

"Constable," he said, holding his grin. He hadn't had this much fun in a while.

"Sorry, Constable, but you're right. I'm here for Señor Manion and Señor Cruz. I understand they were arrested."

"Not arrested," he said. "Just detained."

"Detained? For what?"

"Excuse me, but you said you were an executive vice-president of some such or other?"

"WorldSpan Underwriters."

"So, you're not a lawyer licensed to practice in Colombia?"

"Of course not," Camille said, trying to not let her frustration show.

"Then Señora, I'm not sure how much I can share with you."

"Fine. Can I see the pris—detainees?" she asked.

"No. Visiting hours are over for the day. Come back tomorrow."

"You're keeping them overnight? Why?"

"Let's just say we take killings at the home of our major employer very seriously."

"But that happened before my guys got here," Camille said.

"Well, that's just it. We don't know who did the killing, so maybe your 'guys' know something, or maybe they don't."

"This is not due process, Constable."

"In this part of the world, I say what is due process, Señora. And if you keep running your mouth, you can see your friends, alright. I'll put your fancy French ass in the cell right next to them."

Camille took a step back and held up her hands.

"Good, I think we're done here until tomorrow morning," Constable Munoz said. His smile never left his face the entire time.

Camille turned and left the station. She saw the night desk officer, a woman. She had a stony expression. Camille made sure she gave her a broad smile and a two-finger salute.

She had done business in cities as large as New York and Shanghai and villages as small as this one where one family or company ran the entire show. They all had the same lever that turned "no" into "yes."

She drove back to the rental in Medellin. She plugged in her converters, adapters, chargers, laptops, and sat phones. Her first call was to Lisette Fournier, the top researcher at WorldSpan Underwriters. It was almost midnight in Paris, but she was sure she would be up and eager. She had better be because they had work to do.

19

Carlos "Beato" Pacheo had watched the last three sunrises. It was easy, as he hadn't slept in the last three days.

"Beato" was a moniker from childhood when he earned a reputation for never getting into trouble. That was unheard of in his Peruvian village. A child's prowess amongst his friends was measured by how much trouble they caused for their mother or the nuns.

Beato led that life into adulthood. Rumor had it that he never got a cold, pneumonia, rickets, or any of the other ailments that plagued all the other children where he grew up. It became common knowledge that if someone had some dicey business to handle, and they needed all the luck they could get, then they should take Beato as part of their posse.

This reputation was a gift and a curse that followed him to Colombia.

The gift was that Beato never had to hold a steady job in the fields of the local farms, estates, or ranches, which was the usual path of all the men of his village. Beato became a popular second or third hand of the criminal element. He had more money and more free time than anyone in Venecia Valley.

The curse was what he had to endure. Sometimes he had to live amongst the smugglers on the farms deep in the jungles of the Amazon.

The raped landscape left bare land that failed to grow anything. Ramshackle tin-roof huts on stilts dotted the barren land in the middle of yet uncut jungle. Villagers, who were direct descendants of one hundred generations, roamed the property as aimless slaves where they used to live as stewards of the land.

They had always worshiped and protected the flora and fauna. Now they suffered from mercury poisoning from the illegal strip mining they were forced to do.

They were promised great sums of money but seldom received anything. Others were enticed by a life of good drugs and free sex from village women and children forced into prostitution. If that did not work then there was the threat of death to every member of the reluctant workers' family. The smuggler camps were sad places of ill smells, sickness, and misery.

The boss whom Beato worked for was a woman, Anise Constaneda. She took over the operation from a distant relative who took her under his wing after her father, the magistrate, died. That old man was Beato's first boss.

The old boss had made Anise his sexual plaything. Then he put her to work on the smuggling crews. She learned everything about the smuggling business and then built her own crew and her own network of bribed officials. When the old boss died, she took over the operation. After using her new bribed officials to get rid of some competitors, she was able to run things her way. They were making more money than ever, but the farms were more miserable than ever. After some time it was Anise who made Beato move out to the farms.

"You're too comfortable, Beato!" she told him one day, laughing. "Move out to the farm where you belong. You have people in Venecia thinking you're some kind of boss or something."

That was a year ago. Beato split his time between Venecia and the illegal farms. Anise never said a word to him. Until this week. Three days ago she found him out in the jungle at one of the logging operations.

"Beato, the blessed one, I have a special job for you," she explained, then motioned for them to take a walk into the jungle. They climbed a hill used as a lookout for anyone coming in any direction. The adjoining hills were stripped of trees, leaving just the scrub vegetation. Beato kept his eyes out on the horizon, never looking directly at the guards and their AR-15 rifles.

"The old boss thought you were some kind of lucky charm?" she asked.

"I don't know, Señora. You know how rumors and stories get started in these superstitious villages," he said nervously.

"So, you're not lucky?" she asked. "Are you not superstitious?"

"I don't know," he said, looking down at his boots.

"But it's true that you've never been arrested, shot, or hurt in any way?"

Beato shrugged.

On that hill a few days ago, Anise gave him an assignment. A big one.

"For the next shipment, we need to send over some laundered cash," she explained. "Your trip is scheduled to coordinate with a shipment of illegal lumber arriving in port at that same time."

"I don't mule, Boss," Beato replied. "It's not what I do."

It was true. Carrying smuggled contraband, hot cash, or drugs was the work of the desperate and the young who needed fast cash or needed to work off their drug tab. Then Anise smiled sweetly and leaned in close to him.

"Sweet Beato," she said, reaching up to caress his hot, sweaty cheek with her cold hand. "You do what I say you do."

Now Beato was sitting in the bedroom of his small home in Venecia. The US$50,000 was in twenty-five banded packs. The plan was to duct tape the packs to his body, dress in loose-fitting but casual clothing, and take a plane trip to the United States—New Orleans, to be exact.

His phone vibrated loudly on the rough locally made nightstand.

"Yeah," he answered, his voice just above a whisper.

"Hey, my good luck charm! You ready?"

It was Escoba. He and his brother started in the lumber and mining camps in Peru and different parts of the jungles. They started as laborers and moved up to gunmen who forced the local villagers to work and forced their women into prostitution and slave labor.

Now Escoba and his brother transported the illegal lumber to ships in Cartagena. Beato knew Escoba was called that because he was as skinny as a broomstick, and his hands shook compulsively, a result of the mercury poisoning associated with illegal mining. Beato never knew his brother's name.

"Yeah, I guess," Beato replied.

"You guess?" Escoba said, his voice full of power. "Listen, my friend, when you roll with us, we don't allow any indecision. You hear?"

"Yeah," Beato said.

"We'll be there to pick you up, and my brother and I are going to be positive, happy, no long faces, no bad energy. Understand?"

"Yeah."

"Bad energy can be seen by the police and the NDTC agents,"

Escoba said.

"Bad energy has a stink, man," Escoba's brother said.

"Right."

"Don't get on our truck stinkin', Beato," Escoba ordered.

"I won't."

"'Cause we won't get caught. Understand?" the brother said.

"I remember."

The phone was silent for a few seconds.

"OK, we'll see you soon," Escoba said, then hung up.

Beato looked at himself in the mirror. Thinking about Escoba's words, he smiled his winning smile.

"Of course I'll get through this. I'm Beato! I've been lucky since birth."

20

On the surface, the scene at the Lazaro Coffee estate the previous night looked like Alexandro Lazaro was handling things with an iron fist.

When the local constable took Cruz and Manion away, he had tried to relax but couldn't find what Polonia called a Zen place. Although he would never admit it, all of this scared him. The death of the American, the disappearance of the American's "partner," Antonio's ridiculous wine business, and all these outsiders showing up on his property was just about all the coffee magnate could take.

His father and grandfather had founded and grown the company into one of the most respected business names in the country. Alexandro lived with the fear of being the Lazaro who allowed it all to come crashing down, to not leave a legacy after his death. It was foolishness like this that got people talking, gave his competitors a foothold, and signaled the beginning of the end. If one of his sons would take their legacy seriously, he could get some sleep.

Long after the house was quiet, after his third Mil Demonios Brandy, he was still wide awake. Two hours and two additional drinks later, he washed up on the doorstep of Polonia Meneses. She answered the door in bare feet and the thigh-length, dark-blue silk gown and robe.

Earlier that day she had heard from her cousin—the detective in Medellin—about the American who was looking for his sister, the altercation with Fernando in front of his money-wasting restaurant, and then the Americans showing up at the estate.

She let Alexandro in, but they didn't talk. She helped him out of his suit, made him a drink, and put him to bed next to her. At about 1:00 a.m., she felt him against her back. Still on her side, she shifted her gown and maneuvered her body, and he entered her from behind.

He pushed out his frustration and fear in every thrust. She arched her back as she reached back to scrape her nail lightly against his hips and sides. The last thing she remembered was him showering her neck, cheek, and back with words and kisses of gratitude and raw emotion.

The next morning, she was awakened by the incessant buzzing of a cell phone. She peeked toward the bedroom window. No daylight peeped around the edges of her blackout curtains. That meant it was pre-sunrise, and the call was an emergency.

"Papi, answer your phone. Someone's looking for you," she said, reaching behind her and shoving Alexandro in the chest. He mumbled something unintelligible.

The phone stopped. Then started again a few seconds later. Polonia reached over and answered it.

"Hello?" There was silence. "Who is this?" she asked, perturbed.

"This is Luisa Lazaro. Who is this?"

"Oh, good morning, Luisa, dear. It's Polonia."

"I'm looking for my father. We have big trouble," Luisa said, her voice full of stress.

"Hold on," Polonia said.

By then Alexandro was awake, especially upon hearing his daughter's name. He could even hear her voice in the solemn quiet of Polonia's bedroom. He made hand gestures telling Polonia not to let Luisa know he was with her.

"Alexandro, please," Polonia explained, rolling her eyes and muting the phone. "She just called your phone, and I answered. It's before 6:00 a.m. Now talk to her. She says it's important."

Alexandro rubbed his face in exasperation. He cleared his throat and snatched the phone from Polonia. She shoved his shoulder again, and he bobbled the phone. She got out of bed and went into the bathroom. Alexandro picked the phone up from the floor.

"Luisa, what is it? I'm in a meeting," he said, putting on his best authoritative voice.

"Yeah, I bet you are," Luisa said, barely stifling her chuckle. "Listen, we've been getting some calls from the hedge fund financiers."

"Why? For what?" he asked.

The Ag-Fidelity Fund was a European group of high-end investors who provided bridge loans to coffee growers. They had better rates than commercial banks and asked fewer questions. As long as payments were on time, everyone was happy.

"I'm not sure. It started in the middle of the night, about 9:00 a.m. in their time zone. I got accounting out of bed. We've been going over every account."

"And?"

"Papa, did you get an inspector at the operation?"

"Of course not; I'm not in the fields."

"Are you sure, Papa?"

"Yes, Luisa, I'm sure. Did you check with Paulo?" Alexandro asked, growing more frustrated.

"Of course. The fund managers said they received a scathing report citing the murder and the disruption to operations."

"Liars!" Alexandro shouted. "Someone amongst the field hands is talking!"

"Papa, please. How would our field hands go about calling our fund managers? And why would the fund managers listen?"

"So, what are they saying? They don't want to do business with us?" Alexandro golfed with the largest banker in Medellin every month. He would have no problem taking Alexandro's business.

"Not exactly, but they're voicing concerns from the Teke Manion report they received. We have outstanding loans that could be called up for repayment immediately."

"Wait," Alexandro said, stopping in his tracks. "Teke Manion? What does he have to do with our financiers?"

"You know him?" Luisa asked.

"Just tell me, Miha!" he implored. He could hear Luisa flipping through pages. She gave instructions to someone else in the room. Then she came back on the phone.

"OK, Teke Manion is some kind of insurance underwriter/rater. He works for WorldSpan Underwriters. WorldSpan is a partner to the hedge fund financiers, Ag-Fidelity. They invest premiums for WorldSpan, and WorldSpan conducts investigations of some of their sketchier investments."

"And Manion?"

"He's one of their top investigators. So, Papa, you do know him?" Luisa asked. "You met this Manion?"

Alexandro just hung up the phone and hurried to get dressed.

109

21

For Soledad, It had been the strangest week. A good week but nothing like she envisioned. Waiting on the wine shipment was a stomach churner. Not being able to talk to Antonio was like being on a high wire with no net, but her twin made it better. She was like a gift from heaven, right when Soledad needed it most. Working from the ship Largate was not bad either.

Even Fernando was keeping his word. Soledad hated to admit it, but taking a man along when talking to the quartermaster office personnel and dock managers made things easier. She could have handled it herself, but she appreciated not having to cut through the machismo before getting down to business. Also, the Lazaro family carried weight. Antonio's family shipped a huge amount of cargo through Colombian ports each year.

The sun rose on Cartagena Bay and added a sparkle to the dark water. That luminous energy and the steady rocking of the *Largate* brought her out of her daydreaming and out of bed. She looked out the window and realized they were out to sea.

The *Largate* moved steadily, sending spray over the starboard rails and onto the deck. The vessel's white fiberglass surface seemed to glow in the morning light.

There was a knock on her stateroom door.

"Soledad? You decent?" Anise called out.

"Just a minute."

"Nisa! Get in here already," Soledad said, opening the door and pulling Anise into the room. They laughed, and Soledad noticed that she was hiding something behind her back.

They stood there staring at each other, thinking the same thing as they had since they met.

Wow, it's like looking in a mirror.

"What are you doing?" Soledad asked, smiling and looking playfully suspicious.

"Who's your friend?" Anise asked, standing apart from Soledad, who pointed back to Anise.

They laughed.

"OK, I need a favor," Anise continued.

"Nisa, what are you hiding?" Soledad asked, using Anise's nickname from childhood. The smuggler-gangster gave no one the permission to use that name, but she insisted that Soledad use it.

"I promise you; it's worth it," Anise said. "But my favor first?"

Soledad motioned for her to continue, going along with the show.

"As you see, we're out to sea. We made some upgrades to the engine and satellite systems over the last few days. To get them approved by the Cartagena Maritime Authority, we need to take the Largate out to test the new toys."

"I don't know anything about yachts," Soledad said.

"You don't need to know anything. The deckhands and staff know what to do. Just be on board during the test voyage. I have to go."

"Go where?"

Anise looked at her with the smile of indulgence. "Miha, at some point, I have to show up in the office. If not, my people will run things into the ground."

"I'm sorry. Of course. I knew that," Soledad said, blushing. Anise reached out and hugged her with her free hand.

"I know you do, Sole. It's been fun, right? I enjoyed it too," Anise confessed in a sweet voice. "And I promise: we'll have more of these."

"I hope so," Soledad said, a tear running down her cheek.

"So, you will do this for me? Woman my ship for a day?"

"Of course, Nisa. I don't know how I would have done this without you. Especially with Antonio not being around . . ."

"Aaaahhh," Anise said, then revealed a satellite phone in her hidden hand. She pressed the button to disengage the mute function. "That reminds me. Someone wants to talk to you."

Soledad took the phone from her with a business-like dispatch. She presumed it was yet another question from the dockmaster.

"Sole, how are you, my love?"

"Tonio!" she said, her voice filled with emotion as her eyes spilled over with tears. "Oh my God, where are you?"

Anise eased out of the room. Her smile was reminiscent of a cat that had swallowed the proverbial mouse. She slipped into her stateroom and changed clothes. Then she went with a group of crew members who were similarly dressed in medium gray clothes and caps.

The *Largate* eased to a stop in the waters where Cartagena Bay meets the open sea. Anise and her crew slipped over the seaward side of the ship. She laid face down in a speedboat, a cheap, stripped-down aluminum-hulled vessel about twenty-eight feet in length. The speed came from the twin premium-grade outboard racing engines strapped to the transom. The usual cargo was humans, drugs, or cash, but it always came with hundreds of gallons of gas. Speedboats were used to move precious cargo very fast. In this case, Anise Constaneda needed to get far away from the *Largate*.

Fernando woke up from the drug-induced sleep thanks to the powdered Xanax that Anise had slipped into his martinis.

He found a note from her.

Nando,

You fell asleep waaaay too early but just to bring you up to date . . . Your brother Antonio called on your phone. He is back at the Lazaro Coffee estate. Please use Largate as your headquarters for the next few days while I'm away. Help yourself to anything you like. And, finally, look out for my new sister. I love her. Don't let anything happen to her.

~Anise

That was alright with him. The *Largate* had the best booze and food, satellite communication, modern navigation, the best in comfort. Fernando thought if he looked hard enough, he might even find some decent weed, pills, or other goodies. He just had to get the wine on the ship while managing his brother and Soledad.

He came up on the main deck and realized for the first time that they were out to sea. He could barely see the port of Cartagena off in the northwest. He went to the steering house, and his blood froze. Gypsy was steering the craft and looking out to sea as if he knew what he was doing. The slick ear-piercing artist seemed out of place behind the wheel of the yacht, but Fernando wasn't going to say a word.

A sharp tap on Fernando's shoulder made him jump.

It was Soledad.

"Hey, sister, it seems we have the run of the ship as our headquarters."

"I know," Soledad said with a solemn smile.

"And Anise had to go, but . . ."

"I know," she said, her smile fading.

"Aaaahhhh, but the biggest news is that Antonio is back!"

Soledad held the satellite phone up to him. Her smile was gone. "Yes, I just spoke to him. I told him about everything that's happened, and he told me what I didn't know. How come you didn't tell me Wayne was dead and that Mario was on the run?"

"Like I said, sister, I was trying to shield you and keep you on task."

"But you still didn't tell me about it?" Soledad asked, her eyes accusing and piercing.

"I can explain," Fernando said, his hands up in mock surrender. He took Soledad's arm and led her to seats out on the open deck. "At that time, you and I hadn't met. You had met Father and Luisa, but I was at my club in Medellin. Then, after the shooting, Antonio needed you to focus on getting the shipment out. With what happened to poor Wayne I felt I had to protect you. I promised Antonio we would get the shipment off."

Soledad just looked at him. She knew he was being less than honest, but she couldn't figure out what he was hiding.

Her head was spinning. Anise was gone; Antonio was back; Wayne was dead; Mario was missing, and Fernando was lying. She realized Fernando had been droning on for the last few seconds, trying to explain himself. She held up a hand to stop him. Then she held up the phone.

"Your brother, Antonio, is on the line. He wants to talk to you. Share and improve your fairy tales with him," she said as she tossed the phone into his lap.

Seynah got no sleep the previous night. After departing from the French businesswoman, Camille, she spent the rest of the evening going through the motions in the restaurant. She barely heard her mother's fussy commands or her brother's grumbling.

That night she laid in her small bed looking at the moonlight shadows dancing on the ceiling of the bedroom that she shared with her mother. Andres slept in a room off the back that had been made into a bedroom for him.

The house was quiet save for Zena's heavy breathing. She worked so hard that by the end of the day she had nothing left but to bathe, say her prayers, and fall asleep, listening to the radio. Seynah sometimes felt ashamed of her own thoughts. Zena was her mother, and she loved her to the moon and back. However, every day she watched her work in that restaurant day in and day out, it scared her to death.

This cannot be my life!

She had felt this way before, about four or five times per year, a feeling like her world was closing in on her, so close that it was hard to breathe. When Seynah felt this way, she would get a ride out of town.

Lando was a cousin on her father's side of the family who worked on the Lazaro Coffee estate. Many times he drove truck shipments from Venecia to the docks in Cartagena or into Medellin.

Whenever she felt like she had last night and now this morning, she would look for his truck coming through the center of town and flag him down. He would let her ride into the city with him. If he was working with a partner, she would ride in back of the open-air truck bed with the cargo. She didn't care as long as she got to the city.

Lando would drop her off in the middle town and let her roam the streets, look in the windows, and dream of a different life. Then he would pick her up at the end of the day, bringing her home on his way back to the estate. It would be enough to hold her until the next time.

That morning as she helped her mother open the restaurant, she looked for one of the Lazaro trucks. She cursed under her breath when none of them appeared.

"Seynah, get out of that window, and help your brother stock the shelves!" Zena shouted from the back.

Seynah came out of her daydream and loped off to the storefront portion of the restaurant.

At the other end of Venecia Square, the morning sun illuminated the front of the Lazaro Coffee office building. It was the original courthouse built in the early 1900s with Spanish architecture and clay tile roofing and accents. The walls were a stucco that glowed a soft light coral when the sun shone on it.

The quiet outside façade was in sharp contrast to the human storm going on inside the corporate office.

"Can you please tell me why you dragged me here at this time of morning?" Alexandro started.

He really means, 'Why did I call him out of his secret girlfriend's bed?' Luisa thought.

They were meeting in the office that morning, along with their head accountants and the partners from the firm of Jasper and Jimenez, the Lazaros' corporate lawyers. Ernesto Jasper asked Alexandro to explain in detail what happened at the Lazaro Coffee estate the previous evening.

"So, you actually had them arrested?" Luisa asked. "Papa, what were you thinking?"

"Watch your mouth!" Alexandro shot back. "I told you, I was threatened," he said while studying financial reports.

"You could have just had them removed from the property," Ernesto said. "You actually had them held with no real cause."

"They could have circled back around and slit my throat in my sleep. Or shot me like Antonio's American friend."

"Papa, please. They were here all afternoon, drinking and eating. That sounds like real bandits," Luisa said sarcastically.

Alexandro shrugged.

"It was Soledad's brother? He's a policeman?" Luisa said, continuing to make sense of what happened.

"Did you know this 'policeman' attacked your brother, Fernando?" Alexandro asked.

"Nando was hurt?" Ernesto asked.

"No," Luisa replied, keeping a glowing-hot stare at her father. "I followed up with the Medellin authorities. It was a case of mistaken identity, and they didn't touch Nando. It was the Americans against a couple of bodyguards."

"But I didn't know that yesterday," Alexandro said plaintively.

"Why does Nando have bodyguards?" Ernesto asked.

"He doesn't; they belonged to some woman named Anise Constaneda," Luisa explained.

The lawyer and the accountant looked at each other and then back at Luisa with unmasked surprise.

"Why is Nando meeting with one of the most notorious smugglers in Colombia?" Ernesto asked.

"Smugglers?" Luisa and Alexandro said in unison.

"Do you see?" Alexandro said. "Ever since your brother took up this wine business, we have been besotted with criminal activity." He slapped his hand on the desk in anger.

"I thought Antonio was the son in the wine business," Ernesto said, becoming increasingly confused.

"Fernando has been trying to help his brother," Alexandro explained. "After the shooting . . . it's all been too much."

Mention of the shooting launched a series of comments and interjections between the lawyers, Alexandro, and the accountants, who had been quiet until then, everyone leaping to their feet.

"Can we just stop for a minute?" Luisa shouted. "We're getting off track!"

She snatched the papers from her father's hands. Then she pointed for her father to sit down, not trusting her words at that moment. Alexandro stared back at her large, unblinking stare, her rigid body language, then shot his cuffs and his vest as he slowly lowered himself into his chair. Ernesto and Claudio, the head accountant, pulled visitors' chairs closer to the desk and sat.

Luisa was tired and frustrated with this entire business. She didn't want to be there. She wanted to be on her beautiful gelding and riding in the fields with the morning sun warming her face and arms. She sighed and pulled reading glasses from the front pocket of her Ralph Lauren suit, then silently read the creditors' report from half a world away. When she was done, she took a deep breath.

"Well, at this point the brother policeman is not the issue," Luisa said, looking up from the report. "It's the other one. This Teke Manion?" She cleared her throat. "At about 3:30 this morning, we got emails and phone calls from Ag-Fidelity, the hedge fund that finances a big part of our operations. They expressed concerns. Serious concerns."

"What concerns?" Alexandro said. "We're the surest bet those money-grubbing soul suckers have!" "They wouldn't deal with us if we weren't."

"Yes, and their terms have been better than anything we could get from a Colombian bank. We have bridge loans, operational loans, and loans that never make our books," Luisa said. "That right, Claudio?"

Claudio nodded. "We are not fully leveraged, but we do have some considerable obligations outstanding pending our next shipment."

"OK, so they called and . . ." Alexandro looked to his daughter for an answer.

"They expressed concerns about our operations," she explained. "That's what they said,"

"As of this morning, we are in midterm on loan repayments of somewhere around eight billion Colombian pesos, or about two million US dollars," Claudio explained. "That was the information you requested,

Señora Lazaro."

Seeing that her father's attention was piqued, Luisa continued. "And what about loans that are 'off the books'?"

Claudio looked nervously from Luisa to Alexandro, then cleared his throat. "As you know, the hedge fund allows for discretionary borrowing by the family up to an additional two million US dollars," Claudio reported.

"And how much has been borrowed from that fund?" Luisa asked.

Claudio punched buttons on something slightly larger than a cell phone but smaller than a decent tablet. After a few seconds, he answered. "Off-book loans total $1.138 million US."

"What?" Alexandro said. "There must be some kind of mistake."

"No, Señor Lazaro," Claudio explained. "I double checked this morning before our meeting. I assure you; it's accurate."

"Who borrowed a million dollars off the books?" Alexandro roared, his voice echoing down the hall.

"It appears a large portion of it was borrowed by Señor Fernando. About seven hundred thousand US," Claudio explained.

Alexandro shook his head. "I don't understand."

"Papa, we know what this is about," Luisa said. "What it's always about with Fernando. Gambling, mismanagement, waste . . ."

"No, you can't indict your brother. He is a businessman. He—"

"Papa, it's not about the money! We are here to fix what you did and to whom you did it!" Luisa explained. "Ernesto?"

The corporate lawyer yawned and pulled some index cards from his jacket pocket. He enjoyed these family retainers. They allowed him to live well without hustling like other barristers in Central Colombia. However, the downside was dealing with these "family emergencies" that got him out of bed in the middle of the night or called him home from vacation in Santa Marta.

"It appears that the hedge fund does a fair amount of business with a company called WorldSpan Underwriters," Ernesto explained. "They are a Lloyds of London type of firm, insuring exotic properties and events."

"And what has that to do with us?" Alexandro asked, his apprehension and frustration growing.

"Nothing, until yesterday. When you had WorldSpan Underwriter's top investigator arrested. They didn't like that. WorldSpan did their own homework on your company and found the common connection via the hedge fund."

"So, this is WorldSpan Underwriters applying pressure for putting their best boy in jail?" Alexandro asked.

"We're not sure, but it's likely," Ernesto replied. "All we do know is that the hedge fund administrators were approached by WorldSpan Underwriters, and now they're very jumpy about the loans they are holding with us. Per our agreement they could call all those loans due in thirty days."

"They wouldn't dare!" Alexandro said. "We're one of the oldest coffee estates in South America."

"They don't care, Papa," Luisa said. "When you threw their partner's investigator in jail, you set off a boomerang that is hitting us between the eyes."

"I'm afraid that's true," Ernesto explained. "Whether the concerns are real or contrived, the shooting? The missing American? It's bad optics."

"But how did they even find out?" Alexandro asked no one in particular. "I put him—I mean, Manion and Cruz weren't arrested until late afternoon."

"Oh, I can answer that," Luisa explained. She slid her fingers on the screen of her phone. Then she turned the screen to her father. "This is Camille DeSoronne, a WorldSpan vice-president. She was sitting in Zena's restaurant across the street from here in the central village. Manion works for her."

"Manion works for a woman?"

"Papa!" Luisa shouted in frustration. "She was the one who started the ball rolling that landed us where we are right now after you had them arrested."

"OK, OK, OK," Alexandro said, rubbing his face in fatigue as he tried to think. Then he pounded the desktop again. "I should have never agreed to this wine business! It's been nothing but trouble. These children of mine! None of them listen. Always running off, wanting to do their own thing!"

The room stayed silent after that, but the emotion was palpable.

Alexandro seemed to be on the verge of exploding because his world was turned upside down as a result of all of this nonsense that had nothing to do with coffee.

Luisa had been pulled from Paulo's warm arms in the middle of the night for some of her father's dumb macho tricks. Now he was grouping her with her stupid brothers. She, who is always watching his back on corporate matters but couldn't be given the reins simply because she didn't have a penis.

Luisa didn't know this Camille person. She found out about her from her private sources.

As a child, Luisa had three close friends. By the time they were teenagers, Alexandro made sure they had limited time together. Their families were not the "right" kind of families. As adults Luisa reconnected with Sabrina, Juliana, and Mozella. Unbeknownst to Alexandro, Luisa financed Mozella's Elevacion Salon in the town center. Mozella told Luisa about the beautiful French woman who got $200 in nail services and hung out in town all day, asking questions about the Lazaro Coffee estate in an off-handed way.

A short Internet search and a call to Ernesto Jasper later, and Luisa was able to put two and two together. While Cruz and Manion were at the house, the lady executive had been playing backup. Luisa admired their strategy. She still didn't understand how WorldSpan executives came into play with Deputy Cruz and his sister though.

Either way, Papa didn't see any of it.

There was a knock on the door. It was Edwina, the administrative assistant whom Luisa shared with her father.

"I wanted to let you know. Antonio and his party have returned from the hill country."

"Did they find Mar ?" Luisa asked, her voice rising with hope.

"He didn't say," Edwina replied dryly.

"Well, what did he say?" Alexandro almost shouted.

"He said . . ." Edwina paused like someone with juicy news, her thin red lips flinching as if holding back a smile. "He said he just found out his brother-in-law was in jail, and he was going to bail him out."

"What?" Alexandro, Luisa, and Ernesto said in unison. Claudio just shook his head, suppressing a conspiratorial smile with Edwina.

"He married that American?" Alexandro asked. "I won't hear of it. Edwina, you tell him that I demand he come home."

"No need," Edwina said. "The rest of the message was that Mr. Antonio requests to see you and Ms. Luisa at the estate as soon as he finishes at the jail."

22

Agent Arnie Rutledge's bureau phone rang early that same morning. The surprise was not the earliness of the hour but that it rang at all. His peers in the NDTC detail never initiated calls to him. Arnie always had to call them first. In the dark he could barely find the phone. It was Padilla who, midway through getting dressed in the dark bedroom, opened the ancient flip phone, read the ID, and tossed it to the groggy agent.

"This is Rutledge," he said, fumbling the phone up to his ear. The rest of the call was not much help to Padilla, just a bunch of one-word answers and non-verbal responses.

Padilla had been trying to leave before Rutledge woke up, but now she lingered in the bathroom, listening while pretending to fuss with her hair. Then she fiddled around with her jeans, blouse, and bra. Finally, she rinsed her mouth out with some foul generic hotel mouthwash, but it was better than the sourness of her morning breath.

She heard him hang up the phone just as she was leaning in the doorway between the bathroom and the bedroom. The soft white vanity light shone across her mostly naked body.

"What was that, baby?" she asked with a ridiculously thick Colombian accent. She knew he loved that.

"Things are moving," he said, jumping out of bed and heading to the bathroom, but stopping long enough to bend over and kiss each of her nipples. "Anise Constaneda has a shipment of illegal lumber moving tonight. We have a fix on the shipment and on her."

"She's with the shipment?" Padilla asked.

"No," he said as he swayed back and forth to accommodate his erratic piss stream over the bowl. "She wouldn't be that stupid, but the plan is to pick her up at the same time we make the bust."

"I don't understand," Padilla said, trying not to appear too anxious for intel, but she had to learn the next moves. Rutledge couldn't wait to share.

"First, we pick up the mules with the illegal shipment, taking them both into custody. Second, we swoop in on Constaneda on her fancy-ass yacht. Third, when the mules see video of us arresting their boss, they will realize their only chance is to testify against her before she starts cutting her own deal."

"That feels like entrapment," Padilla said.

"What? No. It's smart police work. Whose side are you on?" Rutledge asked as he turned on the shower.

Padilla didn't answer. She dressed as quickly as she could. She didn't even wave as she left.

What did I say? Rutledge wondered as he watched her go.

It was the first time he thought that maybe sharing information with her was a mistake, but he didn't have time to worry about it. He had work to do. He smiled as he got into the shower. He was an important member of the strike steam.

That same morning in the village of Venecia, it was the morning of my second incarceration in Colombia. JD and I were denied a phone call. We were denied food and water. We were denied a decent reason for being arrested. I was fed up.

I was most fed up with one Juan Diego Cruz. While I was mad enough to drink hot blood, he was sitting in the cell quietly, not saying much. When he did speak to the guards, it was humble and apologetic. I had never heard him speak in such a way. By that morning I wanted to punch him in the face.

"What is your problem, Cruz?" I finally asked. He looked at me quizzically.

"That coffee-growing bastard treats us like crap, and you've been bowing and scraping like some kind of medieval peasant. I never thought I would see you scared."

"Manion, I apologize for asking you to come. I should not have done it," he said, sighing as if he was very tired.

"Too late. I'm already down here, and I care about Sole too," I said, looking at him in the gloomy morning light coming through the jail cell window. "But what about you? Why—"

"It's hard to explain," he said.

"Try me."

"It's not cowardice, but I get that it appears that way. I guess it's culture," he said with a measured tone, as if he was searching for the words.

"I spent my childhood summers in small towns in Mexico, Costa Rica, and Puerto Rico. They were full of old-world landowners like Lazaro."

"And what?"

"These guys run these little places. People are ferociously loyal to them."

"So, you're scared."

"Manion, it's not about being scared. It's about being careful." He stood up. "You've been talking all night about how you could smell fear coming off him. Well, you were right. These guys? These big bosses? They are deathly afraid of their world not staying the same. When things threaten the status quo even a little bit, they can do extreme things to correct it. Believe me; I've seen it."

"But Cruz, we're here now," I said. "He can't get away with anything with us down here."

"Really? Don't be so sure. We got arrested with no charges being pressed. For all we know, Camille has been arrested as well. Before WorldSpan or the State Department can respond, they could make something happen to Soledad and disavow that she was ever down here. Manion, I know what I'm talking about."

That's when I got it. I stayed quiet long enough to hear him. My mind went over what had happened to us over the last few days. We had been stonewalled, lied to, and arrested—twice. The only time we were treated fairly was when Camille came to our rescue.

JD was being careful out of concern for Soledad. We had been there for days and still had not even talked to her. One wrong threat to this Lazaro machine, and Soledad could never come home again.

"Hey, man, we'll find her; I know it, and I want you to know it," I said, placing my hand on his shoulder. He didn't knock it away. He just nodded and looked away, so I didn't catch the desperation in his eyes.

JD and I had never been friends. At times Soledad was the only thing that kept us from slugging it out back in our hometown of White Sand Island, Florida. Back then it would have been worth the arrest.

Looking at the agonized expression on his face at that moment though, I couldn't wait to get my hands on whoever had his sister. We were going to get her back, and then I was going to make sure the Lazaros never forgot us.

"OK, Señors, it seems you have been released," Constable Munoz said, his weirdly obsequious smile as bright as ever. He reminded me of a gun-toting clown at a haunted house. JD gave me a look, cautioning me not to say anything.

Camille was waiting for us when we reached the front of the police station. I had a crazy urge to run up and hug her. Even in the toughest of times, she always had a look of serene coolness, like she was on the verge of smiling or laughing.

However, that morning she looked as stern as a judge, her broad mouth a thin tight line, her bourbon-brown eyes dark and unblinking. I thought about my conversation with JD in the jail cell, and I felt a familiar sense of dread.

"Good morning," she said. "How was your night?"

"Let's get out of here," I answered.

I grabbed her hand and continued walking outside. JD followed us. Going from the dark cells to outdoors, I was blinded by the morning sunbeams just clearing the rooftops of the village buildings.

Camille took the lead as we headed northwest across the center of town. The breakfast customers were thinning out at Zena's, so the three of us found seats quickly. Camille called out to a young man working as a server as if she knew him. She requested coffees and toast with serrano ham, tomatoes, and cheese.

Over the next hour, she explained how she found out about our arrest and explained how Constable Munoz was so "uncooperative."

"I called Paris. Lisette was still online." She was Camille's personal assistant and the best researcher at WorldSpan Underwriters. "Two hours into it, she found a connection. Ag-Fidelity Hedge Fund partners provide short-term financing to Colombian coffee operations. Lazaro happens to be one of them."

"I don't understand," JD said.

"Let's just say that after Ag-Fidelity got a few calls from WorldSpan's directors, the Lazaros got a wake-up call from their money people," Camille explained, giving me a high five.

"You shouldn't antagonize people like them," JD said, looking out the window. He was clearly more nervous, not at all impressed with the silly grin on my face. "At least not before we find Soledad."

"JD, it got us out of jail, man," I said. "It's exactly the kind of leverage we needed. If they know we can affect their purse strings, they won't dare harm Soledad."

He thought about my words, and his face went from worry to guarded optimism. The server, Andres, brought our food. We ate in silence.

A few minutes later, Camille excused herself to take a phone call. I couldn't believe she was getting a signal up there. Just as we were getting a refill of coffee, she returned to the table, an excited expression on her face.

"We've been invited back to the Lazaro Coffee estate," Camille said.

"By whom?" JD and I asked simultaneously.

"Antonio and Luisa Lazaro."

"Antonio. That's the one Soledad has been working with," JD said.

Camille nodded. "Yes. Luisa is the sister. I just spoke with her this morning after our finance friends got them out of bed."

"Great, but what about the old man?" I asked.

"They assure us that he is not in play. No more arrests."

"There better not be," I said.

"Did they say anything about Soledad?" JD asked, his face unreadable.

"They said she's safe. They know her whereabouts, and they'll tell us when we get there."

"Why can't they tell us now?" I shot back. "Why is everything at the mercy of this family?"

"Manion," JD said.

"Yes, I remember what you told me. It just feels like we're being led around by the nose."

"If that's what it takes to get my sister back in one piece, so be it."

23

Beato was up early that morning in the warehouse in Medellin. The luckiest man in Central Colombia had never felt unluckier in his life. He was thinking back to all the times he had felt close to death. His exciting pre-teen years running errands for the Escobar underbosses and dodging the pressure to join the 1990s narco-trafficking militias. He had come through it all, unlike many of his friends.

Everything about this job was off. From the conversation with the boss lady to the details of the trip, it just felt off. He took his time taping the plastic-wrapped money to his body. It started at US$50,000, but last night it was doubled. In addition to girding his midriff, he also strapped laundered cash to his legs, back, and buttocks.

"Are you serious?" he asked one of his handlers. "This isn't going to work."

"Take it easy, Beato," the man assured him. "We got you." They said they had people paid at the airport who knew to let him through.

"Hey, Mr. B, you ready for your ride to the airport?"

It was Escoba, the young skinny kid with the big mouth. Yesterday he had been working in the warehouse, but this morning someone had upgraded him to driver.

On something like this? Beato thought. *What in the world?*

"I was going to take an Uber. You know? Stay under the radar."

"Nope," Escoba said. "The boss says we take you to the airport."

"Aren't you driving . . . the . . .package? The big package? In the truck?" Beato asked, not believing what he was hearing. The truck was full of illegal lumber—mahogany, cedar, and rosewood. Now they wanted *that* at the airport?

"Yeah, so, orders are orders," Escoba said. "Finish up, so we can hit the road."

Thirty minutes later the truck, loaded with illegal lumber attached to illegal papers, pulled away from the warehouse and moved through the morning traffic. Beato was squeezed between the second driver and the passenger door. Escoba was behind the wheel. There were few cars on the road at that time of day. Beato tried to remember what day of the week it was, but he couldn't get his mind to focus. He couldn't get past all the wrong moves they were making.

Just down the street from Anise Constaneda's warehouse, Arnie was sitting in a dull gray Alpha Logistics van. He eased the vehicle into traffic just behind the lumber truck. He couldn't believe how brazen these idiots were. The same truck that he was sure had brought in the illegal lumber was now rolling out with the same lumber on it. It was bundled under some cheap canvas, but it didn't take much to see what they were concealing. The intel was spot on. Arnie smiled in anticipation, thinking about his report back to the States. He wondered what kind of assignment he would get as a result of the bust. Then he thought about no longer having Padilla in his bed three nights per week, and he was momentarily conflicted.

Instead of heading onto the highway for the thirteen-hour trip to Cartagena and the harbor, the truck got off at the airport exit.

"What are they doing?" Arnie asked. His Colombian partner shrugged as he rode in the back of the van with the surveillance equipment. The partner communicated the route to their partners at the harbor in Cartagena.

A team of agents from the NDTC and the Direccion General Maritima were in a nondescript gunboat at the harbor. The minute the smugglers in the truck were arrested and the illegal lumber confiscated, the harbor team would take the *Largate* and arrest Anise Constaneda. Advance teams confirmed that the truck, the warehouse, and the workers were tied to Constaneda's Transportation, Anise's company.

The harbor team confirmed they were still following her yacht from a distance. They had kept telescopic eyes on the *Largate's* deck. A person fitting Anise's description was on board, traversing the deck, eating, drinking, and sunbathing.

On the signal from Arnie's team, after they confiscated the lumber truck, the harbor surveillance patrol would engage.

When the NDTC officers showed the smugglers that they had the queen smuggler in custody, they would fall over themselves to make a deal that saved them and put her away for good. The Americans had even hinted at offering asylum in America for those who cooperated.

Arnie continued to watch the big, obtrusive lumber truck from the parking lot a few hundred feet from the airport terminal. It looked as out of place as bears in a ballet. It stopped in front of the entrance to Copa Airlines. A small-framed Latino man in jeans and a blue satin jacket slowly climbed out of the cab carrying a small gym bag. Arnie had spent the last two years identifying drug mules and money couriers. This guy was so on the nose, he reminded Arnie of the examples in the training brochures.

He had a nervousness to his walk and the way he looked around. He had a small amount of luggage. As he entered the terminal, the lumber truck eased away, moving toward the airport exit and the highway. Arnie's partner contacted the permanent NDTC task force in the airport. After receiving a brief description, they promised to pick up the little guy taking a flight. Afterwards, Arnie sped out of the parking lot to catch up with the truck and its illegal payload.

24

An hour later, JD, Camille, and I arrived at the Lazaro Coffee estate. The gates were open, and Paulo and his friends were nowhere to be seen. A chubby boy in his mid-teens, all smiles and dressed in work clothes, waved us through to the front of the estate. It reminded me of a tourism brochure. However, I couldn't forget what had happened there less than twenty-four hours earlier.

As we passed the greeter, Camille lowered her window, smiled, and said something congenial in Spanish. I could not read JD's expression. My blood was boiling, but I kept telling myself to stay calm, for Soledad's sake. It helped to recall a famous quote that Lemieux, my teacher, often repeated: "A man who masters patience is a master of everything else."

I hated bullies. Everything I saw from the Lazaros told me that they were bullies. That meant even after all this was done, I would want to make them pay.

Petty? Maybe.

It was totally against all of my holistic training, but I didn't care. I let my thoughts boil in hot oil inside my head as we rolled up to the main house.

No matter what JD was, his sister, Soledad, was smart, good, and, yes, beautiful. Along with my brother, Tommy, the guitar prodigy, she was the best thing to come out of our hometown, White Sand Island, Florida.

When I left home seven years ago, I didn't regret leaving anything or anyone. Except her.

Now she was mixed up with these coffee people, and part of me felt partially responsible. Maybe things would have been different if I had been around. I knew that was the thought of an arrogant man, but that's how I felt.

Of course, I did not share this with Soledad's overprotective law-enforcement brother. Nor did I share it with the tall, blonde, uber-smart, mega-beautiful woman with whom I shared an office and a bed. I couldn't imagine what Camille was thinking. I had run off to help my ex-fiancé, gotten arrested twice, and she had to help me both times.

Geez, Manion, what a mess, I thought as I looked at Camille. Her expression was stern; there were lines of worry in her face that I had never seen before, lines caused by me. Whenever we got Soledad back, safe and sound, I was going to have some serious repairs to do to my own situation.

A man and a woman were standing in front of the main house. I could tell they were Lazaro's. They looked like the old man had literally spit them out.

"Juan Diego, my friend, we should have met sooner," the man said, reaching past me to shake JD's hand. "I'm Antonio Lazaro-Alvarez. This is my sister, Luisa."

He was wearing clean, expensive clothes, but his skin had the weathered look of a field hand. His hair was washed but not styled. Antonio was the archetype of expensive, earnest, but casual hospitality.

"And this must be the formidable Ms. DeSoronne," Luisa said coolly.

"Call me Camille."

Luisa just turned and went inside, and the outside temperature dropped by half.

"Don't mind her," Antonio said. "It's been a crazy time for all of us. As soon as I discovered what Papa did, I went to the jail to secure your release, but you were already gone, and—"

"Where's my sister, Señor Lazaro?" JD asked. Antonio placed his hands on JD's shoulders.

"She is safe. She's in Cartagena awaiting our first shipment of wine."

"Cartagena!" JD, Camille, and I said in unison.

We followed Luisa into the house. Soon we were standing in the same room in which JD and I had been handcuffed the previous day.

"I understand your concern, but don't worry. I talked to Soledad just this morning. She is in safe hands with my brother, Fernando," Antonio explained while holding up a satellite phone, his voice full of pride.

The name "Fernando" caused JD and I to exchange careful glances. JD snatched the phone from Antonio's hand.

"The number, Señor?" he said, urgency creeping into his voice. Antonio leaned over the phone and activated the last number dialed. I could hear the ring tone despite the fact that JD was holding it against his face so hard, his cheek was crimson.

"There's still the issue of our financiers that we need to clear!" Luisa said. She was standing at the bar in the corner, holding a drink.

"Are those drinks just for family?" Camille asked casually.

"Listen, I don't know who you think you are . . ." Luisa said, her voice rising.

"First things first," I said. "We need to get Soledad home safe and sound."

"Aaah, yes, you're the investigator, Manion?" Antonio asked. I detected some dismissal in his tone. "Now, if I have this right, you were engaged to Soledad but ran off to Europe, breaking your engagement."

I stared at him. At least I hadn't misread the sarcasm in his voice.

"Did you hear what I asked about the drink?" Camille said, her voice as even and smooth as velvet.

"Of course. I'll pour," Antonio said, still staring at me as he moved toward the bar.

"I'll have whatever your sister's having," Camille said. I could tell by her tone that she didn't like the Lazaros any more than I did.

JD and I declined.

"We've been getting stonewalled, arrested, and attacked for three days when all we want to know is the whereabouts of our friend," I explained as Camille took a sip of her brown elixir. "So, we're gonna continue to ask our mutual financial partners some embarrassing questions about your family's holdings until we get some cooperation."

Luisa began to sputter a response, but JD interrupted her, holding the satellite phone. "There's no answer. Are you sure we're dialing the correct number?"

Antonio walked over and took the large phone from his hand. He dialed the number this time. When it started to ring, he handed it back to JD, who turned to the corner away from the rest of us.

"Where is your father?" I asked.

"That's none of your business," Luisa said.

"Well, he made it our business when he had us arrested for no reason," I said.

"Keep it up," Luisa said, stepping forward. "We can send you right back. Paulo!"

The tall, broad-shouldered brown man with a shiny black ponytail and scary eyes appeared from around a corner with a couple of extra field hands.

"Wait, wait," Antonio said, his arms outstretched as if directing traffic. "Paulo, please stand down. Luisa, stop it. This isn't getting us anywhere. We're all friends here."

"They are not my friends," Luisa said.

Antonio looked at each of us for several seconds. "They will be more than friends soon enough," he said. He dug into his back pocket and pulled out a blue ring box. Opening it, we all saw the princess-cut diamond ring. JD lowered the satellite phone, staring at the ring in surprise.

I stepped forward until I was next to JD, thinking of what this meant to the entire mess. After an embarrassing number of seconds, I felt Camille's eyes on me. At that moment I realized that I looked a bit too invested in an ex-fiancé's love life.

"Excuse me; I need to make a call," Camille said. She cursed about a weak signal and stepped out on the front veranda. I assumed she was trying to reach Paris.

"Tonio, no," Luisa said, her voice a shocked whisper.

"Yes," Antonio replied. "Señor Cruz, this is not how I wanted to do it, but I planned to ask your sister to marry me."

"Wha . . ." JD paused, rubbing his head. "I thought you were just in the wine business. She never said you were . . . seeing each other."

"We have been lovers for almost nine months," Antonio said. "She did not tell you?"

"Are you sure she wants to marry you?" JD asked, his eyes wavering in shock.

"I believe so," Antonio said with a level of confidence that told us there was a lot we still did not know.

"She has told me nothing of this, so excuse me if I withhold my opinion on this matter," JD said through clenched teeth. The satellite phone was still ringing. He switched it off.

"Withhold all you want," Antonio replied. "Perhaps you two are not as close as you think."

There were a few long silent seconds. Then JD, the careful one, lunged with full intention of planting his fist in Antonio's smug face. I was a step quicker, pulling JD away before his fist could connect. We stared each other down for a second, and I could see the old JD I knew (and sometimes hated) but always respected.

134

To his credit, Antonio never flinched, acting like he knew us, knew our lives. Luisa continued to make noises of exasperation.

"Where is your father?" I asked for no reason other than to reenter the conversations.

"Why do you keep asking about him?" Luisa inquired.

"He was the big boss before," I explained. "Now that we have his wallet in a vice, he can't face us."

"That's an insult, sir," Antonio said.

"The insult was throwing us in jail for no reason, Tonio," I replied. "A nice present for your future in-laws."

"You have no say when it comes to Soledad and me," Antonio said.

"OK, you think you know about us, but now it's our turn," I said. "We met your brother, Fernando, the other day. If your brother is with Soledad, why didn't he tell her that her brother was in town looking for her? We haven't been able to reach her on her phone."

"I imagine he did," Antonio said, looking unsure for the first time.

"No, no, man, I guarantee you that if she knew her brother was here, she would have left your vino baking on the dock and tore down half of Cartagena to see him or talk to him."

"When *you* spoke with her, Señor Lazaro, did she mention me?" JD asked.

Antonio paused, and that told me all I needed.

"When we met your brother . . ." I began.

"You mean when you attacked him in front of his restaurant like a couple of hoodlums?" Luisa said.

Antonio looked shocked, but I continued. "He was with a woman named Anise Constaneda. Do you know her?"

Antonio shook his head, but I heard Luisa catch her breath. Paulo and his men reacted as well.

"According to the police, she is suspected of being the number-one smuggler of illegal lumber and wildlife and the top human trafficker in Central Colombia. Now, what kind of business would she have with the Lazaro family?"

"I assure you; she would not. The Lazaro family is an honorable one," Antonio said, though with considerably less confidence.

"Another question: why is Soledad in Cartagena with your brother and not you?" I asked. The silence and the tension shot up in the room.

Camille showed me a note on her phone about village gossip she picked up on the death at the Lazaro property.

"We had some trouble here on the property," Antonio began in ear-

135

nest. "One of my American partners in the wine business was shot and killed. The other partner is missing. I was out trying to find him."

"Wait," JD said. "This is the same wine business my sister is mixed up in?"

"She was already in Cartagena supervising the first shipment when this happened," Antonio explained

JD and I looked at each other, both of us probably thinking the same thing. A dead partner? A brother hanging out with a gangster/smuggler? And this family was too rich, arrogant, and blind to see they were in the crosshairs of something serious.

"It seems we're all catching up on things that were not communicated as they should have been," JD explained.

"I agree with that," Luisa replied.

"Great. Then we all need better communication going forward," JD said, turning to wink at me. Then he turned back and fixed his stare on Antonio and Luisa. "Who's in charge here?"

"What?" Luisa asked.

"Señora, it's a simple question," JD said. "Are we dealing with the organ grinder or two of his monkeys?"

Yeeeaaahhhhh! I shouted, but it was all in my mind.

Just then, Camille came back into the room with an energy that made us all turn to her.

"We need to get back to the central village. We have a helicopter jump to the harbor in Cartagena." She pointed to Antonio and Luisa. "The minute we get Soledad Cruz back, we'll be out of your lives and your pockets."

"I'm coming with you," Antonio said.

25

The center of the village was still that night. Everything was closed and dark except for the police station and Zena's. Large mercury-vapor lights at each corner of the village square burned like mini stars fallen to earth. Despite those monstrous supernovas of light, the darkness lurked all around us. Mountain coyotes hooted and howled. Occasionally, their predatory eyes glowed in the dark, or it could have been a tired farmhand walking home with a flashlight in the shadowy distance.

Earlier that evening in the restaurant, Seynah had literally pushed her mother and brother out the door at closing, promising to clean and do inventory. Her mama was exhausted after stressing over the beautiful French stranger who wouldn't leave her restaurant and who agitated her children and the local folk. Andres was eager to leave, eager to be with his friends, who hung out in the woods and drank homemade liquor like pulque and fruit wines.

Seynah rushed the last customers out while constantly staring out the front windows, looking for her uncle's truck. He drove the Lazaro coffee delivery truck every week. She hoped he would have time and space for her. As day turned to night, and no truck appeared, her spirits turned blue.

Where is he? Today is his day to come, she thought as she wiped the tables for the umpteenth time. The world was starting to feel closed in and hot. If her uncle didn't come through, it was going to be a rough night.

137

The demon in the back corner of her mind was louder than ever, turning her mood dark and brooding. She wished she had never spoken to that fancy French woman about travel, about her dreams. It had awakened a monster inside her.

Zena's didn't sell liquor per se, just a few bottled beers they got from the cantina across the village square. However, there was an ancient bottle of rum on the shelf above the upright freezer. It was used for Christmas desserts and then promptly returned.

The first shot from a disposable paper cup burned all the way down, and Seynah guiltily slid the dusty bottle back into place. With the further weakening of the Internet signal at sundown, her cell phone signal fell to half a bar. Looking at Instagram was painfully slow. TikTok was impossible.

Frustrated, she revisited the brown elixir. On her third shot she felt her "fuck it" gland kick into place in her head. Giving up on the notion of leaving, she would have to sneak into the house without her mama smelling her breath.

She closed the restaurant—checking the burners, pulling the front shades, turning off the lights, and locking the back door. Her backpack with a change of clothes, toiletries, and a book to read was slung over her shoulder. Looking at the ground, she trudged between the buildings toward the front of the restaurant that faced the village center.

She heard it first. Then as she looked forward, she saw the Lazaro Coffee truck pass by.

"Hey! Uncle, hey!" she screamed. She started to run, stumbled, fell, and got up, grabbing her backpack and screaming for the truck to stop. She was loud enough to alert half the people in the town square, including her mother. It was probably the effect of the rum, but she didn't care. She had to get away.

Seynah reached the front of the restaurant and looked right. The truck was stopped at a corner, its brake lights on and a slight white vapor trailing out of the exhaust pipe.

A horn from another vehicle erupted behind her. Seynah realized she was standing in the middle of the street, and she jumped back onto the sidewalk. The horn blower—the lead vehicle in a group of black SUVs—sped by her and turned right down a side street between her and the Lazaro truck.

After the convoy passed, she ran as fast as she could, fearing the truck was going to take off at any minute. She reached the back and flipped the latch open. Her uncle seldom used a lock. He always said coffee was seldom the subject of theft. There was too much of it around, and the sacks were too heavy. Besides, no one would steal from the richest family in the valley.

As she opened the door and jumped inside, she heard a mechanical engine roar in her ear.

More effects of the rum?

The truck engine?

She didn't know. She closed the door and engaged the latch from inside.

She took a deep breath in the darkness of the cargo hold. Seynah had done this a couple of times before, just jumped onto the truck without talking to her uncle. He would find her sleeping in the back and wake her up, a hearty laugh in his voice. The truck began to move, and she stumbled.

Instead of landing on plump burlap bundles of coffee, she banged her ribs against hard wood cases.

"Damn!" she shouted, bent over and rubbing her side. She reached into her back pocket and pulled out her cell phone. When the flashlight app engaged, the cargo hold went so bright, it made her squint. She was surrounded by cases stacked to the roof of the cargo hold. She leaned in close to read the labels. She realized it was wine.

Why is Uncle delivering wine in a Lazaro truck? she wondered. That was her last thought before a large, sweaty hand clapped over mouth from behind her. Her senses were filled with rough skin, body odor, sweat, and a scent she would come to know as fear. She fought against the hand and the arm to which it was attached, but she was held hard against a man's body. Then another hand removed her phone and switched off the light.

"Munch, stop!" Graves shouted as he looked at the passenger-side mirror. Munch was cramped behind the truck's steering wheel. He was tired and irritable. The whole wine-smuggling thing was supposed to be "soooo simple." Now the hulking henchman was exhausted, constipated, and frustrated.

He drove through the night thinking of stupid Nando Lazaro who owed the boss money, and he couldn't pay. For the record, Fernando had been set up to lose that money. Fernando Lazaro was a rich, simple-minded loudmouth. It was pretty easy to use planted players and pretty girls to trick him into betting with his penis instead of his brain. All that just to get him to smuggle loads in his papa's coffee.

Except now they are smuggling our product in this wine!

That was when it all went sideways. First, the Americans caught them loading the product. The crazy assholes jumped them, and Graves shot one of them before he knew what hit him. Then they spent days in the hill country trying to find the other American while also avoiding Fernando's brother, the winemaker, and his workers.

When Graves and Munch called Anise and told her what had happened, she was surprisingly calm. She even laughed like it was something from a movie. Then Munch suggested that they call off the whole thing.

"Nothing has changed," she said with that same low chuckle. "Get my damn product into those barrels and bottles, or you'll never leave those hills breathing."

The two of them doubled back to the Lazaro Coffee estate. Fernando was there grinning like a cartoon character. He had two of his "boys" help Munch and Graves pack the load in the bottles and barrels. The four of them worked around the clock. By the time they finished, Fernando was long gone, getting drunk on the boss's boat. Graves and Munch had to load the truck. Fernando's boys had to go do some coffee thing.

Now that they were on their way to Cartagena, Munch couldn't wait to scrape this part of Colombia off the bottom of his shoe. Medellin was home, but Graves was from the coast. He knew how to get everything in Cartagena, from the best steaks to drugs to hookers.

As they went through the Venecia village square to get on Highway 25 and the long trip to Cartagena, Munch heard what sounded like helicopters. Graves thought it was just Munch's big ol' tired body playing tricks on him. Then Graves shouted for him to stop.

He looked at his side mirror and then rolled his window down a few inches. A team of black SUVs was rolling up behind them. There were no sirens, but it still seemed off to Munch and Graves in their skittish state. They sat in the truck, idling at the intersection, their hearts in their throats. Graves pulled his revolver from his jacket. Munch started to protest, then pulled his own gun. He recognized the helicopter noise overhead. In that little village at that time of night, it had to be the police.

Munch and Graves sat there, their guns in their laps, each of them fantasizing about a gun-blazing death shootout from a movie. For Graves it was *Butch Cassidy and the Sundance Kid*. For Munch it was the bank robber movie *Takers*.

Then the SUVs turned on a side street and disappeared in a dusty haze. A seconds later the helicopter noise also subsided. Then they were alone in silence. They stared at each other for several more seconds, then returned their guns to their resting place and continued out of the village.

26

I watched night fall over Northern Colombia while nestled in the back seat of a Bell 206L-3 helicopter. The pilot and Camille were sitting in the front. I was wedged between JD and the Lazaros—Luisa and Antonio. As stuffy and uncomfortable as I was, the more distance we kept between JD and his future brother-in-law, the better.

It took about ninety-five minutes, from takeoff in an open field behind the park in Venecia's central village, rising to some high altitude over the dark local mountains, to the docks nestled in the lighted cluster of the city of Cartagena.

Four people were standing on the helipad when we landed. One was clearly a member of the Policía Nacional de Colombia . The second one was wearing a uniform I did not recognize. I figured he was Camille's WorldSpan contact. I recognized the third one as Detective Meneses from Medellin. He ducked under the whirling blades and opened the door to the helicopter. The uniformed man secured the aircraft, setting blocks under the wheels. Then he opened the door for Camille. Meneses opened the door next to JD after the Lazaros.

"Come on! I have a room where we can talk!" he shouted before we could ask what the Medellin detective was doing at the Cartagena harbor.

Camille, JD, and I started to follow Meneses. The Lazaros were hanging back, looking reluctant and confused. That's when the fourth person stepped forward.

"Luisa, Antonio, I think you know my cousin, Polonia Meneses," the detective said.

"I'm here on your father's behalf!" Polonia shouted over the roar of the helicopter. She was dressed in another colorful pantsuit, this one purple. Her hair was in a tight chignon that showed off her face with features strikingly similar to Detective Meneses. They could have been siblings.

"Papa sent you?" Antonio asked.

"Tonio, this is probably something we can get done without taxing your father's peace."

Meneses called for the group to follow him, and we all did in single file. A few minutes later we were in a conference room, where the authorities were waiting for us.

There were two of them. One was another member of the Policia De Colombia, but the one doing all the talking was American. He was straight out of federal central casting, badge on his belt and arms akimbo. As we sat, I was close enough to see the ATF insignia.

"Tonight we are executing a takedown of a major smuggler on her own boat. It's part of a multi-year investigation and surveillance," the American agent said. "Now, I understand from Detective Meneses that you have a person of interest in the middle of our operation." He went on to explain that he was Agent Arnie Rutledge of the United States Bureau of Alcohol Tobacco and Firearms and Explosives. He was part of a joint operation between Colombia and the United States to bring down smugglers like Anise Constaneda.

That name caught everyone's attention.

"In the next few hours, right here in this harbor, we'll bust a large cargo of Constaneda's illegal lumber. It's her oldest and most profitable line of business," he explained. The room went quiet.

"We even busted a cash mule at the airport tonight. He had over $100,000 strapped to his body. It was one of the easiest airport busts our customs agents have ever made. We feel the Constaneda Cartel is unraveling. They are ripe for the takedown we have planned."

All the pieces started to come together: the killing of poor Wayne Kowl and the disappearance of Mario Romero, the fight with Constaneda's bodyguards in front of the restaurant in Medellin, and the stonewalling by the Lazaro family. This was a stinking mess, and I could see the dread on the faces of JD and the Lazaros. For the first time, they realized the level of trouble to which their family was connected.

"My brother, Fernando Lazaro, is on that boat along with my fiancé, an American, Soledad Cruz," Antonio said with concern. "So, you can't possibly execute an arrest tonight. It would put them in danger."

I examined my shoes in response to Antonio's entitled comments. I knew what was coming next.

"I assure you we're not looking to harm anyone on this arrest," Agent Rutledge said, sounding like a recorded public service announcement. "Your people should be safe. However, Señor Lazaro, I have to wonder why your brother and fiancé are on the yacht of an international smuggler."

Luisa stepped forward and spoke off to the side in Spanish to an officer who seemed to be the ranking leading member of the NDTC. His name tag read, "Zachary."

Luisa was pleading her case for her brother and extolling the Lazaro family name. Zachary and his second in command responded in a hushed, urgent tone. Then Luisa stopped talking and stood still, looking as if she'd been slapped. She pulled her phone from her back pocket and left the room. Polonia followed her out. A few seconds later, Camille left too.

"You people must understand," Agent Rutledge continued, his face red with emotion and his expression smug with arrogance, "the United States government has invested a great amount of resources in this bust and an even larger amount in Colombian law enforcement. The ATF is calling the shots tonight; we have paid the cost to be the boss."

While I stood there dumbfounded that he had actually said that cowboy crap, JD pulled a picture up on his phone and slid it across the table to Agent Rutledge, who picked it up immediately.

"A picture of my sister, Agent Rutledge," JD explained.

Rutledge took a cursory look and then slid the phone back.

"She look familiar, Agent Rutledge?" I asked. I knew he had a lot going on, but he was not going to dismiss Soledad so easily. I slid the phone back to him.

He took another look and then did a double take.

"They look alike," I said. "We didn't realize that until we got here. That's why we're concerned. It appears that you and your partners are going to take down this woman tonight, on the harbor, on her boat. Soledad Cruz is also on that boat."

"I see a slight resemblance," Rutledge acknowledged. "Your point?"

"My point is, we would like to make sure that the wrong person isn't shot, should it come to that," I replied.

"Should it come to that," Rutledge said.

We sat there in silence, everyone lost in their own thoughts. I wondered what the purpose of the meeting was. It only added to our anxiety.

I remembered the conversation JD and I had in the jail cell. There were nuances to this culture that I did not know. Maybe I was missing something. If that was true, the Lazaros and JD were missing it as well. They looked as lost and despondent as I felt.

The door opened a crack, and I saw Camille's face.

"Excuse us, Agent Rutledge," I said, motioning for JD to follow me out. "Detective Meneses, Antonio, we'll be right back."

The hall was wide, beige, and hot. The carpet carried twenty years of stains and smells. Camille was standing there alone. She looked tired, but her eyes were dancing like they did when she had an idea.

"We need to get out of here now," Camille said, then turned to leave, motioning for JD and I to follow.

"Wait, Mila, where we going?" I asked. She turned back toward me, a look of exasperation on her face.

"We've been sitting here listening to men for three days, and we have nothing but a lot of hot air from an out-of-control ATF agent," she explained. "We need to get JD's sister and the Lazaros' brother back safe and sound, so I can get us back to Paris. Ne pas?"

JD and I nodded.

"Good. With the help of Señora Meneses and Luisa and our resources from back home, we have a vessel."

"OK. We're going to get them?" I inquired.

"Wait! What are we doing?" JD asked. "How?"

"Deputy Cruz, it's the kind of work you and your friend, Tekelius, have done before," she said with a smile that was not warm. She was referring to some unpleasant history.

"He's not my friend," I said, not smiling. I could see JD nodding in my peripheral vision.

"Whatever, Manion," Camille said. "It's not just their lives at stake, here. WorldSpan has been burning a lot of resources on this little side trip—a side trip where we have no client. When we get back to Paris, we better have some results, or we'll all have no friends or jobs. Now come on!"

An hour later, we discovered what determined women could accomplish even though they hated each other.

JD, Meneses, Antonio, and I followed Camille out of the building where we had listened to Rutledge and walked along the harbor, past countless commercial vessels of various sizes from several countries. They seemed like creaking giants, lolling in the water that slapped against giant concrete piers. We eventually crossed into the container terminal, the massive metal boxes forming tall dark corridors, barely lit by temporary lighting.

As we continued to walk, we reached an older part of the harbor filled with rotten wood buildings, older tugboats and personal vessels, and the scratching and squeaking of feral animals. The tall condominiums of Morros City stood in the distance, naval ships from the local base anchored in front of them. There was just enough light for us to see where we were going.

On the side of a rusted metal building set on an abandoned dock was a new SAFE Interceptor 41 patrol boat tied to a concrete pier. Polonia and Luisa were standing next to it looking cold despite the muggy night air.

"Cousin, do we have you to thank for this?" Meneses asked. Polonia nodded.

"So, JD and I are going to get them in this?" I asked.

"I'm going too," Meneses said. "I can drive this, and I'm the only one among us who can legally carry a firearm."

"I'm going as well," Antonio said.

"Tonio, no, I'll go," Luisa said. "Fernando is in trouble, the kind I've gotten him out of before."

"I don't think either of you should go," I said. "Neither of you have experience with something like this."

"And you have?" Luisa shot back.

"Yes," I replied. "Besides, if it goes bad, Señor Lazaro should not lose all his children."

There was a pause as the Lazaros mulled that over.

"Antonio has to go," Camille said.

"Why?" I asked.

"So Fernando will know we are good. The last time he saw you and JD, it wasn't good." Camille was right, like so many other times.

In the end, it was JD, Meneses, Antonio Lazaro, and me. The plan was to get to Anise's yacht and remove Soledad and Fernando before the bust. We thought about reaching out to Fernando or Soledad by phone, but we didn't know the situation on the vessel. It had occurred to me several times throughout the last few days that everything simple on that job was hard.

If Anise was who they said she was, there was no telling what we were going to run into when we found them. Calling or texting could put Soledad and Fernando in more danger. However, we all agreed that if Soledad and Fernando were still on the vessel when Rutledge hit it, they would probably die in the crossfire.

"So, how do we find the Largate?" I asked as I looked around the vessel. The Interceptor was a speedboat used by law enforcement to run down smugglers, drug transporters and human traffickers in the intercoastal waters. Meneses explained this one was modified from the official version.

There were two adjustable seats in the helm. I saw empty bolt fasteners in the middle of the deck.

"There would be additional seats and storage bins here," Meneses explained. "This one just has space, and we'll need it."

"The Largate is out in the bay, along with the Colombian strike team," Camille said.

"The police are not talking to us, but my family, the Meneses, work in every part of this harbor. We have deep ties with every ship captain, weather monitor, and cargo boss on this dock," Polonia explained. "In the next hour we should have the exact position of both of them. We can let you know."

"What's this?" I asked, lifting one of the large backpacks in the open aft area. I handed one to JD.

"That's part of those resources paid for by our friends in Paris," Camille said.

I unzipped the main compartment and pulled out a black rubber suit with flotation pads, snorkel gear, a first-aid kit, and a sports knife. In the front compartment was a small nickel-plated Beretta handgun.

"They are loaded and untraceable, if anyone asks," Camille explained. "They belong to Antonio and Detective Meneses."

"You still want to go on this?" I asked Antonio. He was standing next to his sister, who looked terrified. He didn't answer me, just climbed aboard.

"You ever shoot one of these?" I asked.

"I'm an excellent marksman and hunter," he said proudly.

"Ever shoot and kill anything on two legs?" JD asked. Antonio shook his head. As I thought about it, neither had I.

Meneses fired up the engines, which rumbled with the promise of power. The vessel vibrated, and the multifunction display panel (MFD) lit up detailing the vital stats—sonar, radar, fluid levels, RPMs, and navigation coordinates.

When we were ready, Meneses blew a kiss to Polonia. Antonio leaned over the edge and hugged his sister, promising to come back alive with their brother. I wanted to jump out and kiss Camille, but I settled for a nod and a thank-you. We held eye contact as Meneses backed the boat out of the slip. The engine roar rose.

"Keep your radio frequency open, Manion!" Camille shouted. I noticed her unblinking, glassy brown-eyed stare. It told me all I needed.

As we moved out into Cartagena Bay, we got settled into our equipment and the rubber suits with padding over key areas that would deflect knife thrusts and punches and minimize the damage caused by most bullets.

27

Beato sat in the backseat of a black Chevrolet SUV. It had been two hours since he had been invited to the back room at the airport. They undressed him and found the money in no time flat. Beato had been told there were paid NDTC people at the airport. That was the only reason he had gone along with the stupid, obvious plan.

Who was he kidding? He would have had to do it either way. The boss herself demanded it. That's why Beato had thought the fix was in all the way through. Now he was under arrest and facing jail time for the first time in his life.

Dammit, I'm Beato! he thought as he ignored the NDTC agent who was reciting the charges. Even after all of this, he was sure he was going to be freed, that someone would call on his behalf. Beato had been detained in the past, but it was usually by local police or someone else in the boss's pocket. Then these agents from the United States had come calling.

It was a call over the computer—Zoom or whatever they called it. They couldn't even be bothered to arrest him in person.

"Carlos Pacheo, or would you prefer BEE-AT-TO?" the caller said with deliberate sarcasm. "I'm Agent Arnie Rutledge of the United States Department of Alcohol, Tobacco, Firearms, and Explosives."

"I don't have none of that," Beato mumbled. "Money was not even mine."

"We know that, BEE-AT-TO; it was her money. We don't want you.

We want her. "

"Her? Who is her?" Beato asked, trying to look confused. Rutledge laughed.

"I want to show you something," Rutledge said. He talked to someone off screen. Beato saw movement and a couple of people just outside of the camera's view. Then Rutledge returned his attention to Beato.

"You ready?" Rutledge asked, again with a mischievous grin.

Beato shrugged, acting as if he had no interest.

The screen froze for almost thirty seconds. Beato thought there was some computer glitch. Then a video started.

"Can you see the video, BEE-AT-TO?" Rutledge asked.

"Yes, I see it."

It was night footage at an industrial building. A few seconds later, a truck eased up to the building. It did a three-point move to back up to the building. There was no sound, just green night-vision video.

Then the visual exploded with light and police. They flooded the scene, drawing guns on the truck and yanking two men out of the cab. Beato realized it was the truck that had dropped him off at the airport. The police pulled Escoba and his brother out of the cab, placed them in handcuffs, and forced them face down on the ground. The rest of the officers climbed onto the cargo and removed the ropes and tarps.

"I think you remember your ride to the airport?" Rutledge asked. "This footage was taken a few minutes ago."

"I had nothing to do with them," Beato replied weakly.

"BEE-AT-TO, don't do that," Rutledge said. "This will go so much better for you if you stop playing with us. With you and the bust you see on the screen, we're going to arrest your boss tonight. Gonna drag her sneaky ass right off that fancy yacht of hers."

"I don't know—"

"Anise Constaneda!" Rutledge shouted. "Now, when we take her down—and we will take her down—she's going to start talking about her operation and try to make a deal."

"OK, Agent Rutledge," Beato said. "I'm not sure what that has to do with me. Sure, I had some cash, maybe too much cash, but I don't know about no Anise whoever—"

"Anise Constaneda. As I was saying before you started lying, when she makes a deal with us, she will rat all of her underlings out. People like you. All of you will go to prison, and she will go free."

Then the screen went dark.

"Wha. . . Where did he go?" Beato asked, looking around nervously.

The local authorities and the Colombian airport NDTC agents, who were in the room with Beato, explained the deal. In exchange for his testimony on everything he knew, the luckiest person in Colombia could escape jail altogether. He could go back to the hill country from which he came. Be the stuff of local legend. He could even immigrate to the United States.

Beato thought about how he would never have to go back to the smuggling camps, the misery of men forced into slave labor, harvesting illegal lumber and animal hides and women forced into prostitution, all at the point of a gun or the promise of the next high. Beato knew he was a part of that ugly reality. Until then he was able to ignore it as long as he didn't have to see it every day.

The offer included a timeline. Once they arrested Anise that night, all offers of leniency would be rescinded. They left Beato in the back of the SUV—no contact, water, Internet, or phone and very little light. When they returned an hour later, the luckiest man in Colombia was ready to tell them everything he knew.

28

The *Largate* was slowly moving back into the mouth of Cartagena Bay. The sun's last light was long gone, and the moon bathed the water and the vessels in a light that made everything seem to glow.

Soledad was still lying on the aft desk. She was wearing Anise's cream-colored bathing suit, which fit her perfectly. Her hair was in a ponytail high off the back of her head. She had been there for hours, reading, sleeping, and reflecting.

It was one of the best and worst days of her life. The *Largate* was a luxury craft with a devil-may-care name. Her new friend, Anise, had entrusted her with her beautiful yacht. Soledad had finally talked to Antonio that morning, and she felt ready for the wine shipment to arrive.

Then she remembered Wayne and Mario. Soledad was heartbroken by the news. While she had only met them for the first time the previous week, she felt like they had been friends for years. She thought back to their celebration just days earlier in the casita, eating and drinking their fill.

She was ready to call off the entire order until they found Mario and got Wayne's body back to the United States. She just couldn't believe it, but now she understood why Antonio had empowered Fernando to keep her in Cartagena and help her with the shipment.

Antonio had convinced her to continue the course, get the wine on the ship, and then return to Venecia Valley to finish looking for Mario.

He said that they owed it to Wayne and Mario to finish the job, to get the first shipment of wine on the way to the American market. In the end she had relented. She still felt somewhat guilty for her great feeling that evening; she couldn't help it.

She also couldn't believe how her life was 100 percent different than it had been just a year earlier. She had been working with small producers all over the world, making sure they got a space in US markets. None of them were as prestigious as the Lazaro brand.

In the beginning, Antonio was just a business partner. He seemed like the inexperienced sibling of the Lazaro business empire. He knew very little about marketing anything, least of all coffee and tea. However, he had a dream to produce wine that represented the best of Colombia, a wine that would rival other Central and South American brands.

She poured another glass of the faux malbec, a non-alcoholic version of what was headed to the docks. She reflexively touched her stomach as she watched the moonlight refracted in the purple liquid, like fine crystal or a jewel.

Her mind continued to run over the year's events. She thought back to the test wine flights she had shared with Antonio. The endless samples of Argentinean, Chilean, and Brazilian wines. The idea was to find a prototype on which to base their blended wine. Antonio hated them all, literally spat them out in disgust. It drove her crazy, and she wondered if he was just an arrogant wannabe, a rich man's son pretending to be a vintner.

Then his first offerings were blended and tasted. It was a cool spring evening in one of the casitas on the estate, the freshly born wine paired with smoked salmon, vegetable crudité, and charcuterie meats. That night the wine of his dreams became a reality, and she was there to witness it. They celebrated that night, just the two of them. They talked incessantly about the future of Lalvarez Wines, making notes on napkins after their phones' batteries died.

Business collaboration and friendship turned into more serious feelings, but distance and the delicate fledgling enterprise made them cautious. It would be months before she kissed him. Looking back on it, she realized the night they discovered malbec Test Barrel 1 was the night she fell in love with Antonio Lazaro-Alvarez.

Tonight she felt so fulfilled, a growing business, a man she loved and was proud of, and a new life growing inside her.

"Aaaahhh, now there is a beautiful picture!"

She slowly turned to the voice, but she knew who it was.

"Good evening, Nando," she said with a tranquil smile.

"Not to be a killjoy, but should you be drinking?"

"It's sparkling grape juice," she explained.

"Really?" Fernando said in shock. He was standing over her now.

"We don't make it yet," she explained, "but I commissioned a few bottles because I thought I might need it."

They laughed at the inside information.

"My brother will be so happy when you tell him," Fernando explained. He was in his usual loose-fitting slacks and open-collared shirt, both made from expensive material and in a light pastel color. Tonight's color was "café con leche." He had been sipping some clear liquor, either gin or vodka, over ice all day.

"You really think so?" she asked. "I mean, he has a lot on his plate right now."

"Are you kidding?" Fernando said, followed by a small hiccup. "Look, you know how he is, proud Colombian from a proud family, etcetera, etcetera."

They laughed in agreement.

"So, to that end, he will be over the moon with the extension of our 'bloodline,'" he continued, standing over her.

"Only if it's a boy," Soledad said.

"Doesn't matter. He is proud but not a dinosaur like Papa."

"And what about your papa and Luisa? I don't think she likes me very much."

"Luisa doesn't like anyone," Fernando said, and they laughed at the familiar often used line to describe Luisa.

Soledad thought it was good to see him laugh. Fernando was a man who smiled a lot but never seemed genuinely happy. He laughed like someone who was trying to convince other people of his happiness. But at that moment it seemed genuine.

"Besides, yours is a good secret," Fernando said.

"Yeah," Soledad said

"My family is full of secrets. For instance, my papa has a secret lover, the lady who runs the roasting house."

Soledad gasped in surprise.

"He thinks we don't know, and we let him have his little secret. It's good for him," he explained with a pelvic thrust, and they laughed again.

"And Luisa?" he continued. "She doesn't realize I know she is seeing our head field manager, Paulo. If Papa knew about that . . ."

They giggled over that one. Soledad remembered seeing the handsome man with straight hair, riding tall in his saddle next to Luisa on many days. Soledad could see the attraction clearly in her mind now, but she had never put two and two together.

"And what is Fernando's secret?" she asked.

"Oooh, my sister," he said as his smile went from humorous to reflective. "Mine is no secret. I am the family disappointment on so many levels. A gambler, a lady's man, a drunk. Everything but the deserving heir to my father's coffee legacy."

"But the restaurant and coffee shop. You could be on to a new commercial market for Lazaro coffees, commercial contracts," Soledad said.

Fernando laughed as if remembering an old joke. "You know, sis, I floated that same idea. The coffee shop was . . . uh, what do you Americans call it when you want to test something?"

"Proof of concept?"

"Yes!" Fernando exclaimed. "But when Papa learned of the additional capital outlay to upgrade operations in anticipation of supplying restaurants, he refused."

"I'm sorry," Soledad said, and they were silent for almost a minute.

"You know, I actually had a lot of ideas for the company. About growing the beans? Sales? Packaging? But in the end, it's Alexandro Lazaro's company, and he lets you know every day that you work for him."

"So he preferred Luisa over you?" Soledad asked.

"No, Luisa does what he says, exactly how he says, but he will never make her the successor."

"Because she's a woman?"

Fernando shrugged.

"And Antonio never wanted it," Soledad said, remembering conversations from the past.

"Nope," Fernando said with a wide grin that seemed out of place. "Little brother wanted to forge his own path, and he did."

They clinked glasses.

"To Lalvarez Wines," they said almost in unison.

"Are you hungry?" she asked. "I am."

"I think we're on our own. The service staff seems to be gone," Fernando explained.

"Who's driving the boat?" Soledad asked, a hint of worry in her voice. After all, Anise had said she was in charge. She should have been asking such questions before then.

"Relax," Fernando said and hiccuped again. "I've seen a few crew members floating around, the guys in the gray shirts and black pants? But everyone else left with the owner."

"C'mon, brother," Soledad said, getting to her feet and wrapping her silk-printed cover-up around her waist. She put a hand on Fernando's shoulder. "I'm gonna fix us some dinner. Then we'll find out from the crew when we're docking. My wine should be at the harbor by now.

They found the galley and one of the remaining crew. He was a small man with a pleasant smile and ruddy skin. He offered to prepare something for them. Soledad searched the various coolers and found the ingredients for a niçoise salad. The crew member, who said his name was Pablo, offered to cut up peppers, onions, and mushrooms.

Soledad worked on the tuna and green beans. Fernando and she stood over the stove looking out at the harbor lights through port-side windows. She talked nonstop about the future wine shipment, its arrival in the States, and the anticipation of the first feedback from the customers. Fernando answered eagerly, enjoying the conversation. Pablo worked quietly and offered to refill their drinks. They were so engrossed in their conversation that they never saw the white powder that Pablo poured into their glasses.

29

NDTC communication transcript between the land strike team headed by American ATF Agent Arnold Rutledge (code name: Jaguar) and the NDTC marine strike team monitoring the private vessel owned by suspect Anise Constaneda (code name: Piranha). Maritime Authority—drone aerial surveillance (code name: Toucan)

Piranha, this is Jaguar 1. What's your position?"

"Jaguar 1, this is Piranha. We are at the mouth of Cartagena Bay. Coordinates coming via geo tracking."

"Piranha, we have the illegal payload in sight. Engagement and apprehension in less than thirty minutes. Do you have eyes on the prize?"

"Affirmative. The Largate is in sight. We have visual confirmation of the suspect. Off-white bathing suit, lounging on the aft deck."

"Excellent, Piranha. The prize vessel is headed in what direction?"

"Jaguar, the vessel is stable. Appears to be anchored for now."

"Piranha, you're keeping a surveillance distance? We need to maintain the element of surprise."

"Affirmative, Jaguar. Surveillance confirmed via Toucan in the sky and long-range visual reconnaissance."

"Any other vessels in proximity of the prize, Piranha?"

"Negative. Traffic is light and transient. Vessels are coming and going. None suspicious."

"Affirmative, Piranha. When we take control of the load, we'll give you the go to take the Largate. Jaguar out."

"Piranha out."

30

The Interceptor cruised slowly out of the old harbor where we had left Camille, Luisa, and Polonia. Then Meneses opened her up to about thirty knots in the outer waters. We headed straight out to sea until we could look back and see the entire coastline surrounding the harbor. Polonia had promised to use her contacts to pinpoint the exact location of Anise's yacht. It was called the *Largate*. We waited and watched through night-vision binoculars.

"Here is what I don't get," I said as we sat in silence. "Why is Soledad on that boat?"

"My brother was keeping an eye on her for me. At my request," Antonio explained.

"Right. But why is he keeping an eye on her on a smuggler's yacht?"

Antonio shrugged.

"You don't know?" JD asked. "Señor Lazaro, that seems like the answer to a lot of your questions. You don't know who shot your business partner. You don't know why your brother is hanging out with criminals. You don't seem to know much."

"Deputy Cruz," Meneses said, "I understand your concern, but we need to keep our heads at this moment in time."

"Easier said than done, Detective," JD fired back.

"Very true, and your questions are quite valid. I just want us to remain a focused unit for now."

"Thank you," Antonio said sulkily.

"Don't thank me yet, Señor. You Lazaros seem to have your rich, pampered hands in a lot of shady stuff. When this is over, your family will have some explaining to do from Venecia Valley to Medellin to Cartagena."

We were quiet. All of us were in our wetsuits, checking weapons and gear. However, my mind kept racing about the events surrounding this crazy week. Over time, I had found that if I picked at something from all angles, I could find the piece that unraveled the fabric of the crime or deception, the thing I was missing.

I walked up to the wheelhouse where Meneses was leaning against the console, smoking a cigarillo.

"Sorry about my friend," I said. "He's just worried about his sister."

Meneses took a long drag and let the smoke slowly stream through his nose, looking at me the entire time. He seemed to be sizing me up, but I didn't care. I stared right back.

"Yeah, no worries," he said, finally breaking eye contact. "I'm starting to worry about my cousin as well."

"Oh yeah," I said.

Meneses cast a pensive look at Antonio. "Not sure who all knows, but my cousin, Polonia, has been seeing the old man for some time. I don't think he's into anything illegal, but the kids . . ."

"Fernando," I said.

"Yeah, a first-class fuck-up, you know? A life full of excess—gambling, women, booze, and blow."

"So, what do you think his thing is with Constaneda?" I asked.

"I don't know for sure. We've been watching her for years, but it's only in the last week or two that Fernando has been pinging in her sphere of influence. If there's a connection, and there seems to be, then it's for all the old reasons."

"Like?"

"He owes her money? He's starting to mule for her—be her pusher with the rich and elite of Colombian society?"

We sat in silence, thinking that over.

"What about the sister? And the kid over here?" I asked.

"Naw," Meneses said, shaking his head. "Luisa is just a female version of the old man. Family and firm first and always. Antonio is the baby. Got his head in the clouds about selling wine but seems to be totally legit."

That was good to know. I didn't want to think we were bringing a double-crosser to this fight.

"About Constaneda . . ."

162

"Manion, you ask a lot of questions. Are you sure you didn't want to be a cop at some time?"

I laughed, but Meneses waved for me to continue as he took his last drag and tossed the cigarillo over the starboard side.

"Why hasn't she been caught before now?" I asked. "Even the Americans have been down here for years."

"Yeah, the Americans?" Meneses said with a small laugh. "Rutledge had to be someone's attempt to get rid of a problem. Maybe someone back home hoped he would get shot in the line of fire."

"So, it's incompetence?"

Meneses shook his head. "As much as I would like to blame it on the Policía Nacional de Colombia, I truly believe the problem is at the local level. Constaneda has moles in every local police department across Colombia, constantly feeding her information. Any information shared at the local level eventually finds its way back to her."

"Even in your department in Medellin?"

Meneses nodded.

"Do you know who?"

"I think so, but I haven't been able to prove it. A fellow detective, female, called Padilla. She always seems to be hanging around the edge of conversations or just outside the conference room doors. The rumor around the department is that she's keeping time with an American federal agent."

We fell silent for a minute, lost in our own thoughts.

"If she's a rat," I said, "let's feed her some cheese and see if she bites."

Meneses gave me a quizzical look and then nodded.

We spent the next few minutes using the ship-to-shore communications and texting from Meneses' phone to track down some IT night staff who could be trusted, someone to set up phone tracking. Meneses proved as resourceful as his cousin. If I was right, we would go a long way toward shutting down smuggling in Colombia. If we were wrong, we needed someone we could trust to bury the call tracking setup, so it never saw the light of day.

CELL PHONE TEXT EXCHANGE: Detective Mateo Meneses and Detective Ramona Valez (a.k.a. Padilla)

Meneses: Hey, you on duty tonight?

Padilla: Not really, but I can be.

163

(no response to build anticipation)

Padilla: What's going on? Where did you go?

Meneses: I'm here. Things are moving on the Policía Nacional de Colombia task force with the Americans.

Padilla: What? Tell me!

Meneses: Maritime Authority intel says raid on smugglers tonight.

Padilla: Really?

Meneses: Additional hands may be needed. If you're around tonight, big catch by the NDTC and the Americans.

Padilla: Who they got on the hook?

Meneses: The Big one. Constaneda herself.

Padilla: What? You coming in to help?

Meneses: Nope. Found out too late. Had other commitments, but I thought of you if you were on duty.

Padilla: Thanks for the heads-up.

Meneses: Be discreet. I don't want them knowing I told you. I wasn't supposed to know myself.

Padilla: Yeah, yeah, I got you. Gotta go.

I looked to the back of the boat. Antonio appeared to be showing JD pictures from his phone. Both of them were smiling, JD shaking his head in disbelief. I assumed he was proving the level of his connection to Soledad. For a moment I allowed myself to imagine them as in-laws, as a part of this Lazaro family. It didn't seem likely, but Soledad had found her place down there, and JD would do anything for his sister.

164

I couldn't help but think about my own situation, my connections to other people. Camille? My brother? Would I do anything for them? I was sure I would, but was that love or duty? Or was it just a desire to always be the answer for everyone's problems? I knew what I wanted to believe, but I really didn't know.

Without realizing it, I had started down a long road of jumping into situations midstream, untangling the knots, and jumping back out before I got too invested. It made me good at this job but maybe not so good at other things. I had told myself many times that those other things didn't matter. My ability to "fix" things made up for my lack of emotional attachment. That night on the boat, though, I wasn't so sure.

31

Where is everybody? Fernando wondered as he moved through the yacht. The sleeping dram that Pablo had given them was working. Soledad fell asleep first, in the middle of her salad. One minute he was talking about Antonio as a kid, and then she was out. Fernando knew pregnant women went through things, but this seemed off. Besides, he was starting to feel strange as well.

He called for the crew to help him move her from the galley to one of the lounging areas. He had to keep her busy and away from the loading area until the wine got onto the ship. That was the deal he made with Anise. She had people on the docks and the ship to take it from there.

No one responded, so he went looking for the crew. The wine shipment would be in Cartagena by now. He wanted to know the minute it was loaded. It was time for him to get off the boat.

He had done his part. The way he saw it, while the authorities were watching Anise's look-alike on the *Largate*, the real Anise would be moving their product onto the ship in his brother's wine bottles.

Fernando wondered how they would get their product once it arrived in the United States, but Anise said she had that covered. Fernando didn't care. He just wanted to be out of the vulture bitch's debt.

He went looking from room to room, deck to deck. No one was around. He got down to the room just off the engines. It was so hot that he was sweating through his clothes. He stumbled over his own feet and caught himself on a closet door handle. Then he realized it.

We've been drugged, he thought, his mind going frantic with worry. *Why would they drug me?*

He got to his feet and tried to remember the way he had come. His vision doubled, and fear kept him from thinking clearly.

"Hey! Hey!" he shouted. He continued to stumble down the hall, again grabbing a door handle. According to the sign just to the right of the door, it was the head.

Get some water on your face, so you can focus, he told himself.

It was a tiny room with a toilet and a hand bowl, similar to an airplane lavatory. He held the faucet lever down with a shaky hand as he pooled water in his other hand and threw it in his face, hoping the force and the cool wetness would bring him back around.

The little guy, the cook, he must have spiked our drinks.

All he could think about was getting out of there. He thought he remembered where the life rafts were, but he was conflicted. Should he try to get Soledad out or not?

He knelt to look in the cabinet beneath the small sink for a towel. That was when he saw it, and it sent him out of the bathroom in blind terror. It was why he didn't see Pablo's foot extended out to trip him. He fell hard, his chin bouncing off the floor. The uncontrollable sleep was coming over him again. He barely registered his arms being tied and his mouth being gagged.

32

Things were quiet out on the bay. Meneses, JD, Antonio Lazaro, and I just watched each other and the lights on the dark sea. We snacked on the provisions included with our gear—water and some kind of protein bar. We all peeled out of our wet suits at least once to pee. It would be another hour before things got going.

"Come in Interceptor. This is ground support." It was Polonia, her voice over the radio breaking the long silence.

She was being generic for security reasons. Smart. Over the next few minutes, she gave her cousin the coordinates and directions to where the *Largate* was anchored in relation to our position. Meneses pointed the Interceptor in the general direction. I took a look through the night-vision binoculars, but I could only see hulking shadows on the water.

JD and I suited and strapped up while Meneses guided the Interceptor in the direction that Polonia had conveyed to him. As I looked back, I saw Antonio slipping a gun into the waterproof inner pocket of his wet suit. I looked at JD, who waved me down as if to say, "It's alright."

Hmph. I guess they're partners now, I thought, hoping the wine maker would not have a reason to use the gun.

"Humans and bears conspire, unwittingly, to conquer the mountain lion," Rudolph Lemieux was fond of saying from time to time during our Zen discussions of natural forces.

Looking back over the starboard side, I saw the shadowy shapes that resembled watercrafts. All of them were moving slowly through the bay, a small guide light on the bow of each, but one, a luxury cruiser, rocked idly in the water off by itself. There were dim lights in the wheelhouse and inner cabin. I could see figures moving around the deck. All men. It was the one.

Meneses slowed the engine to a crawl and slowly turned our starboard side to the *Largate*. We were several hundred feet away from the right aft corner of the mega yacht.

"OK, let's get this done," I said, feeling a mixture of excitement and fear about what was coming.

On the port side of our vessel, we deployed the inflatable Zodiac raft. Its surface was painted to appear aged. It was extra wide and deep. When we were ready, JD and I laid on the floor of the small watercraft.

Meneses and Antonio stripped their wet suits down to their waists and put on old T-shirts and reflective vests. They sat toward the rear of the Zodiac with a shrimp cage and fishing poles between them. Lastly, we hung a rusty sign off both sides that read, "Bocagrande Fishery," an ancient operation run by a Meneses cousin off the Cartagena docks for half a century.

As we anchored the Interceptor, my cell phone pinged. It was a text from Camille.

"Communication link set up. Engage the earpiece communicators."

I showed the text to the other three, and we did as it directed, fitting the ear communication pieces and tapping the small button to engage. There was white noise for a few seconds, then . . .

"Good evening gentlemen. Am I coming through clearly?" Camille asked in a calm voice with a slight French accent.

I looked at JD, Meneses, and Antonio. Each one gave me a thumbs-up.

"You're loud and clear, Command. How are we?" I responded.

"You're clear. We hear you and see you're ready to engage."

"Ten-four. You got eyes, Command?" I asked, looking around.

Just then a helicopter flew near our seaward side. As it banked away, I read a sign that said, "Cartagena Helicopter Tours" and saw a hand waving from a side door.

"Just a romantic night tour of the Cartagena skyline," Camille explained into our earpieces. "We can't get any closer. Airspace over the bay is restricted. They really mean to make a show of that bust."

"How much time do we have?" I asked.

"No idea, but I would get on with it. We have eyes on the US customs' strike ship. It's sitting in the slip, but there is a lot of activity on it."

"Keep your eyes on that ship," I said. "If it heads out toward the Largate, let us know."

"Ten-four. And Manion?"

"Yes, Command."

"Do what you do, but don't get dead."

"Roger that, Command."

With that the tour helicopter passed on our port side, banking away from the bay and into the city, giving a wide berth to the restricted airspace.

Then we were off in our fake fishing raft. The space was hot and close. Every minute or so I lifted my face to the edge of the Zodiac to feel the night air on my skin. I looked over at JD, who was lying so still I wondered if he had gone to sleep.

"Halfway there," Meneses said. He was steering the small engine on the back of the Zodiac. He handed the rudder stick to Antonio who was doing a good job of looking like a tired, bored fisherman. They spoke to a couple of fellow boaters as they passed in the night. When we cleared them, Meneses slipped back into the top half of his wet suit.

The closer we got to the *Largate*, the more my nerves began to pulse. In a perfect world, we would gain access unseen. Most likely we would be seen as we approached, and then we would play it by ear. If they were cool, we would be cool. If they opened fire . . .

I patted the pistol in my front pocket.

Fifty feet out, JD and Meneses slipped into the water. They floated next to each other as Antonio and I moved away in the Zodiac. I was going to approach the *Largate* from the other side to board her or at least to distract whoever was on the deck long enough for JD and Meneses to board the yacht.

I took the rudder from Antonio and gave the *Largate* a wide berth, moving around to the yacht's bow. The ship cast a dark shadow on the water in the moonlight. I eased the Zodiac right against the front tip of the hull, hidden from anyone on deck.

Antonio and I ducked down in the Zodiac, staring down the starboard side. In a few minutes, the water's surface broke as two face masks appeared next to the access platform for jet skis and boat access. One of them gave me a short wave. JD and Meneses were about to board the yacht.

Antonio and I moved slowly around the *Largate's* bow. I eased down the port side of the yacht. For almost a minute we were back in the moonlight and could have been clearly seen by anyone had they been looking on that side. There was no access ladder on the port side. We had to use a grappling rope thrown and hooked onto the railing.

"Team 1, what's your position," I whispered to Meneses. No answer.

I looked around and saw Antonio standing with his pistol in his hand. I waved for him to put it away, but he shook his head.

"Team 1, your position? Over," I whispered again.

"Team 1 is on deck. Encountered no personnel. No sign of the packages yet," Meneses responded.

From the Zodiac, I gathered my rope and grappling hook. I threw it well over the port-side railing and onto the deck. Just then Meneses appeared at the deck rail just above us. He secured the grappling hook to the rail and then waved me up.

"I want to come with you," Antonio whispered with urgency.

"No. We talked about this," I said. "Someone has to stay with the Zodiac."

"OK, you stay, and I'll climb up. It's my brother and my fiancé," he said, throwing my history with Soledad in my face, but I was laser focused and emotionally numb at that moment.

"Antonio, if things go bad up there, your father could lose both of his sons tonight."

That made him pause.

"Also, if you're approached by the authorities, I expect you to use your name and position to buy us time."

That also made him think. I patted his shoulder and then grabbed the rope. Meneses reappeared looking down from the deck. He was quiet but waved frantically for me to hurry up. I did the yank test on the rope. The hook was secure on the railing with Velcro straps.

I would never put the following in my final report to WorldSpan, but . . .

As I scaled the side of the massive yacht, I thought about Batman and Robin. In the 1960s live-action version of the superhero show, starring Adam West and Bruce Ward, there were scenes in which they scaled the sides of buildings with comic relief along the way. I hadn't thought about that since I was a kid. It's crazy, the stuff that comes to mind when I'm scared.

Just as I reached the rail, I heard Meneses talking to someone.

"Hey, my friend, it's OK. We heard there was a distress call . . ."

Two shots cracked the night quiet. It wasn't that loud, but the ping off the metal railing and the visual of Meneses diving to the deck registered more in my mind.

His face was even with mine, his against the deck floor, mine just over the rail hanging off the side of the *Largate*. His eyes were fixed on the danger as he continued to babble his way out of the situation.

I didn't hesitate. Holding the rope with one hand, I unzipped my front with the other hand and pulled the Beretta APX Compact out, flipping the safety off. I pushed hard off the side of the hull swinging away from the rail but giving me a brief look on deck. I saw a dark shape with a gun in his hand stepping toward Meneses, whose eyes were clamped shut. He seemed to be waiting for the third shot to hit where the others had missed. I pulled the trigger once and shot three times.

The first shot embedded in the deck between Meneses and the crewman in gray, who was holding a shiny nickel-plated pistol. The second shot got the gunman in his upper leg, just below the hip. He spun around, losing his gun in the process. My third shot went wide and shattered glass on the main salon.

I swung back into the side of the *Largate* so hard that I let go of the rope. I started to fall, but the safety harness engaged, and I stopped. The jerk made me feel like my back had been cracked.

I reached up and grabbed the railing with my free hand, refusing to drop my gun or put it away. With one arm over the rail and trying to lift my leg to meet it, I was pulled onto the deck. I rolled over and came up on one knee, sweeping my gun in every direction. The gunman was lying on the deck holding his leg and looking around for his gun.

The hands that pulled me over squeezed my arm and forced my gun down. I looked up at Meneses, who was smiling at me with unblinking eyes. He reached over my gun and engaged the safety.

"Command, we are good. One obstacle struck, injured but not dead," Meneses said into the communicator.

"Strike team, I need a full status," Camille said, urgency in her voice.

Strike One was Detective Meneses. I was Strike Two. JD was Strike Three. Antonio was Strike Four.

"Find his gun," I whispered to Meneses, indicating the crewman who was trying to get to his feet and slink away, his blood spreading over the deck.

"Stay down," Meneses said as he swept his foot under the gunman, sending him sprawling to the deck and grabbing his leg in pain.

"Strike One, Two, and Four are good," I said, my voice a little shaky and breathing hard as if I had just run one hundred meters against Usain Bolt. "No eyes on Strike Three but will follow up once the prisoner is secured."

"Prisoner? There's no plan for prisoners," Camille said.

Then we heard heavy footsteps, slow and steady. I brought my pistol back up.

"How many of you are still on board?" I asked the crewman. He mumbled something in what sounded like Portuguese.

Meneses leaned over and asked in his language, punctuating his words by popping the man on the back of his head with his gun. The gunman said something in reply.

"He says he doesn't know," Meneses said. He asked the man where Soledad and Fernando were being kept and got the same answer.

"The footsteps are getting closer," I said as I eased next to the door that led to the ship's lower levels.

Meneses cursed under his breath. He took a measured swing and delivered a knock-out blow to the crewman on the deck. I looked at him as if to say, *What the hell?*

"I'm going to find some rope to tie him up and tie off his wound. You gotta handle any crew members who come up," Meneses said. "Just a piece of advice, Manion. Squeeze the trigger and then release, so you control the number of bullets coming out."

"Got it," I whispered.

"And if you have to shoot, try not to kill anyone. Remember, we're trespassing."

"Got it," I said with a wave.

Then we heard more footsteps. I waved him away from the door.

"Command, let us know if you hear police chatter over the gunshots," I whispered into the communicator as I focused on the job at hand.

"Ten-four," Camille replied.

I stood next to the door, my pistol in my right hand. I could hear Meneses opening and closing hatch doors looking for rope.

"What's going on?" Antonio kept shouting up from the Zodiac.

"Shut up!" Meneses shouted back.

Two minutes passed. It seemed like hours. Sweat was pouring from every part of my body. I wish I would have pulled my wet suit down, but I was kind of busy.

Then the footsteps started again, getting closer. It took so long, I thought maybe I should have gone to meet the person coming up. Maybe that's what they wanted. As long as we stayed up there, we had the advantage. These guys were killers, and if things went wrong, Soledad and Fernando could get dead.

"Command, Strike Three present!" JD finally said over our communicator. Just then, I could hear him simultaneously on the stairway. "Manion, where the hell are you?" he shouted.

I moved down the steps, my pistol to my side. It was a square spiral and steep. I willed myself not to stumble. On the third turn, I found JD leaning on the banister.

At his feet was a little crewman who had been beaten black and blue. Over JD's shoulder was the long-missing and unconscious Soledad Marie Cruz. She was in an off-white bathing suit with a semi-sheer cover-up.

"Watch this clown while I get Sole out of here," JD said, stepping over the guy. "Little joker tried to stab me."

"Is she OK?" I asked. "Did you find Constaneda or Fernando?"

"Sole's just knocked out. I think she's been drugged," he said, moving up the stairs. He stopped and pointed to the little crewman on the landing. "He says Constaneda's gone, along with her gang. Please tell me Meneses wasn't shot?"

"No, it was another crewman."

"You kill the crewman up top?" he asked, kicking the crewman who was lying on the floor.

"No. Leg shot. And what makes you think I shot him?"

"Cuz I know you. Plus, I can smell the cordite off your gun," he said as he moved up the steps. "Command, this is Strike Three. Coming up with half the package."

He started up the steps, then turned back to me. "As soon as I get up top and get her on the Zodiac, I'll send Meneses down with you to bring up this piece of trash and then find Fernando."

"Got it," I said.

"Manion, wait for the backup," JD said as he climbed the steps, Soledad's head bouncing off his back with every step.

Then I was alone with the little guy. His name patch read, "Pablo."

I leaned down close to him. He tried to scoot away, but I grabbed his shirt and pointed my pistol at him. "Now, I'm going to ask you some questions," I said through gritted teeth. The stairway was hot and stuffy, but my senses were on high alert. "I just shot your boy upstairs. I can give you the same. In for a penny, in for a pound? Right?"

He nodded nervously.

"How many more of you are there on board?" I asked.

"N-not sure," he said. "At least one more."

"Where is everybody? It takes more than three men to run this ship."

"They left with the boss," he said, looking around.

"When did she leave? When is she coming back?"

"She ain't coming back as far as I know."

I gave him a long look.

"I swear. I don't know. We were waiting for instructions."

"And what were you supposed to do with the girl and Fernando?"

"Just keep them on board, especially the girl."

"Why?"

He rubbed his face, taking stock of the bruises he got from JD as he considered his answer.

"Strike Team, this is Command," Camille said in our earpieces. "The NDTC team is on the move. You need to find the packages and quit the vessel."

"W-w-wait a minute; I heard that," Pablo said, struggling to get to his feet. "The police are coming?"

"Right, where's Fernando?" I asked, also standing.

"I have to get out of here," Pablo said, trying to limp upstairs. I grabbed him by the back of his collar, dragging him back to me.

"Not until you tell me where Fernando Lazaro is," I said, then shook him so hard his teeth rattled. I realized Meneses had not made it down yet. "To hell with this. Let's go, lil' man."

Still holding onto his collar, I half guided, half shoved him down the stairs. We continued down to the next level. I heard noises down the hall—a chair scraping, fabric rubbing together, breathing. I had to push it, remembering the NDTC agents and the Americans were coming.

"Command, this is Strike Two. What's the ETA for the NDTC agents?" I asked.

"Less than twenty minutes, Strike Two," Camille said. "Get a move on!"

"Have you found the additional package? Have you found my brother?" Antonio asked.

"Working on it," I replied.

"I'm coming to help you," Meneses said.

"No," I replied. "We don't have time. You need to get to the Zodiac. When I bring him out, we have to boogie out of here."

There was a pregnant silence.

"Strike Team, do you copy?" I asked.

"Copy that, Strike Team Two," JD said. "We are retreating to the Zodiac. Awaiting your extraction."

"Strike Team, the NDTC is fifteen minutes out," Camille said.

I moved down the lower-level hallway, looking left and right, Pablo out in front of me. I heard what sounded like crying but didn't trust my ears.

"Fernando! Fernando Lazaro!" I shouted. "I'm here to take you out of here!"

No answer. I hear sobbing. It was a man. I continued moving forward. As Pablo and I approached the end of the hall, he began to squirm, trying to escape my grasp.

"What's wrong with you? Settle down!" I said, struggling to hold his collar.

"I have to get out of here," Pablo said. "I can't be here right now!"

He ripped his shirt open in the front and shrugged out of it, leaving me holding what was left, and took off down the hall. Just then another crewman stepped from behind one of the last doors in the hall.

"Fredo, it's me! Don't shoot!" Pablo shouted, but it was too late. The crewmen didn't hesitate. His pistol was up as he stepped out from behind the door. He fired three shots. Two shots hit Pablo in the neck and head. The third whizzed past my head.

As Fredo stood there, shocked by his mistaken identity, I fired two shots of my own, hitting him in his arm and lower torso. It knocked him back, but he didn't go down. Instead, he took off down the hall and through another door. I checked Pablo as I stepped over him. He was done, lifeless eyes staring back.

"Strike Team, in pursuit of third combatant," I said into the communicator. "He may be coming up to your level from the opposite side. Heads up!"

"We heard shots!" JD said.

"Affirmative," I replied as I continued down the hall, looking from side to side. I had my pistol up in case other crewmen were still out there. "I hit the third combatant. He's injured but still on the move."

"Strike Two, where is the combatant I left with you?" JD asked.

"Pablo is dead."

"Dammit, Strike Two," JD said. "Did you kill him?"

"No!"

What's his deal? I've never killed anyone around him.

The hall was filled with the smell of gunfire and smoke. My ears had a low-level ring in them. I could still hear the sobbing, but I couldn't make out where it was coming from. That was how I almost passed the room where Fernando Lazaro was being held.

33

The Lazaro Coffee truck with Lalvarez wines inside arrived at Cartagena Harbor. Just like Anise had promised, there were smugglers working as loaders. Munch and Graves visibly relaxed. They were ready to get rid of their cargo. Munch was convinced the load was bad luck, both of them still convinced that the helicopter they heard in Venecia was meant for them. Now it was someone else's problem.

"You guys are late," one of the loaders said. Munch recognized him as a guy named Ray.

"Yeah, well, we had some delays, but we're here now," Graves said. "The sooner you get this loaded, the better."

"I agree. Then we're going underground," Ray said. "I advise you two to do the same."

"Underground?"

"You haven't heard? The boss's shipments have been getting busted all over the place. Beato was trying to fly with one hundred thousand dollars in his underwear. The lumber shipment was also busted."

"Whaaaaat?" Munch said. "Someone must be talking."

"You think?" Ray replied. "Help us get this wine on the ship. Then we can get off the grid."

"And then what?" Munch asked no one in particular.

"We stay there—until we hear from the boss," Graves said in his trademark flat tone.

They moved around to the back of the truck, preoccupied with talk about where they were going to hide out afterward.

That's why they weren't ready for what came next.

As they swung the doors open, a stack of wine cases six feet tall fell out toward them, knocking Munch back into Ray.

"What the fuck?" Munch said, trying to regain his balance and unsuccessfully grabbing the cases to keep more bottles from breaking. Wine and pieces of glass bounced off the pavement, adding to the confusion.

A young girl jumped out of the truck and took off running up the lane toward the main street that led away from the docks. The smugglers and Munch were confused, but Graves was as cool as ever. He was a detached emotional being who was incapable of love, warmth, or even camaraderie, but it made him an excellent killer.

While the loaders and Munch were flailing with the cases, Graves pulled out his favorite piece, a long-barrel Colt revolver, and drew a bead on the back of the girl who was running away. They had to contain this situation, and that started with keeping her from leaving.

That was when Mario Romero eased from between the remaining cases in the back of the truck and buried the sharp edge of a broken bottle of malbec into Graves' neck, right in his jugular vein. The glass stuck in Graves neck, protruding like a strange growth. Blood flew out of his neck with the rhythm of his heartbeat.

The minute Mario saw the man who shot his husband, he went on automatic pilot. The dock was dark, but Mario's sight and aim were flawless.

Graves slowly lowered his gun, Seynah long gone up the road and around the corner. He looked back at Mario, who was momentarily stunned by the spectacle he had created. Munch and the other smugglers were getting to their feet. Mario could feel the effect of the surprise attack waning. He had to make a move.

Mario jumped on Graves's back, and they began to spin. He wrapped his legs around the killer, who was still disoriented by the attack. Mario grabbed Graves's gun hand. They staggered around, bouncing off the back of the truck.

Mario felt beside himself. He was no tough guy, but the events of the last week had thrown him into this crazy bloody existence. The trip started as a dream vacation with Wayne in the beautiful hills of Colombia, and it would end here.

He pointed the gun at Munch, Ray, and the other smugglers, then fired two shots just over their heads. Ray and the other loaders took off running in every direction. Munch, however, was made of stronger stuff. He was more afraid of Anise Constaneda than this little gay guy with the gun. There was product to get loaded. Graves looked done, but Munch had been taught to stand by his work partner.

So, he stood there, his hands up, staring at Mario. Graves fell to his knees, the blood continuing to spew from the wound in his neck. Mario leaned over Graves but kept the pistol aimed at Munch. There was a humid silence save for a sound like a hissing breath. It took Mario a second to realize that noise was him, crying hysterically.

"Man, I'm sorry for your . . . uh . . . man," Munch said. "We didn't want to kill him. You took us by surprise that morning. Fernando said no one—"

"What? What? Fernando? Fernando Lazaro?" Mario asked through his sobs.

Munch realized he misspoke and stayed quiet.

Mario looked around, confused, like he suddenly didn't know where he was. He looked down and grabbed the glass extending from Graves neck and forced it in as far as he could. Blood spewed in all directions. The back half dug into Mario's hand, but he was beyond feeling it.

Good for Mario that he did. Graves was prepared to fight back. He had slipped his seven-inch Bohler blade in his left hand and was poised to stab up at Mario. He never got close. With the last thrust into his neck, he seemed to melt to the ground and was dead or close to dead.

"What's your name?" Mario asked, turning his attention back to Munch. His demeanor was as light and airy as an icebreaker exercise at an Amway convention.

"They call me Munch."

"OK, Munch," Mario said, his teary eyes wide with manic emotion. "Your boy here is done. He shot Wayne like a dog in the street."

He stopped talking long enough to wipe his eyes and blow his nose on his sleeve. Munch tried not to look nauseous.

"Munch, I won't shoot you on one condition: that you tell me two things."

"Sure, anything," Munch said.

"The truth," Mario said, pointing the gun at him.

Munch nodded.

"First, did Antonio Lazaro have anything to do with this?"

"The little brother? The wine maker? No. The plan was to smuggle our product in the wine. Fernando owed the boss a lot of money. This was his way of paying his debt."

Mario slowly crouched next to Graves's body and vomited between his feet. When he looked up again, Munch was running down the lane. Watching him, Mario thought he moved fast for a big man.

He looked down at Graves's pistol in his hand. It seemed the most natural thing to do. He took aim and shot at Munch's back seven times. He wasn't sure how many hit the mark. He stood there for what seemed like a half hour thinking that the police would show up in response to all the gunfire. When they didn't appear, he went back into the truck's cargo box.

He broke several wine bottles until he found one without the smuggled product stuffed into it. When he found one, he drank from it. He remembered the times when they discovered the small batch wine. He called it "world-class, world-changing wine."

"Changed my world all right!" Mario said, unable to hold back a sickening laugh.

Mario took another long pull on the malbec. It was just as amazing as it was the first time they tasted it, but now it might as well have been bargain Lambrusco. He opened another one and continued to drink. On his third bottle, he pulled out his phone. He still had a small charge. He had kept it off most of the time he was on the run in case someone tried to track him.

On the day Wayne was shot, he had escaped the killers running into the hills. There he found a private zipline that took him a mile away in seconds.

He traded his credit cards and cash with a local farm family, who hid him for several days. Their oldest son knew the Venecia hills like no one else took Mario through the jungle back to the edge of the Lazaro estate.

From there he hid out, watching and waiting for his chance to strike back. Realizing what they were doing with their wine, he stole away in the trucks behind the flexitanks until the right time.

Now it was over, but he still felt miserable and alone. He found a familiar number and called it.

"Hi, this is Wayne Kowl," the recording said. "You've reached my voicemail. Please leave me a message at the beep, and either I or Mario, the wonder, will call you back. Later!"

That's what Mario was still doing when the police and Seynah returned to the dock to investigate what she had reported.

34

On the *Largate* I found Fernando sitting on the floor, handcuffed to a stainless-steel table bolted to the wall. He looked like crap. I knelt next to him. He seemed like a deflated balloon version of the one we had met and fought with in front of his restaurant just a few days ago. His monochromatic cream-colored shirt and pants were drenched with sweat and smudged with dirt on the knees, thighs, cuffs, and elbows. His face was sweaty and slightly bruised, but it didn't seem to be from fighting. He seemed like he had been drugged. His head lolled up and down as he fought to focus on my face.

"Command, Strike Team, this Strike Two, I—" I stopped short. Despite all his lolling, Fernando's sweaty hand shot up and covered my mouth. I knocked it away and pointed my pistol at his face. He put a shaky finger to his lips. Never taking his eyes off of mine, he pointed to my ear where the communicator piece was live and picking up every sound. Then he slowly moved his finger back to his lips.

"Strike Team, this is Command. The maritime authority and the NDTC officers are nine minutes out!"

"Strike Two, this is Strike One. What's your status? Who did you find?"

I watched Fernando's face for several seconds. It was pleading.

"Strike Team, this is Strike Two. Still working through the last rooms. No sign of the package yet," I said. I pulled the communicator from my ear, switched it off, and placed it in my front pocket. Fernando deflated even more with relief.

"OK, we gotta get out of here. The NDTC is coming to shut this down and take everyone on board into custody," I said, pulling a tool out to break the handcuff or the table leg to which it was connected.

"That won't be necessary, Manion," Fernando said with a groggy voice. "I'm not leaving."

"Lazaro, stop with the bullshit," I began, but he raised a hand for me to be quiet. "We don't have time," I said.

"Less time than you think," Fernando said, pointing under the table.

I am not an explosives expert, but I had watched enough disaster-relief training and action movies to be sure it was a pack of C-4 with an electronic trigger. The timer read 18:22.

"Jesus!" I said, crawling backwards. "We're out of here! C'mon, Fernando. Your brother's waiting for you topside. Your sister's on the docks."

"No, no you have to go. Leave me here." His swollen red eyes refilled with tears. "Listen to me. I know you have no reason to believe me, but just listen."

I stopped working on the handcuffs to hear what this pompous asshole had to say. Explosives two feet behind his head, and he wanted to grandstand, to make some kind of statement. This crazy family that Soledad attached herself to was one piece of work.

"First, I didn't know what the plan was. This plan? To blow up the ship when the Policía Nacional de Colombia comes. I just found out in the last two hours."

"Anise Constaneda? What does she have on you?"

"Money," he rasped. "Pure and simple. I ran up a gambling debt. A big one."

"More than you can pay? Or your family can pay?"

"Papa paid last time. I couldn't stand to have him do that a fourth time," he explained, showing some of that old family pride.

"So, what was the plan?" I asked, glancing nervously at the bomb attached to the table.

He proceeded to explain the entire plan. The debt. The plot to smuggle illegal prescription medicine into the US.

"She wanted to send it in Lazaro Coffee sacks," Fernando explained. "I couldn't do that, but—"

"You thought no one would pay attention to your little brother's modest little wine shipment," I said, filling in the next step.

He nodded as I glanced at the timer: 17:33

"Until Anise's people killed the American?" I asked.

"Stupid fools. I found out Antonio moved his packing schedule up, but before I could get to them, the Americans found Anise's people putting product in the bottles. Instead of just knocking them out, tying them up, and contacting me, the assholes shot one of the Americans and drove the other one into hiding."

Fernando gave me the *Reader's Digest* version of how, after the shootings, he offered to get down to Cartagena and handle the wine shipment and Soledad for Antonio, who took a team of men into the hills to find the other American.

"You were playing the supportive big brother when all this time you were trying to get illegal drugs in his wine shipment."

"I was trying to get her out of my life!" Fernando said, getting frustrated. He raised his hand in apology. "Please, Señor Manion, we don't have much time." He sat up straight. "Have you noticed that Anise Constaneda and Soledad could be twins?"

"Right, right. That's why we approached you in front of your restaurant."

"Well, I thought it would be fun to introduce the two of them, hide out on the Largate, and keep Soledad distracted while we got that wine onto the ship. Once it was on the ship, I was in the clear."

"What was the plan when it got to the States?" I asked.

"First, it wasn't the entire shipment—a little less than half. Anise said she had people who could get to it while in the US customs hold or while en route to the American distributor's warehouse. It was my understanding that she was setting something up with the Chinese. This was a test run."

"Well, I'm sorry, but she's gonna fail," I said, working on the handcuffs again.

He headbutted me, pushing me away.

"Hey, Fernando, don't think I won't really leave your ass down here," I said.

"Now you're catching on, Manion."

"You want to die? Why?" I asked, not believing what I was hearing.

"You were right; she did fail," he said, holding up his phone.

On the screen a breaking news story about US and Colombian customs agents making hits on Anise Constaneda's operations from Medellin to Cartagena. It also included a bloody scene at the harbor involving a damaged wine shipment.

"I'm done, Manion. When this all comes out, it's prison, shame on my family. I won't survive that. I'm not built for that. I'm going down with the ship."

"Man, are you crazy?" I said, working the file on the handcuffs. "Your little brother is here risking his life for you. Your sister helped put this rescue together. You think they care about all this other stuff over your life?"

"But I'll see it in their eyes, in my papa's eyes, every time I see them from behind prison bars. Anise Constaneda is wanted in three countries, including the United States. I can't do time outside of Colombia, without my family's influence."

"But she's not even here," I said. "Where . . . why?" Then it hit me. I looked down at Fernando, who wore a smile with no warmth.

"That's cold, right? I just put it all together myself," he said by way of explanation.

"From the moment she met Soledad, she had a plan to use her as bait. She demanded that I keep her on the ship. Keep her away from the docks until the wine was loaded. The whole time she was a look-alike to the NDTC agents watching the yacht."

"So, they busted her shipments, and when they came to take her look-alike into custody, boom!" I said, putting the pieces together.

"I think the idea was to kill Soledad and make it look like Anise died in the blast," he replied, nodding. "She was going to disappear and operate underground."

It was insane, but it all made sense. I could barely wrap my mind around it, but everything locked into place.

Just then I heard the sound of another small motorboat.

"That's the last of the crew," Fernando said. "Probably the one you shot. He made it to the escape boat. Won't be long now."

"Wait a minute," I said, trying to think while my inner survivor was shouting for me to break out. "She was going to leave you here to die as well?"

"Probably. I told you the bitch was cold," he said, looking at me with pitiful eyes that turned hard. "It doesn't matter anymore."

I just sat there with him because I didn't know what else to do.

"Dammit, Manion. They said you were the smart one. None of this is about smuggling. They've been trying to bust Anise Constaneda for over ten years. Then, all of a sudden, she got caught in multiple raids? She set it up that way, so they would come for her right here."

"Jesus," I said. "As far as the world would know, she would be dead."

"Yeah, but she didn't know or count on you or Soledad's brother. I didn't even know she had a brother who was in law enforcement. That tells you everything you need to know about this sorry operation."

I had heard enough. I checked the timer under the table: 16:05. I had to think about Soledad. That was who I had gone there to get. Everything else was . . .

I went to work on the handcuffs again and immediately felt a stab in my upper arm.

"Are you crazy?" I asked, then punched Fernando. He was sitting there with a stiletto blade, looking more alert than he had since I found him.

"Manion, I know you think I'm crap, and you may be right, but I love my brother and sister. Just say you couldn't find me. Can you be a stand-up guy and do that for me? For me and my family?"

I couldn't even speak.

"If not, and you keep trying to free me, well, me and my little blade here will do everything to stop you. It might not be so bad to have some company on the way to see the devil," he said. The look in his eyes scared me. He was serious.

I looked him in the eye and nodded, then glanced at the timer: 14:09.

I stood up and took one last look at him. He was sitting on the floor, his legs crossed in front of him. He stared straight ahead like he was watching a video that was only running in his mind.

I turned and ran up the hall, then hit the steps two at a time. I stopped long enough to pull out my communicator earpiece. I turned it on to a cacophony of chatter.

They were all on the Zodiac waiting for me, as we planned. It seemed that Meneses wanted to leave, but Antonio and JD wanted to stay for their own reasons. It broke my heart listening to the kid talk about his brother, and I couldn't believe I was hearing JD sticking up for me.

I made it to the deck and started talking fast and loud. "Command and Strike Team! Command and Strike Team! This is Strike Two. Back on the deck."

"Strike Two, where have you been? Where's the other package?" It was Meneses, but I knew he was only asking what was on everyone else's mind.

"Strike Team, this is Command. Collect your team, and quit the vessel. Now! NDTC vessels are four minutes out!"

"This is Strike Two. The Largate is packed with C-4 explosives set to detonate."

"Ten-four, Strike Two. Quit the damn vessel! Now!" Camille said, her voice full of emotion.

I crossed the main deck and headed down the portside access to the boat launch. I saw everyone in the Zodiac. Soledad was still unconscious, cradled in her brother's arms. Antonio was the only one standing. He was looking up at me expectantly, and I felt my insides go heavy and my scalp shrink. I jumped into the Zodiac. Meneses engaged the engine and pulled away from the *Largate*. We were on the sea side, hidden from view of the encroaching NDTC vessels.

"Manion, what's your status? And what is this about explosives?" JD asked.

"C-4 packed in at least three places with a timer scheduled to go off in the next few minutes" I yelled over the engine. I lifted my phone to show him a closeup picture I had taken of the first C-4 pack I found. JD was ex-military and trained to recognize, if not use, high-grade explosives. His face went pale.

"Get us outta here, Meneses!" JD shouted. "That stuff has a blast range that's out of this world. It will be raining hot metal for a mile in every direction."

"Wait! What about Fernando?" Antonio shouted over the raging engine. Meneses had us on an open sprint back to our own ship, which was still anchored just beyond the curve of the shoreline. The helicopter overhead barely registered.

"I didn't find him," I said, shaking my head.

"What?" Antonio said as if he was expecting any answer but that. He was standing now, barely keeping his balance as the Zodiac roared across the bay.

"That was why I took so long! I went through the first time—"

"When you shot another crewman," Meneses said.

"Right. But I went through the lower level multiple times, even the engine room. Your brother wasn't there."

"That can't be! He was supposed to stay with Soledad," Antonio said, pointing to the unconscious woman in her brother's arms. "He wouldn't have left her alone on that ship."

"I found Sole by herself in the galley in this condition," JD said. "I never saw or heard Fernando. I was calling both their names; that's how that little jerk almost stabbed me."

Everyone looked at me.

"One of the crew, the little one, Pablo, said Fernando may have left earlier with Anise," I explained, trying to infuse my voice with relief. "The important thing is, he's not on the Largate right now."

Antonio pondered that for a moment. "I just wonder, where he could be. What should I tell Luisa and Papa?"

I looked around the Zodiac. Everyone was in their own thoughts. JD was still staring at me. I couldn't read his gaze. Did he smell the liar's sweat coming through my pores?

When we reached the Interceptor, Meneses jumped from the Zodiac onto the deck. He pulled me up next. I assumed that was to help the others get aboard.

Then he found a gaff and pushed the Zodiac, with the others in it, away from the Interceptor's hull. We all gave him a puzzled look.

"If we don't do something to slow them down before that C-4 detonates, NDTC agents will die," he said. "My fellow officers will die. They'll reach the Largate just as it explodes."

"We can get a call in to them. From Polonia. From Camille. Tell them of the danger," JD said.

"Would that stop you if you were the NDTC chief and the American federal agents about to execute a plan you've been working on for months or years?" Meneses shouted as he cranked the Interceptor's powerful engines. "We would also have to explain how we know about the bombs."

"So, what's the plan?" I asked. He smiled as if he wasn't sure I would sign on to whatever lunacy he had in mind.

"Wait a minute," JD said. "What are we supposed to do? Sit out here in the open water in this raft?"

Meneses was on the verge of laughter. He pointed behind them. We all looked in that direction. The twinkling lights of the Cartagena shore filled the night. High-rise condos loomed in the muted light.

"The Zodiac has more than enough fuel to make it to the Morros City coast," Meneses said. "Manion and I will tell my cousin and Señora Lazaro where you are. They will pick you up from there."

We sat there for a few seconds, no one having anything to add.

"Good luck, mi amigos!" Meneses shouted as he whipped the Interceptor's nose into the open water. One moment, I was waving to JD and Antonio. The next moment, I was thrown onto the boat's floor as Meneses gunned the engine.

For about thirty seconds we were speeding in pitch darkness, the MFD our only light. I got to my feet and held onto the back of the chair in which Meneses was sitting. He was working the switches with one hand and steering with the other. The whole time his attention was laser focused over the bow. Eventually, he found every light on the vessel. We were a nautical Christmas light torpedoing into Cartagena Bay on a crazy mission.

"Manion, what's going on?"

It was Camille in my earpiece. I looked at Meneses, who heard the question in his earpiece as well.

"Command, we—"

"Stop that 'Command crap' and talk to me, Tekelius!" she said, just as the helicopter flew overhead. "Why are you headed back toward the Largate?"

"It's going to explode—"

"I heard you the first three times, but why are you going back in?" she shouted.

"We're going to slow up the NDTC patrol to keep them back," I explained.

"What does that look like?" she asked.

"Not sure!" I shouted over the engine's roar. "If you have any rabbits in your hat, please try to get through to Arnie Rutledge and the NDTC team to pull up on the full charge."

"Tekelius!" she shouted.

"Mila, we have minutes, or a lot of people are going to die!"

Silence

"I gotta go!" I said.

More silence

"I love you!" I said.

Silence. Then . . .

"Get on with it! Command Out!" she said, breaking off communication.

I turned back to Meneses, who was staring at me, the boat's radio mic in hand.

"Just do what you can, cousin," he said, speaking into the mic.

For the next few seconds, we continued to speed back into the bay. The vessels were dark shadows as we passed them.

"So, you and the boss, the elegant French lady?" he said, keeping his eyes out on the bow.

"It's a special relationship," I said with what I am sure was a goofy grin.

"I bet," he replied, shaking his head and smiling. "Manion, you're either the genius of the age or the luckiest man I have ever met."

We continued for another minute or two, the spray soaking us and the deck. Then he throttled down.

"It's the point of no return," he said. He pointed to his right. The *Largate* was sitting as still as when we left it. I stared at it, hoping I would see some sign of movement, that Fernando had had a change of mind. As we passed it on the left, we saw a wide band of lights coming our way. The NDTC team. They seemed close.

"Are we too late?" I shouted.

"Nope! They look about a half mile out but closing fast. Take the wheel, Manion!"

"What? No! I can't drive a boat."

"Twelve-year-old boys can drive a boat, Manion," Meneses said, standing up. He forced me down into the seat. The Interceptor started to veer to the right, and I caught the wheel.

"Stay on this course," he said, placing my right hand on the speed control. "Pull back to go faster and pursh forward to slow down. You turn the wheel hard and coast to a stop in the water. No brakes."

"OK, got it," I said as I focused on the bow. "What are you going to do?"

"Try to keep us from getting shot on sight," he said. When I turned to look at him, he had a smile on his face. "Keep your eye on the bow, Tekelius!"

That's exactly what I did. Keeping my speed at what I later learned was about forty knots, I headed for what seemed like an "armada" of law enforcement vessels. As we got closer, I saw Colombian and American flags. I stayed on course even when they started blowing their massive horns.

That was when Meneses reappeared behind me. He stepped on the side seats and onto the bow as we were going along at forty knots!

It didn't seem to bother him, but it scared all the macho out of me. If I accidently threw him into the bay, I was cooked since he was the only one who knew the plan. I pushed the speed lever forward just a bit.

He placed a white flag in the holder on the tip of the bow. Anyone looking at us would see we were flying the universal symbol of noncombatants.

Then he placed an old jacket on the bow and secured it with rope fed through the sleeves and tied around the windshield. In that moment it was easy to see that he was from a long line of mariners. I looked over the windshield at the jacket. It had the Policía Nacional de Colombia shield on it.

He jumped back into the Interceptor's passenger compartment.

"Tell me again why we don't just reach out to the NDTC vessels by radio," I said, pointing to our vessel's radio.

"Polonia is working on that right now. She's working with the central dispatch to get the word to the lead vessel. However, it's a covert NDTC mission, which means they're on their own radio frequency. Few people have access to it. Every minute we spent trying to talk, the closer they would be getting to that bomb."

I nodded. Even if we could make radio contact, I doubted if Agent Rutledge and his friends would stand down based on our word. The arrest had been a long time coming.

"OK, it's all luck now," he said. "Manion, on my mark, make a hard right. We're gonna cross in front of them and hope they know we come in peace and don't start shooting at us."

"What if they do?" I asked nervously.

"Then pull the speed lever back and get out of the way," he said, looking at me as if I was missing the obvious. "On my mark! Three . . . two . . . one . . . turn!"

I turned the wheel hard. Maybe a bit too hard, as I had to adjust out of a U-turn. Nevertheless, we were moving through the water perpendicular to the path of the oncoming law. I glanced over my shoulder to see what my partner was doing. Meneses had stripped out of his rubberized suit and was sporting a dark blue uniform shirt. I recognized it as the uniform of his officers in Medellin.

"Manion, in another ten seconds, whip us around and go back the way we came!" he shouted.

I was in the zone by then. I even felt in pretty good control of the Interceptor.

I counted down in my head, then performed a 180-degree turn going in the opposite direction but still crossing the oncoming slew of vessels with guns. I stole a glance back at the *Largate*, which was sitting in the water like a silent tomb.

I made similar turns four more times, ignoring the warning horns. Then we were in their huge searchlights.

"Slow your speed by half!" Meneses shouted as they shouted at us in Spanish. I didn't need an interpreter. They were telling us to get our nuisance asses out of the water.

That was when Meneses stepped out beyond the windshield and kneeled next to the jacket that was lying flat against the bow. With the white flag and the jacket, it was starting to come into focus. I slowed our vessel just a bit more. That was when Meneses held his detective badge straight into the air and held that pose.

What if it seems like he's aiming at them in the dark? What do I do if they open fire? The questions came to mind, but I kept them to myself.

We did this for three more passes, me turning and reversing. Eventually, their searchlights shone in our faces and reflected off Meneses' badge.

They were so close, I could hear them yelling from their decks.

"Just keep doing what you're doing, Manion!" Meneses shouted over his shoulder.

Then things went quiet. It took me a few seconds to realize that the NDTC ships had come to a stop. Then three horn blasts sounded from the lead vessel.

"Unidentified vessel, this is Captain Zachary of the National Directorate of Taxes and Customs! You're in breach of civil water command. Remove your vessel immediately, or we'll employ extreme force to remove you!"

Meneses lowered his badge and scrambled back onto the deck next to me.

"OK, we got their attention! We did it, Manion," Meneses said. "Now what—"

I didn't hear the rest because, at that moment, the *Largate*, a forty-meter Baglietto superyacht, went up in a massive explosion.

The sound was deafening, and the sky was full of debris, most of it aflame. The good news was the NDTC vessels slowed to a stop. Alarms went off, and lights swept across the water, personnel scrambling on the decks of the oncoming ships.

Then boat parts and water rained down on all of us. I heard it landing on all the vessels, including ours. Meneses and I ducked beneath the dash in the lower storage area. The air filled with the sound of debris splashing into the water.

The noise seemed to go on for an hour—the sirens, the engine noise, the falling debris, the yelling of law enforcement officers, and the ringing in my ears from the explosion. The communicators were knocked out either from the blast or from the interference from all the other vessels, or maybe it was just too loud to hear. I could barely make out the noise of a helicopter. I knew Camille was out there watching over me.

"Alright, you clowns can come out!"

It was Agent Rutledge speaking through a bullhorn. I peeked over the Interceptor's rail. He was standing on the bow of one of the NDTC vessels, dressed in tactical gear, a flak vest, and the shiniest black military boots I had ever seen. In one hand was the bullhorn. His other hand was on his heavily belted hip. A collective of agents was standing behind him, representing Colombia and America.

With the lights and the activity all around us, Rutledge seemed like a character playing out a scene in a movie. Then I heard laughing in my earpiece. I looked over and saw it was Meneses. I frowned at first. Then he pointed to Rutledge, and I realized he was thinking the same thing. Then I started to laugh at how ridiculous he looked.

We laughed at Rutledge. We laughed because we were alive. We laughed because we had saved a lot of people from dying. Then I remembered Fernando, and my throat got thick, my eyes filled with tears, and my chest heaved with emotion, but I never stopped laughing.

35

In the end, we were all arrested—Meneses, Polonia, JD, Soledad, Antonio, Luisa, and me. The Colombian and American governments wanted their big fish. They thought they had been looking at Anise the whole time, only to realize they had been duped. They had Anise's lumber, her cash, even her prescription drugs, but not her.

Instead, they had a ragged band of individuals telling them an amazing story that entertained but didn't answer the only question that mattered: where was Anise Constaneda?

Technically, it was jail, but in actuality, we were held in that same building where we had met Agent Rutledge the previous day. Or it may have been the day before, as I was sleeping a lot. There were desks and couches but no television or music. They brought in cots for us to sleep on with thick army blankets.

We were allowed to charge our cell phones, which were returned to us, but I'm sure they had tracking and cloning software installed on them. Meneses, Polonia, and I were kept in one room. Antonio and Luisa were in an adjoining room. JD and Soledad were in a room on the opposite side.

On the first day of our confinement, I did not worry. I was confident that Camille and good ol' WorldSpan were working on an exit strategy for me, and I wouldn't have come that far without JD and Soledad. Meneses and Polonia had connections all over those docks. I was confident they would be released soon.

I thought back on all the simple things made hard on this case. Was it even considered a case now?

I laughed at myself, thinking back on the plans I had as JD and I flew down there. I was going to watch JD scold his little sister like I had seen him do so many times in the past. I was going to laugh as she gave him as good as she got. Then I was going to see some of Colombia on my own. Now I couldn't wait to get out of there.

I thought back to White Sand Island, where I grew up. The last time I was there, I couldn't wait to leave. It seemed when I was around folks from home, there was always trouble.

Over the next twenty-four hours, I heard JD and Soledad having some heated conversations about why he had never heard of this "wine dude who thinks he's her future husband."

Soledad was shocked at the news that Antonio was going to propose.

Way to go, JD.

I did hear him ask what kind of man would leave his fiancé in jail. As it turned out, the Lazaros were the first to be released. A savvy-looking lawyer named Ernesto Jasper showed up, and Luisa and Antonio were gone within the hour. As far as we knew, the kid never made a peep of an inquiry about Soledad.

Listening to them, I realized that, along with spotty phone service, some things as simple as pride, ego, and fear of disapproval had also led to our difficulties. If JD didn't criticize his sister so much, maybe she would have been more forthcoming about the wine business and her relationship with Antonio. Maybe he wouldn't have included me in this mess at all. If the Lazaros weren't so proud and dismissive of anything non-Lazaro, maybe we could have arrived at a solution that was less . . . like this.

Meneses and Polonia were released the next morning through the efforts of their extensive family connections and the Policía Nacional de Colombia.

That left the three Americans. They put us in a large room together. I wasn't sure how much longer it would take, but I could tell things were in the works. The quality of food improved immensely. We even got our choice of alcohol.

Eventually, I got the chance I wanted. JD was taking his supervised daily walk around the complex they afforded each of us once a day, leaving Soledad and I alone for the first time.

"Soledad, I—"

"How are you here?" she asked as if I was the last person she wanted to see.

She looked very different from what I remembered the last time I had seen her, about a year ago. She looked more developed. Maybe it was just the clothes. She had graduated from her workout, sweat-suited, snug-fitting, boyish attire. She dressed like a young businesswoman, a dark blue wrap-around dress with heels. Her hair was shorter and parted on the side. She was also wearing makeup, full makeup. The Soledad I remembered was a tanned, sun-kissed beauty without any artificial adornments.

"Your brother asked me to come, Sole. I just wanted to help."

"And yet here we are in another mess," she said, looking at me with an expression I couldn't read. "I can just imagine what Antonio is thinking right now."

"So, it's true? You and Antonio? Why didn't you tell JD?"

"Wow, now I have to explain myself to my ex? Do you know how long I've had to spend explaining myself to men, getting their OK, clearing my next steps with a man, be it my brother or whoever?"

Things weren't going the way I wanted. I moved to the other side of the room and made myself a drink, a locally distilled aguardiente over ice. Colombians usually mixed it with something fruity, but I always added a splash of rum. I offered the container to her, and she shook her head.

Then it hit me. The secrecy? This ferocious attachment in a relationship that didn't seem to be that long? The way she turned down a drink, as if she wanted one but thought better of it?

"Oh my God, Sole. You're pregnant!" I could tell I hit the mark by the expression on her face. She crossed the room until she was within inches of me.

"Who told you?" she demanded, clearly pissed.

"No one," I said, my hands up in mock surrender. "I guessed."

She slapped the drink out of my hand and punched me in the mouth.

"You're a damn liar, Teke," she said through clenched teeth. "The only two people I've told are on the run from the law," she said. "So, you're lying now, and you were lying about Fernando when you said you didn't see him on that boat."

"Anise? You told Anise?" I asked.

"And Fernando, and you didn't answer my question. Who told you?"

"No one."

"Bullshit, Manion," she said, jabbing her index finger into my chest. "Anise left that ship earlier that day. When I blacked out, Fernando was still there. You know about the baby, which means you talked to Fernando."

I started to reply, but she kept talking over me.

"Nobody believes your story about his not being there. Fernando didn't leave me on that ship the entire time. Then you're saying at the eleventh hour, he took off? I don't believe it, and the Lazaros don't either."

She didn't know how close she was. Out of all the people involved in this mess, I mistakenly thought I would be able to confide in her. She knew Fernando and had spent time with him on the Largate. Now I saw she was just as invested in the Lazaros as Antonio said they were.

"First, don't hit me again," I said. "I mean it."

I picked up my glass, which hadn't broken, and made another drink as I explained. "The pregnancy call was a guess based on a number of things, such as the way you and JD have been fighting about Antonio."

"Eavesdropping, huh?" she said with a smirk. "Always the investigator."

"Always. I've never heard you talk back to him like that, especially over a man."

"True, not even over you," she said.

"I wasn't worth it," I replied, ignoring her attempt to hurt my feelings. For the umpteenth time in the last two weeks, I was regretting ever getting on that cramped-ass plane with JD.

"Second, we have had great alcohol for about twenty-four hours, and you haven't touched a drop," I said, draining my glass this time and building my third.

No sarcasm that time, just folded arms, cold stares, the sound of ice bouncing around in some fairly nice Ralph Lauren low-ball glasses.

"And third," I continued. "I remembered how Antonio talked about you when we were trying to find you. You know? He and JD almost came to blows because you never confided in your brother. He had to find out about all this from strangers."

She still didn't have a snappy comeback, so I continued. "He thought it was a lie because there was no way his little sister would have all this going on and not tell him. It's why I'm here. Why would JD ever ask me for anything unless he thought it was life or death?"

That made us both laugh.

"God, I could use one of those right now," she said. I held my glass out to her.

"Manion!"

"Sorry," I said. I finished the drink and put the glass away. I opened two bottled waters and handed one to her. She rolled her eyes but took it.

"You have to look at this situation before the bottom fell out, before Anise Constaneda," she began, taking a long sip of water. "I was going to tell JD after this trip, after the shipment. I was going to tell him about the business, Antonio, and the baby—once I told the father, of course." She plopped down in one of the chairs. "I just wanted to make sure there was something to tell. This business venture was a long time in the making. A lot of things could have gone wrong, from a bad harvest to contamination in the processing to no interest from distributors."

I took a sip and nodded, giving her time to talk.

"But it all went well. The winery is going to work. It's going to be my biggest client to date. Antonio and I, well, that was the icing on a perfect cake."

"Then things went south," I said, squeezing her shoulder.

"You got that right," she said and gave me the first smile since we found her. "Most of it I didn't know was happening. Fernando kept all that from me. He didn't even tell me JD was in town. Anise had me snowed. Have you seen a picture of her?"

I nodded. "We met her."

"Oh yeah. JD told me about the fight in front of Fernando's place in Medellin. Anyway, she had me thinking we were sisters, and she was going to take me under her wing. Ha!"

I shrugged. "She fooled a lot of people."

"Yeah, but I'm not gullible, Manion," she said, the shame spreading across her face. "But she got me. Between the wine business, Antonio, and the beautiful Colombian hill country, I was gone!"

She stopped as the tears ran down her beautiful face. At that moment I felt every disappointment she had ever felt. I felt the death of her mother and her stepsister. The betrayal of the men in her life, like her stepfather. Like me.

"Was her plan really to kill me? To make it look like she died?" she asked. I nodded solemnly.

"Was Fernando in on it?"

"I don't think so," I replied. "Fernando was a customer of hers. He owed her a lot of money and was forced to put her drugs in your wine shipment to work off his debt."

"God, Antonio must be broken-hearted that his brother would do that to him," she said, shaking her head at the mess.

"What does JD think?"

"My brother suspects all of them. He even thinks Antonio had something to do with it."

"Big brothers are like that. He's always been a little crazy when it comes to you," I said, thinking about the two crowns he knocked loose in my mouth when I broke up with her.

"What do you think?" she said, her eyes full of hope.

I walked over and knelt in front of her. "I think that, despite some ferociously bad luck, you've done some good things here in Colombia. I hope the wine can circumnavigate this bad news, and I hope you and Antonio can work this out. The guy is madly in love with you."

"You think so?" Soledad asked, her eyes twinkling with tears and positive emotion. "I trust your instincts, Teke. Be honest."

"Oh, yeah, he loves you, and in that proud Spanish way. He didn't flinch when JD challenged him," I said, laughing. "Your boy is serious. He's just hurting now. The Lazaros are a proud family, and Fernando is . . ."

"Yeah, I guess so," she said, not sounding very convinced.

"You better know it, Soledad," I said, getting to my feet. "You marry that guy, you marry that entire family with all their history and tradition. Because he needs you. They all need someone like you."

We both laughed at that. Then she reached up and grabbed my hand.

"JD told me how you all came to my rescue. Thank you."

"You're welcome, Sole," I said, returning the smile.

I finished my water and walked over to make a real drink before I returned to my cot to watch Netflix. As I was stirring the mixture, I felt her behind me. I could smell her familiar scent. I glanced over my shoulder and saw her face behind my right shoulder blade. I returned my attention to the drink table.

"Teke?"

"Yeeeesss?"

"Tell me the truth. You never saw Fernando? The Lazaros are out of their minds with worry."

"I didn't," I said, making sure I kept my voice slow and conversational and my face turned forward, so she couldn't see it.

"Antonio still feels guilty about not going to look himself," she said. "I talked to him earlier today."

"We were trying to protect the Lazaros in case things went really bad. Besides, I knew Fernando from before."

"But if he isn't with Anise? Where is he?"

"Sole, the guy was facing racketeering, money fraud, accessory to murder, and association with suspected international smugglers. He was going to prison despite his last name. It made sense that he would run away."

"But if he knew about the Largate, about Anise's plan, he wouldn't have left me there," she insisted.

"I'm sure he wouldn't have," I replied. Then I turned around to face her, looking down into her eyes. She put her arms around me, and I hugged her back.

"He was lazy and a gambler and a womanizer," she said. "But he wasn't evil."

"Just a guy who got in over his head," I said. "That was the only reason he would agree to put that crap in the wine shipment. He thought he had no other way out."

I felt her nod, her face buried in my chest.

"Just promise me you checked everywhere. He could have been drugged like me and unconscious. He may have put up a fight."

"Sole, if I had found him, I would have brought him out even if I had to drag him out by that hoop earring of his."

Then there was a knock on the door. A moment later, it opened.

"Look who I found in the hallway," JD said, smiling. Seeing Soledad and me in half embrace brought a frown to his face and a quizzical expression to Camille DeSoronne.

"Camille, hey," I said, pulling away from Soledad. "What's the latest?"

"Hmm . . ." she said as she stood in the doorway. She was in her signature cool green pastel pantsuit with a short bolero jacket. She smiled at JD and patted him on the shoulder.

"Juan Diego is right. Looks like we're getting out of here. Manion, we need to prepare for our final briefing with the authorities."

36

JD and Soledad were told they were free to go as long as they immediately left the country. The authorities put them on the first plane back to the States. Soledad threw a bit of a tantrum. She wanted to go to Venecia Valley and see Antonio, but the Policía Nacional de Colombia and the American State Department were not having it.

Camille and I, however, had a few more hoops with our names on them.

We were among the investigative professionals in this scenario. Suspicions were high on all sides. They still had no idea regarding the whereabouts of Anise Constaneda. Camille and I checked into the Hotel Cartagena Plaza. Camille had new suits delivered for me, a blue wool single-breast and a tan sharkskin.

"I wasn't sure what would work best, so I got both of them," she said with a small smile.

"Thank you," I replied, not knowing what else to say. It was our first chance to be alone, but she was still in business mode.

As she walked back and forth in the hotel suite, setting up laptops and secure Wi-Fi, she had the cool efficiency of someone I didn't know. On the third pass, I grabbed her arm and pulled her into me.

"Hey you," I said, "what's going on?"

I tried to kiss her and got her cheek. Then she seemed to think better of it and kissed me on the mouth as good as I had ever gotten from her.

If it wasn't for all that had come before it, I would have been fine. Now it felt false, as it probably was, but I let it go.

The rest of the day was spent preparing my briefing for the Colombian authorities. It had to be run by the partners at WorldSpan first. Aside from a few minor changes, they approved it. Still on the high from my previous assignment in which we recovered a fortune in gold for Spain and the partners, they were willing to forgive this side trip. However, they did admonish both of us for the cost of this "off books" operation.

The next day, Camille and I had an Air France flight out of Nunez International Airport with connections in Bogota and Madrid and continuing on to Paris. Due to the outlay of WorldSpan resources used to date, Camille felt the last thing we should request was a private jet to get us home. Nevertheless, before that twenty-one-hour flight ordeal, we had to report out to the locals.

I thought it was uncanny that we were back in the same room we had met in almost a week earlier. When Camille and I entered, Meneses was there. Also on our side of the table was Adam Samuelson. Adam was an old-world statesman, a State Department veteran of seven administrations.

"Mr. Manion, you're the most colorful American citizen I have had to work with since 'Daddy Bush,' but I couldn't pass up a chance to assist the 'golden boy of WorldSpan' in another entanglement."

I shook his hand and sat down. I had never known him to be a happy person, so his persona threw me off.

"Adam is having a renaissance at the US State Department since the gold find," Camille whispered in my ear. "See? This is what was waiting for you if you had just brought your heroic ass home to Paris."

She delivered that last part with a smile, but there was no joy in it. I shook hands with Meneses, who was back to his cool reserve. His smile seemed genuine, though, like we were two people who had been through a crisis and lived to tell about it.

On the other side of the table were some familiar faces, including Agent Rutledge from the ATF.

Now there were more players, some in police uniforms, some in suits, but all Colombian judging from their lapel pins to their framed photographs in the hallway of that very building. Also on the other side of the table was Alexandro Lazaro, the patriarch of the Lazaro family, and his attorney, Ernesto Jasper.

"Señor Manion, we appreciate you meeting with us before you leave," said Captain Horace Nacio of the Cartagena Division of the NDTC.

Captain Nacio had been involved since the beginning, but until then he had not been able to talk much, thanks to Agent Rutledge.

"Thanks, but it didn't seem like I had a choice," I said, trying but failing not to come off like I had an attitude. Camille showed some emotion for the first time in the last two days. She kicked my leg and jabbed me in the ribs. Her expression was very much, "Stop messing around."

"Señor Manion, if you can get on with your report, the Colombian government does not wish to retain you any longer than you wish to stay."

This came from one of the suits whose photographs graced the hallways. His name was Wilfredo Salvatore, the Minister of Maritime Customs enforcement.

I sat there in my chair, Camille on my left and Meneses on my right, and looked at everyone and everything around me. I placed my folder on the table in front of me. The Cruzes were gone, and they were the reason I was there. Suddenly, I also wanted to be gone.

"We understand you have a report you want to share," Ernesto said.

I wanted to cry foul, but I remembered JD's advice about families with influence and how they could make one's life a living hell.

"I would," I said, then stood up. "I'm going to tell you a story, and at the end of the story, I'll take any questions you have."

Agent Rutledge rolled his eyes and started to protest, but the minister motioned for him to be still. Rutledge sat back in his chair. I looked at Camille, who was not making eye contact. Adam from the US State Department gave me a thumbs-up.

"This story actually goes back about twenty-three years," I began. "Alexandro Lazaro and his coffee estate friends convinced a local judge to aid them in acquiring small tracts of land owned by smaller farmers. They did this through tax lean buyouts and other legal maneuvers. This allowed them to grow their operations into the large coffee operations we know today.

"When they got what they wanted and were pretty much running the Central Colombia coffee industry, Lazaro and his friends ran that same local magistrate—Hector Constaneda—out of office and into obscurity. One of his daughters was Anise Constaneda.

"Going from a fairly well-connected family to abject poverty, she felt her only choices were to leave Colombia hired out as a domestic, fieldwork in the coffee rows, prostitution, join the drug-selling machine, or smuggling.

"She had an eye for authentic goods and fine quality, so she eventually formed her own crew. The two suspects, Munch and Graves, were her oldest recruits."

"These are all unsubstantiated statements!" Alexandro shouted, leaping to his feet.

"Señor Lazaro, you have no jurisdiction here," the minister said. "You're here as a courtesy of the Colombian government. If you can't stay silent, you will be removed. Besides, all of this can be fact checked before acceptance into the record."

"Fast forward to this year," I continued once the minister advised me to do so. "Anise Constaneda is now the number one smuggler in Colombia. She is moving everything from illegal lumber to animal hides, laundered cash, and human cargo. She has narrowly eluded prosecution two ways. She has never gotten into the drug trade directly.

"While authorities were chasing the Escobar drug wannabes, she was able to build total control over that which she did well. She also made a strong connection with smugglers working in the Amazon across Peru, Ecuador, and Colombia. She paid for connections in local and national law enforcement in Colombia and the United States.

"Then two things happened. First, Anise was approached by Chinese crime syndicates to move illegal prescription drugs through her network and into the States. Oxycodone, Fentanyl, Valium, and Xanax. The money they were offering was too good to pass up.

"Second, she recognized a name in the crowd of loud, lazy rich men in one of her illegal gambling dens. It was Fernando Lazaro-Alvarez. He was the worst, bragging about money he didn't have, pushing women around, making stupid bets, and then getting into fights when he lost. Then he would leave her holding IOUs for months.

"Fernando had run up a substantial bill about a year ago. He threatened not to pay. Anise threatened to tell his father. She wanted to look at that smug old man as she showed him what a worthless son he had.

"But then she got paid. A tall black man who worked for the Lazaros came to her and paid her in full, then paid her extra for her silence. In turn, Anise paid some bribes amongst the Lazaro fieldworkers. She found out the payment was actually authorized by Luisa Lazaro-Alvarez, the sister. The father had no idea.

"Then Fernando was again running up an insane debt. Only worse. She had seen enough.

"With the Chinese, she had a chance to get more money than she ever had, maybe even quit the lumber, animal hides, and illegally mined minerals. The US Justice Department had started an entire division dedicated to wiping out her way of life. US agents were crawling all over the illegal mining and lumber camps. Her suppliers were drying up.

It wouldn't take long before federal agents climbed up the chain and reached her.

"Then she got her idea. She would find a new way to move her Chinese product. While authorities were crawling all over her underground distribution lines, she would move the drugs out under the most protected, above-board product to come out of this part of the world using a name that was above reproach.

"Over the next few weeks, she launched her best girls on Fernando. They goaded him into betting wildly and covering food and drink tabs on everyone in the house. He wasn't an addict, but Anise noticed what he liked and gave him as much of it as he could stand. Even sent him home at the end of the night with a sample of cocaine, weed, and bag of date-rape pills. She didn't sell it or distribute it, but she kept some around, just like any other tool in her business. To get people to do what she wanted.

"When he was into her for almost one million Colombian pesos, or about US$250,000, she applied the squeeze slowly. Men like Fernando are like overripe fruit. Squeeze too hard, and they go out of control. He would go crying to his family with a pitiful story. Then they would come after her with all their political might.

"Instead, she became his friend. She explained how important he was to her operation. How he brought in all the VIPs on his name alone. Now what would happen to her business if it got out that he had to be bailed out by his family? Again?

"She had a way they could all recover their losses. She never mentioned the Chinese, but she said she had product that needed a ride to the States in his father's coffee sacks.

"Of course. Fernando scoffed at it with all his bravado. She let him have that, then slowly weened him off of everything: the girls, the weed, the gambling, the action. After spending a boring week at home with his girlfriend, he was practically begging to take the Chinese product on board.

"When it came time to do the deed, Fernando threw a curveball into the mix. Instead of putting the Chinese payload in the coffee sacks, he instructed Munch and Graves and their crew to hide it in the Lalvarez Wine shipment. At first it pissed her off. The rich lazy boy thought he could fake her out. On second thought, she realized it was better this way. She could move her product in the wine as easily as the coffee. Besides, when the time was right, after she had moved millions of dollars of product through the Lazaro name, she could shame two sons instead of one. At that point Anise Constaneda was just as guilty of bad judgment as Fernando. Her typical careful business sense was muddled by her desire for some long-overdue revenge on the Lazaro family.

"On the day of the transfer, everything went wrong. Fernando assured Anise that the wine would be available to pack, but Munch and Graves found the Americans, Wayne and Mario, already in the warehouse starting to prepare the shipment for transport. A fight ensued, and Graves decided to shoot both of them. Wayne jumped Graves, and they struggled. Wayne took multiple shots to the body, which gave Mario a chance to flee. Wayne died at the scene. Luckily for Soledad, she had left a half day early for Cartagena to accept the shipment when it arrived.

"At that point, Fernando wanted to call the whole thing off, but Anise was too far in for that. The Chinese product was on the Lazaro property. Either it went in the wine or in the coffee. Anise was ready to put a bullet in Fernando to make it happen.

"About a week after Soledad left for Cartagena, Fernando stepped up as the big brother. He suggested Antonio go into the hills and find his friend, Mario. Then Fernando would make sure the wine was loaded and delivered to Soledad in Cartagena. Antonio was grateful and took him up on his offer. Antonio felt responsible for his friend's death. He didn't understand what could have happened that led to this.

"It was just about that time that JD Cruz and I arrived in Medellin looking for Soledad. Following information about the Lazaros, we headed to Fernando's restaurant. We came face to face with a woman who looked just like Soledad. We fought with her bodyguards and Fernando and were arrested for our trouble."

Meneses cleared his throat. I nodded to him. "We were released and decided to try our luck at the Lazaro Coffee estate," I said. "We were arrested again. It was clear we were being stonewalled by the Lazaro family.

Alexandro stood again to protest, but the minister waved for him to sit. Everyone was laser focused on me. The minister motioned for me to continue.

"Meanwhile, Fernando met with Soledad, and convinced her to wait on the yacht owned by his friend, Anise Constaneda. Noting their striking similarities in physical appearance, he thought it would be fun. Soledad had no way of knowing that Fernando and Anise had a secret plan to keep her away from the wine shipment that carried the product from the Chinese until it was safely on the ship.

"Anise was fascinated by her doppelganger appearing before her very eyes. She took it as a sign and decided to use Soledad to further her cause.

"Anise knew she was always under surveillance by Colombian and American law enforcement, so her first thought was to use Soledad as a decoy, a look-alike while she pulled off crimes all over the world. She wined and dined Soledad, shared her clothes and jewelry with her, and told her intimate stories of struggle and mistreatment. In the end she gained Soledad's trust.

"Despite the fact that this was what Anise wanted, Soledad's trust in Anise disgusted her. We learned from those closest to her that she felt Soledad's trust was a weakness, pure and simple, and her plan evolved.

"Anise wondered, what if she could use this simple-minded look-alike to stage the ultimate deception, and fake her own death? If Anise Constaneda no longer existed, she could run her new operations with the Chinese for years as a ghost.

"She even added juice to the plan. She set up easy take-downs at the airport and at one of her warehouses. She made it easy for the authorities to collect evidence and witnesses. They were going to come after her, and she needed them to come for her—or the woman they thought was her. The look-alike, Soledad Cruz, who had no idea.

"When the NDTC officials had the evidence and testimony they needed, they would come after the woman they saw on Constaneda's luxury yacht in Cartagena Bay. When they did, the Largate would explode, taking some agents with them. Then people would assume that Anise Constaneda was killed in an explosion on her own boat. The amount of C-4 on the Largate would assure no DNA evidence would be found because the ship would be blown into small fragments and land in salt water.

"It would have worked, but we got Soledad off the yacht prior to the explosion."

37

When I finished my narrative, the room was full of shocked expressions. The minister recovered first.

"Señor Manion, that is quite a tale, and I look forward to reviewing your supporting documents. First, do you have any knowledge that would lead us to the whereabouts of Fernando Lazaro-Alvarez?"

"I do not," I said, trying my best to look sincere, my eyes staring straight ahead, but I think I flinched when Ernesto and Alexandro made a show of rising from their chairs and stalking from the room. My stomach grumbled, and I worried that Meneses and Camille could hear it.

"Señor Manion, second question: do you have any idea of Anise Constaneda's whereabouts?"

"I do not," I replied. "I think if you question her co-conspirators, you may get a line on that."

"Well, those who are still alive," the minister quipped. "This entire exercise left a lot of dead bodies in its wake."

"I may be able to help with that, Minister," Meneses said as he stood to be recognized.

I looked at Camille, who shrugged. Then I looked back at Meneses, who winked at me before sitting in front of one of the microphones on our side of the table.

"As of nine o'clock yesterday morning, we took into custody one Ramona Valez, a former detective in the Medellin Region of the Policía

Nacional de Colombia."

The room murmured with talk. I looked at Meneses and mouthed, "Pa-dee-ya?"

He nodded solemnly.

"If I could continue, Minister," Meneses said into the microphone as he handed sheets of paper across the table. "We have phone tracking, text messages, voicemails, and photo evidence that Detective Valez was in touch with the suspect, Anise Constaneda, for at least three years. We believe they were lovers. It is our contention that she had been feeding sensitive law enforcement intel to Constaneda during that time, including information on the NDTC raids."

"But she wasn't a part of the task force?" the minister asked.

"Yes, we believe she 'befriended' someone on the NDTC task force who may have been feeding her information unknowingly."

The room erupted into a cacophony of chatter, protests, and questions. I would never have thought it, but in the middle of all that, Agent Rutledge got up and slowly moved to the rear door. He turned to look at us, his face pale green and his eyes wet with tears. I turned to Meneses, who looked back at me like he had just caught the biggest fish in the lake.

Epilogue

How did I get so much background information on Anise Constaneda?

It turned out that even though Mario shot Munch seven times, the big thug didn't die. Somehow, while Mario wasn't looking, he crawled away and managed to call some nefarious connections he had in Cartagena and got most of the bullets pulled out of his back, neck, and leg.

Munch needed to make a deal. He knew Anise had connections all over the police department, so forget them. While healing underground, he read in the paper how the fake death thing blew up in her face. Graves was dead, and the authorities had the Chinese product.

In the end, he contacted Polonia after seeing that her cousin, Mateo, the detective, was working with an insurance investigator to work things out. Within half a day we had Munch in our control and under a doctor's care. He was ready to answer any and all questions. He corroborated Detective Valez's connection to Anise Constaneda. In exchange we negotiated his passage to the United States. He was happy to do time there versus Colombia.

In addition to Munch, the US Justice Department and the ATF/FBI task force with the NDTC made a record number of arrests down the supply chain to illegal mining and lumber operations across three countries. They also arrested and seized property up the supply chain from various customs departments, distributors, vessel captains, and high-end customers in Colombia and the United States. There were news stories of expensive animal hides, wood furniture, and wall hangings being confiscated from investment fund managers, movie stars, and social media influencers.

None of that saved Arnie Rutledge, who was relegated to permanent desk duty for compromising the operation. The public did not know it, but the Colombians knew that a US agent had allowed himself to be compromised, and the embarrassment could not stand.

Ramona Valez, a.k.a. Padilla, was released on conditional bail. The idea was that at some point she would lead them back to Anise Constaneda. Three weeks after her release, she was found dead in an alley behind a gay bar in Medellin, a single bullet hole in the back of the head. While everyone assumed it was Anise cleaning up loose ends, I read the official report from the minister's office. I thought it was interesting that she was killed with a Speer Gold Dot nine-millimeter bullet, the same issued to US federal law enforcement. I wondered if anyone had checked on the whereabouts of Agent Rutledge that weekend.

The Lazaro Coffee company went through a major shake-up. Alexandro was forced to step down as CEO. He was never the same after Fernando's betrayal and disappearance. He spent a fortune over the next six months on detectives, trying to find his son.

Decision making was passed solely to Luisa and Antonio. They hired a CEO to run the place. He was the number-three man from one of their competitors. That way Luisa could work in the field like she wanted. She continued to see Paulo when he was free. Polonia Meneses hired Mr. Diallo to run her roasting house. He also ran the coffee shop and restaurant that belonged to Fernando. Initial reports are that he is doing quite well.

After the initial shock, the news of a new Lazaro baby was welcomed all around. Antonio was so proud. Even Luisa thought it was a good thing, especially when Soledad agreed to stay in Colombia.

They had a large outdoor wedding with meat on spits, wine from the vineyard, and vegetables from Luisa's garden, and JD brought a few folks from White Sand Island. He also escorted Soledad down the aisle.

The wine business was kept out of the news. The first shipment was delayed, but that worked. Antonio and Soledad took over the wine distributorships in the States. After Wayne was laid to rest, Mario went into a rehab/rest facility. He was not sleeping due to nightmares caused by what happened to Wayne and what he did to Graves and Munch. Antonio and Soledad pledged they would be there for him no matter what.

As for me, I didn't get to go home with Camille. I had to make another stop in Washington, DC, to meet with the Department of Justice, the FBI, and the ATF and repeat my report. There was much less fanfare, just me, a stenographer, and one overworked assistant to the assistant director of the ATF.

Two days later I caught a direct flight to Paris. I called Camille, and it went to voicemail.

When I got home, she wasn't at my apartment. Nor had she been there. We had a habit of stopping at each other's place to get it "ready" when the other was coming home from a trip. It included a meal from our favorite restaurant, great wine for her, and single-barrel bourbon for me. This time all I was met with was a dusty apartment. I was sure I was in trouble. For the last few days in Colombia, we didn't talk much unless it was about the case. When I tried to reach out to her, it was like holding a limp fish.

I agreed that she had multiple reasons to be furious with me. I was mad at myself. I didn't think my side trip would have turned into what it had. The WorldSpan partners were already grumbling about the bill. Plus, the directors didn't like having their name mentioned in the same news articles as international smugglers. As the boss and my "handler," Camille has taken a fair share of the heat for that. All this so I could go save my ex-fiancé. Way to go, Manion.

I hadn't been sleeping much. Fernando Lazaro kept appearing in my dreams. Sometimes he was pleading for me to come and get him. Sometimes he showed up in the newspapers giving interviews about the American who left him to die.

On my first night home, I decided to go down to the Café Alhambra and get a bite to eat, maybe catch the last music set, sip some warm bourbon. I didn't want to be left in the apartment with just my thoughts. It was late fall in Paris. Cool and wet. I found my three-quarter-length suede jacket and headed out.

I opened the door, and Camille was there. She looked amazing, wearing a glittery silver raincoat, her hair spiked in that cool way I loved, and those big brown eyes. She had a bag from the local market in one hand and a bag of liquor bottles in the other. There was a young girl with her, about twenty years old. She was carrying a cardboard box.

"You leaving?" Camille asked, surprised.

"Oh, uh, no, just to get some dinner," I said.

She held the food bag under my nose as she walked in, smelling like my favorite perfume. The girl followed her. She was in blue jeans and a sweatshirt with a bomber jacket. Her face looked familiar. She looked young to be a WorldSpan intern, but what did I know?

"I tried to call, but it went to voicemail," I said.

"Yes, baby," she replied with an accent that seemed extra thick. "I was busy. Hands full."

She held up the bags again as if it should have been obvious. She instructed the girl to place the box in the corner window seat. After the girl dropped the box, she left with a friendly wave.

My Teke senses were in full drive, the senses that made me good at what I do, the senses that should never be used on someone I love, so I shut them down.

We had dinner, and it was great. Camille had pâté de campagne and mussels mariniere. I had escargot in garlic butter and poulet scallopini. All of this was paired with a variety of side dishes and our favorite Tattingers champagne.

I didn't realize how much I missed Paris, our local haunts that made the best food, the whole scene in my apartment. It dawned on me that I had been away for well over a month. We sat on the long, wide sofa facing the Paris skyline, the casement windows cranked open to the night air. When the rain started, I built a fire in the large, ancient hearth. The heat from the flames mixed with the wet air created a beautiful, cozy micro atmosphere where we sat. Somewhere on my third glass of cold Hibiki Japanese whiskey, I was immersed. Smugglers, coffee farms, proud, snobbish families, and exploding yachts all faded away.

I am the first to say that I know I have a good woman because I get what I know I don't deserve. At some point I tried to bring up why I did what I did—running off with JD with no word and work reason to go, the scene with Soledad and me in a half embrace, what I really found and left in the bowels of the Largate—but she shut it all down with a kiss that melted me into the couch. Without breaking the lip lock, she pivoted on top of me, straddling my waist. She placed one of my hands inside her blouse where her fully erect nipples met my palm. Pulling away long enough to look me in the eye, she placed the fingertips of my other hand in her warm, wet beautiful mouth. Then she guided my hand to other places on her body, and I would have been a fool not to understand her meaning and intent.

The rest of the night was a beautiful blur. She left before dawn the next morning. I slept in late and arrived at the office at about 10:00 a.m.. I knew I had some level of "counseling" coming from the directors, but I was in no hurry to get it.

Walking down the WorldSpan executive hallway, I usually got to Camille's office before my own. I walked past her space twice before I realized it was empty.

"What is this?" I said as I stood in her doorway.

"Aaahhh, Tekelius, welcome back," Marcel LaRoche said from behind me. He was the managing partner for WorldSpan's Paris Division.

When I started several years ago, I barely understood his English, but I always thought his accent was cool. I knew he was happy with my work. It was Marcel who created the position I now held as the "expeditor."

"Marcel, how are you?" I said absently. We embraced and brushed cheeks. Before I could turn back to the empty office, Marcel took my arm and led me into his office.

"Camille's reassignment has gone through," Marcel explained.

"What? Where?"

"Not important," Marcel said. "She's where we need her for now. The important thing is that we keep you on track. New assignments are coming in every day for someone with your unique skills."

I started to apologize for what I later found out was being called "L'aventure Colombienne" or the "Colombian Adventure." Marcel waved it off.

"It is true we incurred a few expenses, but you will make it up to us, n'est-ce pas?" he said, smiling confidently. I agreed heartily. Marcel threw his hands up and turned to leave.

"But I don't understand," I said. "What was so important that you had to split up Camille and me? We're a good team."

Marcel looked at me like I was crazy.

"Tekelius, I don't understand your response. We thought you knew about this."

"Well, I didn't," I said. Marcel looked embarrassed and at a loss for words. "What, Marcel? What am I missing?

"I don't know if it's for me to say, but, well, this move? Your reassignment? It was Camille's idea."

In Colombia, Antonio Lazaro-Alvarez and Soledad Marie Cruz, at the strong urging of the Lazaro family, decided to have a December wedding. It was a beautiful affair on the grounds of the Lazaro Coffee estate. It was about more than Alexandro demanding the marriage precede the birth of his first grandchild. It was a rebranding of the names "Lazaro Coffee" and "Lalvarez Wines" to distance the family from the sad news earlier in the year.

The entire estate was festooned with large white, yellow, and lavender flowers. Rose bouquets of various colors were on all the tables. There were two large oil portraits set on pedestals in the main hall. One depicted Victoria Alvarez-Lazaro, Alexandro's wife and Antonio's mother, who died years earlier. The other one was a rendering of Fernando, who had not been found. Some presumed him to be dead, but the Lazaros never gave up hope.

At some point in the middle of the reception, Antonio and his close male friends, dressed in formal black tuxedos, retired to the grand library to smoke.

Alexandro was holding court on the rear patio with gentlemen closer to his own age.

Soledad, dressed in a fitted white lace-sleeved dress, was with the ladies of the family. Antonio's aunts on his mother's side were wonderful, funny, and tender. She felt more loved than she had in a long time. Polonia was also included in the group.

Just after sundown, Soledad excused herself to go look for her new husband. She was tired, and the baby was moving like butterfly wings inside her. Luisa found her in the grand hall way just off the foyer.

"Sister, can I have a word?" Luisa asked, a humorless smile on her face. They were getting along these days, but they would never be affectionate. Luisa was not the type to have close friends.

"I'm looking for Tonio," Soledad said impatiently.

"Great, I'll take you to him," Luisa said.

They entered the smoking room. Everyone was gone except Antonio and Daniela Jasper, Fernando's girlfriend.

"Come in, Sole," Antonio said. He smiled, but like his sister there was no humor in his eyes. "You remember Daniela."

Soledad made pleasant noises to the lady who looked as miserable as the last time they met. That was when Luisa told her that Fernando was missing and either presumed dead or on the run from the authorities.

"Daniela, please show my wife what you showed me," Antonio said.

Daniela stepped forward and placed an item on the counter. It was a gold earring.

"I have always been suspicious of the story they told us about Fernando," Daniela said. "If he had left the Largate and was on the run, I would have heard from him by now."

"His *family* would have heard from him," Luisa said, defiance in

218

her tone.

"Of course, Luisa," Daniela said, raising her hands in a conciliatory gesture.

"Let her finish, sister," Antonio said, his voice tight.

"The Cartagena Maritime Authority said they didn't recover anything from the explosion site," Daniela explained. "The bay was too deep, the particles too small, the effect of the salt water . . ."

"OK," Soledad said, nodding.

"Well, I just paid a private company skilled in recovering gold from shipwrecks at the bottom of the ocean. They pulled up everything from the bottom of the bay at or near the explosion site. This was there," Daniela explained, pointing to the earring. She tapped on her phone to find a file. "A few days before the explosion, Fernando posted this photo on his Instagram page."

It was a picture of the day on the ship. Soledad remembered that day. Everyone was making fun of Fernando. Anise forced him to get his ear pierced as punishment. He was drunk and went along with it. The post showed Fernando posing with the large earring hanging from his bloody lobe. The caption on the post read, "A Tiffany Pirate!"

"What are the odds that we find a Tiffany hoop earring on the floor of the bay right where that ship exploded?" Daniela asked.

"Soledad, my wife, my love, I have to ask . . ."

"Yes, Tonio, I remember that day very clearly," Soledad admitted. She flinched when Antonio banged the table. Luisa broke down crying.

"I knew it. I knew it," Antonio said. "My brother was on that ship when it exploded. This proves it."

"I think so too," Daniela said. "If he were still alive, we would have heard from him by now."

"This isn't over," Antonio said, his face a mask of anger. "Teke Manion lied to us. I don't know why, but I'm going to find out."

"I think he killed my Fernando!" Daniela said.

"Wait, why would Teke kill Fernando?" Soledad asked. "And he didn't blow up the boat. That was Anise Constaneda."

"But I asked Manion multiple times, and he said Fernando was not on the ship!" Antonio almost shouted. "As to the question of why he would lie, I intend to ask him that exactly."

"But we need to know where you stand, sister," Luisa said, her voice dripping with sarcasm. "We know you and Manion have history."

"Why would you have to ask?" Soledad asked, an edge to her tone. Over the last few months, she and Luisa had entered into a phase of mutual respect, if not love. "I'm a Lazaro now. I want to know what happened to Fernando as much as you do."

Antonio came around the desk and held his arms out. Soledad folded into his chest, allowing him to embrace her.

"See, Luisa, Daniela? I told you. We're all on the same page here. One heart. One vision." Antonio released Soledad, then turned and picked up his glass of wine. "To Fernando and to the truth!" he shouted. Luisa and Daniela repeated the words after him. Soledad just mouthed them. Then she excused herself.

Walking back through the hall, she fought to keep her cool. She had come to understand this proud, loving family into which she married. Her child would be a Lazaro. The business was taking off, and Antonio was taking his place as one of the future leaders of Lazaro Coffee and the voice of Lalvarez Wines. She was his partner and his wife.

She found her brother sitting outside with Paulo and some of the other field bosses. She told him what had just happened.

"Sole, they may want to interview me. I was down there too. I didn't see him either."

"But you didn't search every room," she explained. He nodded in agreement.

"But why would Manion lie?" JD asked. "He's not my favorite person, but he's the best at this sort of thing."

"What should I do?" she implored.

"Nothing. Let your husband handle his business. Manion is a big boy."

She kissed JD goodnight, claiming fatigue. As she headed to her room, she remembered Fernando during those days on the Largate. He was fun and helpful and supportive, but he was as insincere as an off-brand timeshare presentation. He seemed more like a troublesome younger brother to Antonio and Luisa as opposed to the firstborn of the siblings.

The truth of the matter was that he knew of Anise's plan to smuggle prescription drugs in the wine. He actually set it up to pay off his debts, but the Lazaros totally ignored that. The family PR machine pushed out the story that Fernando was working undercover to expose Anise when he learned about her plans. He wanted proof before he went to the police. She doubted if anyone outside of the family actually believed that tale.

She wanted to scream about the mendacity of the entire exercise, but she stayed quiet. For the life she dreamed of with Antonio, she stayed quiet. For the baby inside her, she stayed quiet. For the sanity of JD, who wanted to snatch her away at a moment's notice, she stayed quiet. Families are not perfect. The Cruzes had more than enough drama.

She understood the grieving process, having lost her mother at a young age. Therefore, this witch hunt for Teke to get answers would be at best an understandable indulgence of a family with almost unlimited resources and still in the depths of grief.

On the other side was Teke and that earring. Although she tried to put it out of her mind, Soledad recalled what Teke had said that day while they were still in confinement. He said he would have "pulled him out by that corny earring."

But Fernando didn't have that corny earring until well after his run-in with Teke and JD in front of his restaurant. How did Manion know about it to comment on it?

The baby fluttered again, and suddenly Soledad was very nauseous.

December 23, 2019
Phonexay District of Luang Namtha, Laos

Anise Constaneda sat in front of a bank of monitors watching the news, true-crime documentaries, and reruns from the 1990s. Her first months in exile had been busy. She continued her business—the lumber, the animal hides, and the human trafficking—using well-paid contract agents. The cost ate into her profits immensely.

She was anxious. She had finally made a connection with the Chinese, who were sending a representative to work out what had gone wrong and what would happen going forward. She was scared for her life, living in fear of apprehension and death.

They could be coming to kill her now. She knew that, but it was the chance she had to take. She was bored in that apartment, sending out for everything, and she was running out of money. What she had learned while in hiding was that she had to pay three times the price for everything, from food to toilet paper to underwear.

She had hired some local muscle to watch her back, but at best they would give her a chance to defend herself and get away.

The knock on the door was familiar, but the door opened before she could respond. The muscle came in with his hands up.

"Señora Constaneda, I mean no harm. I am your appointment for today," the voice said, very English, very American.

"Put your hands down, and get out of the way," Anise said.

The muscle complied. The American returned the gun to the muscle and shooed him outside. He didn't ask Anise if he should leave; he just

221

left. Anise rolled her eyes and took stock of the visitor.

She was American, a redhead, close to forty years of age. She was well-endowed up top but had the shoulders to pull it off. The rest of her was slim and slickly dressed.

"Come in," Anise said. "I made tea. You don't sound Chinese."

As the woman stepped closer, Anise got a good look at her face.

"Great, a fucking grifter," Anise said.

"Pardon?" the redhead asked.

"I can tell by the dancing eyes and the too-perfect smile for all seasons," Anise said. The redhead smiled. "And how did you get in the middle of this?" Anise asked.

"I always was," the redhead replied. "I was the one who brought you to the Chinese. I'm a fan of your work."

"You got a name, grifter?" Anise asked, clearly deflated as she sat back on her cushioned sofa.

The redhead shrugged. "I go by a lot of names."

"Then I'll call you Red," Anise said.

"Call me Molly. Teke Manion and Soledad Cruz knew me by that name."

That brought Anise to her feet.

"I had dealings with them years ago. They cost me a lot of money. I've been lying in the tall weeds for a chance to pay them back. Soledad's brother, JD, too."

"And you were planning to use me to do it?" Anise asked.

"I know. It's a delicate process. I knew you had Fernando in your grasp. Fernando was brother to Antonio, who was Soledad's lover and business partner. Through you I could get close enough to exact my revenge. Either I would do it myself, or you would do it for me; I didn't really care."

"Sounds flimsy to me," Anise said.

"It was the beauty of the plan. A lot of things needed to go right to be successful, but you were wrong on two points."

"Oh?" Anise asked.

"First, I'm not a fucking grifter; I am an exceptional grifter. I had you pegged. I planted the idea to smuggle the Chinese product in the Lazaros' cargo via a thousand hints sent by your people, your friends, your hangers-on."

Anise just stared at her, not quite believing what she was hearing. Then she had to laugh. It all made sense. She flopped back in her chair, plucked a cigarette from her box, and lit it.

"OK, Molly, what was the second?"

"Your idiotic plan to fake your own death. Really?"

Anise shrugged. "Seemed like a good time to do it."

"You watch too much TV," Molly said, pointing to the true-crime show on the television.

They sat there in silence for a couple of minutes, Anise smoking and smoldering, Molly sipping her tea and looking around at the drab apartment.

"So, where does that leave us?" Anise asked. "The Chinese obviously want the value of their product back."

"Not at all. I squared your debt with the Chinese. They have another job for you if you can stick to the plan. It will go a long way toward restoring your place in the smuggling game, and yes, erase your debt to me."

"Cool, I'm ready," Anise said, feeling that old excitement. "What is it? More medicine?"

"Not quite," Molly said. She pulled a slip of folded paper from her inside pocket and handed it over to Anise. She read it, frowning like it was written in code. Then she turned the paper over and back several times.

"Is this a joke?" she asked. "Five million hospital masks and five million units of hand sanitizer?"

"Be patient and have faith," Molly said as she sat back and crossed her long legs. "Something is coming. I don't know what, but the Chinese assure me that in the next one hundred days, those items will be worth more than gold."

Made in the USA
Columbia, SC
26 September 2022

67772465R00124